HOARFROST

(Whyborne & Griffin No. 6)

JORDAN L. HAWK

Hoarfrost © 2015 Jordan L. Hawk
ISBN: 978-1511415620

All rights reserved.

Cover art © 2016 Lou Harper

This book is a work of fiction. Names, characters, places, and incidents are products of the author's imagination or are used fictitiously. Any resemblance to actual events or locales or persons, living or dead, is entirely coincidental.

Edited by Annetta Ribken

This book is dedicated to

Rhys Ford

*without whom none of this
would have been possible.*

CHAPTER 1

Griffin

PA WAS DEAD.

The wind blew in from the ocean, breeze stiff and touched with October cold. It smelled of salt and fish, seaweed and decay. Moonlight sparkled from the waves, and lanterns lent false warmth to the scattered rock of the strand. But a part of me could see only the flat plains of Kansas, the rich earth of the fields, the fresh-painted house where I'd grown to manhood.

At least others stood with me. Whyborne had asked me if I wanted to be alone, but I'd numbly said no, because what sort of wake had only one mourner? So Christine and Iskander rode out here with us in a carriage borrowed from Whyborne's father.

I'd been so excited when Ma's letter appeared in the mail. I hadn't received any correspondence from my adoptive parents in over two years. Surely it was a sign they'd changed their minds, chosen to accept my love for another man after all. Or, at least, decided they loved me more than they hated what they saw as my sin. Perhaps they even wished me to visit. I was already considering train schedules as I tore open the envelope.

But instead of a new beginning, the letter contained an end.

Pa was dead. Heart trouble. Don't come for the funeral.

For two years, I'd thought he might change his mind. Believed, on some deep level I hadn't even recognized, he would. He'd come to understand I loved Whyborne, see our relationship wasn't just some venial sin, some perverse gratification of the flesh.

It was too late. He'd never forgiven me.

And now he never would.

There came a soft splash from the heaving ocean. I'd guessed, when Whyborne chose the beach at night as the location for the wake, he meant to summon others. A surge of gratitude went through me nonetheless to see two ketoi rise from the waves. They were thin and wiry, their bodies nearly sexless beneath the scant covering of gold and jewels. A forest of tentacles, like the stinging arms of an anemone, sprouted from their heads in place of hair, and row upon row of shark's teeth filled their mouths.

"Bloody hell," Iskander whispered from his place beside Christine, well back from the incoming tide. Christine shushed him.

One of the newcomers approached me with no hesitation, her stride made awkward by long, batrachian feet. "Griffin, my dear boy," said my mother-in-law, and embraced me. "I'm so very sorry for your loss."

Her skin felt like a dolphin's, sleek and firm. "Thank you, Heliabel." I blinked rapidly; I refused to cry. Not in front of this gathering, intimate as it was. "Niles sent a card of condolence."

It was a stupid thing to say, and I cursed myself immediately. I didn't know if she thought often of the man who had been her husband on the land, the father of her four children, but I shouldn't have brought it up in case the reminder were in any way painful for her.

She drew back and ran a clawed hand gently over my cheek. "I'm not surprised. For all his faults, Niles always wished to do right by his family."

"Yes," I said, glad not to have hurt her. And she was right; despite their damaged, angry relationship, Niles never tried to separate Whyborne from me. Attempt to convince Whyborne to enter into a convenient marriage with an heiress and keep me as a lover in the shadows, yes. But from Niles's point of view such an arrangement would only be practical. Many would agree with him.

Pa wouldn't have. He believed in the sanctity of vows spoken before God. But he would never have believed the vows Whyborne and I spoke to each other on this very beach last year to be anything but blasphemous.

Heliabel stepped away to greet Whyborne. Persephone, Whyborne's twin sister who had been raised beneath the sea, paused before me. Although I'd seen her regularly over the last year, I didn't have the same easy relationship with her as with Heliabel. "Brother's husband," she said in her odd, formal fashion. "Mother says it is polite to offer condolences. I am sorry your father-who-raised-you died far from the sea. What will become of his body?"

How many times had I stood in the little graveyard outside the church, flanked by Ma and Pa while mourners lowered some unfortunate into the cold earth? Women who died in childbirth, children from sickness, people of all ages and sexes from accident. The occasional elder whose time had come in its fullness, rather than succumb to the harshness of life on the prairie.

"They'll bury him beside his brother," I said.

"In the earth?" She looked revolted. "And they will not eat his heart, so his spirit may remain with them, to be born again in its time?"

A part of me wanted to laugh. She looked like a barbarian queen, nearly naked and carrying a dagger of bone at her waist. Clearly, though, she thought us the savages.

"Persephone, please," Whyborne said, before I could formulate a reply. "Not now."

He looked very somber in his black suit and top hat. Macassar oil slicked his unruly hair, or tried to; it already stuck up on the sides once again. I was unspeakably glad to have him with me tonight. For him to have arranged this...whatever it was. Ceremony, perhaps. A farewell, certainly.

"I only wish to understand your customs," she replied. Given her inhuman nature, it always startled me how much she and Whyborne still managed to resemble one another. Both had their mother's eyes, but it was more than that. A similarity in nose and cheekbone, perhaps, or in the way they held themselves. "How else shall I know what is appropriate?"

"There's nothing for you to do," I said. "Other than be here. Thank you for coming."

"Of course." She joined Heliabel, who conversed quietly with Christine. Iskander, who had heard us speak of the ketoi but never before seen them, had a slightly gray tinge to his brown skin. I couldn't blame his reaction; at first glance I'd thought the ketoi monstrous as well.

Odd, how familiarity changes one's perceptions.

"What do you wish to do, darling?" Whyborne asked quietly.

I took a sheaf of letters from within the pocket of my overcoat. I'd wanted, very badly, to do *something* to mark Pa's passing. A funeral of sorts, even if the only thing I had to bury was hope. "What I mentioned. Perhaps it's foolish, but..."

"Only if you deem it so." His fingers brushed lightly against mine. Scars covered the back of his hand, branching down to the very tips of his fingers, like a pattern of frost on a windowpane.

"This blasted wind is freezing the life out of me," Christine complained. "Can we open the whiskey yet, Whyborne?"

"Christine!" Whyborne said, giving her a glare.

I laughed, though. "Yes," I said. "Please."

Iskander took the whiskey from the small basket we'd brought and poured us each a dram. When he passed a glass to Persephone, she took a cautious sniff of it. Her hair-tentacles retracted sharply, and she made a face. Did ketoi have alcohol? I'd never thought to ask.

Whyborne went to a small pile of driftwood, laid by Iskander while we waited for Heliabel and Persephone. He said nothing, only looked at it for a long moment. The dry wood crackled, then burst into flame. Within seconds, a small fire burned merrily on the strand.

"Thank you for coming," I said to them all. "I know most of you never met Pa, so this has little meaning for you."

"We're here for you, dear," Heliabel said gently.

Tears pricked the back of my eyes again. "I suppose under ordinary circumstances, this is where someone would say a few words, or we'd all exchange stories about the deceased."

"Well," Christine said dubiously, "he seemed...nice...enough. But honestly—"

"Christine, this is a funeral," Whyborne interrupted. "In other words, the last place for your brand of honesty."

"My brand of honesty? What the devil do you mean?"

"Please, both of you!" Iskander exclaimed, looking scandalized.

"I only meant to say Griffin is a fine fellow," Christine objected. "And if—"

"Christine!"

"Oh, very well." She scowled.

I found myself smiling, despite everything. "Thank you, Christine," I said. "I do appreciate the thought." I clutched the letters in my hand tighter. "The truth is...the truth is, Pa was a good man. He worked hard to provide for his family. When he and Ma couldn't have children, they took in a frightened Irish lad from the orphan train and raised him as their own. He told me to keep my birth name, so I wouldn't forget my parents, but he never treated me for a moment as if I were anything but his blood son."

Damn it. I refused to cry. I might show my tears to Whyborne and Christine, but not to the rest. Even though, God knew, they'd never judge me for them. I still had my pride.

"He saved me from the asylum, where they put me when I tried to warn them about monsters beneath Chicago," I went on. Of course, I'd never have gone to Chicago in the first place if I'd not been caught with the neighbor lad. If Pa and Ma hadn't agreed it would be best if I left, while Benjamin Walter married a local girl as quickly as possible. "I won't pretend he was perfect, but I owed him a great deal. And I wish..."

I trailed off. Wishes didn't matter now. It was too late.

"Then let us remember the good," Iskander suggested, raising his glass.

The whiskey went down smoothly. Persephone made a choking sound, then offered me a grin to cover her lapse, exposing rows of serrated teeth.

The gathering should have seemed stranger to me than it did. Pa would have been horrified: two ketoi, my sorcerer husband, and a brown foreigner, all drinking to his memory. He'd simply never been certain what to make of Christine, but the rest...

I handed my empty glass to Whyborne and walked to the fire. The flames crackled merrily, their heat on my face something of a comfort. I shuffled the letters in both hands, looking at the envelopes. Each held a letter I'd sent to him and Ma, all of them returned unopened. Two Christmas cards, birthday wishes, even the announcement card for our wedding, printed by a very discreet stationer I knew from my days in Chicago. *Return to Sender* had been written on each one in his firm hand.

"I want to believe there's a life beyond this one," I said aloud. "And that, if there is, the smoke will carry my words to him, and he'll finally understand. So things will be different, when I see him again."

"God rest his soul," Iskander murmured.

"May the dweller in the deeps speed his rebirth," Persephone added solemnly.

Whyborne looked faintly uncomfortable, but he didn't believe in gods of any sort.

I tossed the letters into the fire, one at a time so as not to smother it. The paper curled and blackened, flames devouring my words. As the final envelope burned away, I glimpsed a line of writing in my own hand, the rest of the message already going to ash. *I love you.*

Whyborne put his arm around my shoulders, and I leaned into him. Iskander quietly refilled my glass and pressed it into my hand. In silence, the six of us stood and drank, until the fire burned down and nothing remained but ashes.

The dusty tunnel stretched before me, dry air biting my skin. Pain burned through me, like hooks sunk into my flesh, dragging me forward. I had to make it stop.

I squeezed through the passageway that had been my only home, my refuge from the burning light of the sun. Once I had stretched my wings and flown through it, but now my form was crushed and distorted by the enclosing walls. But I was fast, fast enough to stop the creatures I had been awakened to kill.

Fast enough to stop the pain.

There—they ran before me, their misshapen bodies awkward. They looked back at me, their two eyes hideous, horrifying. They screamed and jabbered, incomprehensible sounds, but I ignored the noise and focused on one. If I killed it, the pain would end. I could sink back into sleep, into nothingness. I could forget I was alone.

I jolted awake, my hands clenching the blankets to either side of me. Where was I? What had happened to the dry stone passage? My heart pounded and my head ached.

A body stirred beside me. One of those who had been running away from me in the dream. In the nightmare.

"It's all right, darling," Whyborne murmured, his voice slurred with sleep. He slid his arm across my chest, and flung a leg over my thighs. "You're safe. You're in our home, in our bed. I'm here."

Whyborne was used to me waking him at odd hours of the night. The horrors I'd seen in a basement beneath Chicago, where my partner Glenn had died so terribly, would have been enough to give anyone nightmares. Coupled with the time I'd spent in an insane asylum, while the doctors worked to cure me of both delusions and desire, and the attendants...

I'd ended writhing in fits, unaware of where I was, convinced I'd been transported back to that terrible time. Instead of rejecting me for weakness, Ival embraced me, did everything he could to lead me back through the thickets of my own mind to reality.

It helped. Time helped, in its way. The fits grew less and less frequent, until more ordinary nightmares took their place.

Then we'd gone to Egypt, and I'd accidentally awoken the monstrous guardian of a curious gemstone. It had hunted us through underground passageways, and only daylight had saved us. Even so, it had come perilously close to killing us all, and Whyborne nearly sacrificed his life stopping it.

After that, the dreams changed.

I ran my hand down Ival's arm, tracing the scars lightning had inscribed on his flesh. "I'm sorry," I said.

His arm and leg tightened around me. "Shh. You have nothing to apologize for." His lips pressed a soft kiss onto my cheek. "You're grieving. Tonight you said goodbye to the man who raised you. Bad dreams are to be expected."

Emotion constricted my throat. He'd always been so understanding. Never impatient with being woken in the night. Never pushing me to speak of what haunted my dreams.

Perhaps I should ask his opinion. But I'd already burdened him so much. He'd been my rock through everything, from my fits, to my falling out with my parents, to Pa's death. I couldn't ask him to worry about something that was probably just some strange quirk of my mind.

Because in my dreams of Egypt, I wasn't fleeing from the daemon, as I had in reality. Instead, I was the monster hunting us.

CHAPTER 2

Whyborne

A WEEK OR so after the passing of Griffin's father, I perused the morning paper over coffee and cereal.

Our breakfasts as of late had been quiet, ever since Griffin received his mother's letter in the morning post. Our dinners had been quiet as well, to be honest. I could only prattle on so much about my work at the museum, after all. Griffin ordinarily would discuss his cases with me, but he'd dismissed my questions with a few terse words before lapsing back into silence.

I scanned the paper for headlines that might draw him out. PRINCE TUAN BANISHED TO SIBERIA blared one. THREE OTHERS SENTENCED TO DECAPITATION FOR ROLE IN BOXER UPRISING.

"It looks as though the Chinese Emperor will return to Peking," I remarked. "And supposedly a wealthy Filipino is paying a bounty on American ears. I wonder if he's a sorcerer looking for body parts. Although I suppose nothing but ears would be rather useless."

"I see," Griffin said absently.

I lowered the newspaper just far enough to peer at him over it. He sat with his coffee cup forgotten, staring off into the distance. Mourning dictated he wear a black tie and vest, rather than his usual more colorful clothing.

I suppressed a sigh. Damn James Kerr for doing this to Griffin. I'd always been instructed not to speak badly of the dead, but Griffin's gloomy mood left me increasingly angry with the fellow. How could anyone raise a man like Griffin, only to abandon him for falling in love with the wrong gender? As though my sex somehow outweighed all the good Griffin did in the world.

But Griffin didn't need my anger, even if it was on his behalf. He needed me to find some way to engage him, to get him interested in the world and out of his own thoughts. Easy enough to do in bed, of course, but the effect only lasted until the next morning. What Griffin needed was a case challenging enough to demand his full faculties. Perhaps it would give him the space to heal, to lessen the immediacy of his grief.

The soft clack of the mail slot falling closed echoed through the house. "I'll get it," Griffin said, rising to his feet. "Finish your breakfast before you're late for work."

"I'm going to try to remove the curse from Dr. Gerritson's pearl this morning," I said.

For once he seemed to hear what I said. Stopping, he frowned at me. "Doesn't that one kill people?"

"Only Polynesian chiefs."

He still looked dubious, but didn't argue, only left to get the mail. Over the last month, I'd studied infusing magic into objects, in the vague idea I might be able to place some protective enchantment on Griffin's wedding ring, for when his cases took him to dangerous parts of town. It occurred to me, if one could put a spell on something, one might equally be able to take it off again. The Ladysmith's trove of cursed objects seemed as good a place as any to test the theory. If I made the museum a slightly less deadly place to work, it would surely be for the better.

Griffin's tread sounded in the hall. "Anything interesting in the mail?" I asked.

"A letter from Ruth, a flyer for Pears' Soap..." Griffin put a package wrapped in brown paper on the table between us. "And this from my brother."

Griffin's two older brothers had been adopted separately from him. While he hadn't yet located the eldest, he'd managed to track down the middle brother, renamed Jack Hogue by the couple who adopted him. Jack had joined the other stampeders in the Yukon, and the two had exchanged lengthy letters over the past year.

"Perhaps it's gold?" I suggested.

Griffin hefted the package. "It is heavy, although not heavy enough, I think." Retrieving a penknife, he cut the twine around the parcel and slit open the paper wrapping to reveal a letter and a battered cigar box.

We exchanged a puzzled look. "What does the letter say?" I prompted.

Griffin unfolded the paper and read aloud:

Dear Griffin,

I'm sending this from St. Michael, where I intend to stay until I get your reply—I hope soon. When I last wrote, I mentioned my intention to spend the year in what we've dubbed Hoarfrost camp, way up in the mountains north of the Yukon River. Although others have found gold, I think Nicholas and I discovered something far more valuable. I've enclosed a photograph—it looks like some sort of broken column, buried deep in the permafrost.

Griffin frowned and opened the cigar box. A photograph lay atop the straw packing. I leaned forward and peered at it with him. Although the poor lighting it had been taken in failed to show details, the photo revealed a deep pit dug through layers of gravel and dirt. At the bottom rested a jagged bit of broken rock, which looked like the base of a stele. Other fragments of rock lay in a jumble around it. Some appeared to have carving on them.

It doesn't look anything like what the natives make. They don't have any kind of writing, and this column or what have you has some strange words on it, although I couldn't tell you what it says. I showed the fragment to a couple of Tagish I know. They said the entire area is bad medicine, so I'm guessing whatever is here hasn't been disturbed by anyone in a long time.

Nicholas knows a little about these things and said it might be from an unknown civilization. I mentioned you're friends with the lady archaeologist and Dr. Whyborne, so he suggested I send this to you to show them. Or maybe you know some collectors who would be interested?

Keep the fragment I sent with this letter, whatever you decide. After finding this, Nicholas has taken over the saloon, instead of working the claim, in case there's more to it. If the weather holds, we plan to continue digging through the winter and see if we can find anything else. Let me know if we should wait for you or the lady archaeologist.

Sincerely,
Jack

"Do you think there's anything to this?" Griffin asked.

"It certainly looks like something," I admitted, putting the photograph aside. "Let's see what your brother sent us."

Griffin removed the straw packing to reveal a small, flat rectangle of greenish stone. It had been carefully polished on two sides and what appeared to be a rounded edge. The other three sides were rough and broken. Although weathered, the signs of carving remained clear, including a series of dots and lines I thought I recognized. Where had I seen them?

Oh. Oh dear.

"The pattern. It seems familiar, but...no. Never mind," Griffin murmured, a puzzled frown on his face. "What do you think? I know you're not an archaeologist yourself, but your philological studies have given you knowledge of at least some ancient peoples."

"I have seen something like it before," I said. "In a book in the library. One of those kept under lock and key. You said it seemed familiar to you?"

"I...no." Griffin shook his head. "It was just an odd feeling, nothing more. You said you've seen similar things among the restricted tomes? That isn't good."

"No," I agreed. "It probably isn't."

"Is the artifact dangerous?" His face paled sharply with realization. "Jack. He's in St. Michael now, but what if he returns to Hoarfrost, where he found this? Do I need to warn him? Would he even believe me if I did?"

"Griffin." I put my hand on his, stilling him. "I don't know. But I promise you, I will find out."

CHAPTER 3

Whyborne

AN HOUR LATER, I settled behind the desk in my office in the Nathaniel R. Ladysmith Museum. After years exiled to a windowless office in the basement, I now occupied a rather nice space on the second floor, complete with large windows to let in the light. I'd also gained a personal secretary, in the form of Miss Parkhurst, who came in quite handy for preventing visitors from disturbing me.

Rather than immediately turn to the library for answers as to the fragment Griffin's brother had sent, I decided to wait for Christine's expert opinion. She'd not been in her office when I stopped by, so I made a mental note to round her up for lunch, then set myself to the work I'd planned to do before the arrival of the package.

Not that removing the curse from one of the museum's possessions constituted my work in any official capacity.

The cursed pearl lay in front of me on the desk, wrapped in silk. Although Dr. Gerritson swore it only killed Polynesian chiefs, I had decided to treat it with great caution. After all, there was no knowing what might in truth activate the curse. A certain bloodline? Sorcery? What if the chiefs in question had been ketoi hybrids and the thing decided to attack me as well?

I removed the silk wrapping carefully. The pearl looked innocuous enough, its luster shining against the dark cloth. Hopefully removing the curse, assuming I even could do such a thing, wouldn't damage it in some way. My salary was generous for my needs, as I lacked a wife or children to support, but it would hardly cover the destruction of a large and presumably rather valuable pearl.

I closed my eyes for a moment, opening my senses. Magic whispered far beneath me, flowing through the lines of arcane power that converged here in Widdershins in the form of a gigantic magical vortex. Now that I'd become attuned to it, I felt the slow rotation under my feet, the pulse of power along the scars on my right arm.

I sensed nothing from the pearl. Either the curse didn't actually exist, or I would have to touch the blasted thing. Taking a deep breath, I hesitantly poked it with my forefinger.

A little tingle ran up my arm. There was something here after all.

Hoping I wasn't about to do something foolish, I picked up the pearl in both hands. I felt the arcane energy trapped within it, quiescent for the moment. Waiting for the wrong person to wander past, no doubt.

I ran my fingers over its smooth surface, hoping to feel the shape of the spell. The *Liber Arcanorum* had spoken of drawing or painting certain sigils, wrapping the magic about the object to be enchanted like a net, and letting it sink within. If I could find the warp and weft of the spell, I might be able to pick it apart, like pulling just the right thread to unravel a sweater.

I might as well have been trying to read Monsieur Braille's system of letters. There was *something* there, but what I couldn't even begin to make out.

Very well. This enchantment hardly seemed like a thing of great power, despite its effect on certain chiefs. If I couldn't untie the knots, perhaps I could simply cut through them.

My scars ached hotly as I drew power from the maelstrom beneath me. I'd spent almost three years honing my will into an instrument of sorcery. I found a place where the spell seemed thinner, for lack of a better word, and focused all my concentration on forcing it apart.

The enchantment responded. I *felt* the edges unravel, the spell fail as it shattered beneath my will. My fingers burned, arcane energy releasing from the pearl directly into my skin, my blood. A tingle ran through me, and I hardened beneath my trousers.

"There you are, Whyborne!" Christine exclaimed, flinging open the door.

I dropped the pearl: it fell to the desk, rolled past the clutter of piled books and notes, and tumbled off the edge onto the carpet.

"Blast it, Christine." My cheeks and ears went red, and I scrambled under the desk in search of the pearl. "At least have Miss Parkhurst announce you."

"What the devil for?" She strode in. Iskander followed her, looking a bit more uncertain. I was surprised to see him here. On the strength of his experience in Egypt, he'd done a bit of work for the museum, cataloging items and the like, but didn't have a full position on staff.

I found the pearl, thankfully unharmed. The power still sizzled beneath my skin, but at least my rather inappropriate erection had faded. "I was doing delicate work," I said, brandishing the pearl at her.

"Is that Dr. Gerritson's cursed pearl?" she asked.

Iskander looked alarmed. "It's cursed?"

"Not any more." Perhaps I sounded a bit smug, but surely I was allowed.

Christine was far less impressed than I'd hoped. "Don't let the director hear you say that." Indeed, Dr. Hart seemed under the impression a vast assemblage of cursed objects drew crowds rather than drove them away. I had to admit that thus far, he'd been right.

I put the pearl safely in a drawer so I could return it later. The power I'd taken from it still seethed uncomfortably, aching through my scars, but I ignored it. "I have something for you," I said, pulling out the cigar box.

"We're getting married," Christine blurted out.

I blinked. Iskander beamed, and Christine looked...well, slightly terrified, but mostly happy.

The announcement didn't come as a surprise. After all, Iskander had relocated from Egypt to join her here in America. I rose from my seat and went around the desk. "I'm extraordinarily happy for you both," I said. Iskander was a fine fellow, and I thought his sensible approach to life would do Christine a great deal of good. I shook his hand, then embraced Christine. "Have you set the date?"

"Not yet." She returned my hug. "I'd be happy to go before a judge, but Kander wants something more elaborate."

"Is it wrong of me to want to mark the occasion with ceremony?" he asked.

"Of course not," I said, feeling as if I ought to stand up for him.

Christine twisted her hands together. "Whyborne, I know...well, it's terribly silly, but will you give me away?"

Her request warmed me, even though I knew it must be painful for her and Iskander, both. "I'm sorry your father—"

"Bah!" Fire flashed in her eyes. "Devil take my parents, if they can't accept having a half-Egyptian for a son-in-law, no matter how good a man he may be. They're no better than Griffin's accursed father. And even if they would deign to come to the wedding, it's you I'd want to stand by me, anyway."

"I understand," I said, and I did. Christine was my sister, more truly than any who shared my blood, even Persephone. "Of course. I'd love to be a part of your wedding, in any way you wish."

She arched a brow. "Even if I asked you to put on a dress and be my bridesmaid?"

"Even that, although you would be better off with Dr. Gerritson in such a role." I considered Dr. Gerritson a personal friend as well as a colleague, but he did have an unfortunate penchant for dressing in women's underthings at work. Although I admired his independent spirit, I had tried to point out a dress would be a more appropriate choice for a professional setting. He claimed the skirts and neckline inhibited his thinking. "He probably already has the gown for it."

"No doubt." She sat in the visitor's chair. "Now, are you going to tell me what's in the box?"

I handed her the artifact and photograph. Iskander leaned over her shoulder to study them, and a line sprang up between his thick brows. "It can't be one of the Eltdown Shards—they were pottery—but it rather looks like them, doesn't it?"

"The what?" I asked.

Christine frowned as well. "That sounds vaguely familiar."

"The shards were discovered in southern England...oh, it must have been twenty years ago now." Iskander settled on the arm of Christine's chair. Her eyes strayed to the seat of his trousers, and I hoped she was paying attention to the discussion instead of her fiancé's attributes. "I primarily remember them because I'd already developed an interest in archaeology, despite my young age. I collected every newspaper article I could find about them."

"Do you remember any of the details?" I asked. "The culture that created them?"

"That's just the thing." Iskander shifted slightly, his brown hands resting lightly on his knee. "They didn't seem to have a connection to any previously known archaeological finds. The man who dug them up —sod it, I can't recall his name at the moment—swore they were genuine, but given the depth of the stratigraphy, they far predated any known human habitation of the isles."

"A hoax?" Christine asked.

Iskander shrugged. "Impossible to say for certain, but that seemed to be the consensus. It's probably why you've never heard of them. Where did you get this, Whyborne?"

I sank back into my chair, uncertain what to believe. "Griffin's brother sent them. He claims to have found the stele while digging for gold in Alaska."

Christine straightened. "Do you think the find to be genuine?"

"I don't know. I can't imagine what he could gain from a hoax."

Her dark eyes flashed with excitement. "What if the Eltdown Shards were real? Can you imagine—evidence of an ancient seafaring culture that spanned the Old World and the New!"

"Er," I said. This wasn't what I'd intended at all.

"Just think!" She held the artifact up, as if in triumph. "An unknown civilization, and within the borders of American territory! Buried beneath the permafrost along with mammoths, undiscovered and unsuspected until now."

"That would be...something," I agreed, a bit alarmed by her enthusiasm. "The thing is, Christine, I believe I recognize some of the symbols. And not in the context Iskander knows them from."

Iskander frowned. "What do you mean?"

"I'd have to go to the library, but I'm almost certain I've seen them in some arcane writings."

"Oh." He pursed his lips.

A horrible thought occurred to me. "Do you know anything about sorcery in England? What happened to the shards? Eltdown is near Cornwall, isn't it? Could the Endicotts have them?"

His eyes widened in alarm. "Dear heavens, I've no idea! I didn't even know England *had* sorcerers until Christine wrote me about your cousins."

"There's no point in worrying about it now," Christine said with a wave of her hand. "What's important is we might have genuine evidence of an ancient civilization no one else even realizes existed! Seafarers like the Polynesians, perhaps, who might have traveled over vast stretches of the earth. We must investigate further."

Blast, why hadn't I anticipated this? After losing the firman to excavate in Egypt last year, Christine had devoted her time to writing a definitive history of the Sixth Dynasty. I should have guessed she'd long to return to the field and its accompanying thrill of discovery. "But if there's magic involved, it could be dangerous."

"Then what are we dawdling here for, man?" she exclaimed. "We must get to the library and find out if this will revive my career, or kill us all in the process!"

CHAPTER 4

Whyborne

"Ah, Percy, there you are!" exclaimed Bradley Osborne in an overly jovial voice.

I bit back a sigh. Christine and Iskander had taken the fragment for photographing. Once done, she would join me in the library and look through the archived journals for every mention of the Eltdown Shards. I'd gone ahead, as I knew nothing about camera or lighting, and would likely only get in the way.

I'd almost reached the library without encountering anyone save for a few curators. For a moment, I considered pretending I hadn't heard Bradley, but past experience taught me he'd only keep calling until I gave up and acknowledged his presence.

Midmorning light streamed through the high windows lining the outer wall, glowing from the polished wooden floor and glittering on the chain of Bradley's pocket watch. He smiled as he advanced on me, but like his greeting, the expression seemed far too forced, like an actor badly playing a part.

In most of the years I'd worked at the Ladysmith, Bradley found me an easy mark for his jokes and cutting words. Someone he could view with a sort of easy contempt, whom he didn't have to spend much time thinking about otherwise. Now I possessed a better office than he did. Not to mention the ear of the director and museum president, should I choose to have them. Exactly the things Bradley most wanted for himself.

I worried contempt had turned to jealousy, which was far more dangerous.

"Good morning," I said. "Did you need something? I'm in a bit of a hurry, you see."

"Only to bid you a good morning and ask after your health." His smile took on a brittle edge. "And Mr. Flaherty's. How is he these days?"

A whisper of cold slicked my spine. The battle against my brother in the museum foyer revealed me as a sorcerer, but I feared it had also revealed something else. Stanford had not only called me a disgusting sodomite, but shot Griffin with the obvious intention of hurting me.

Everyone present considered the episode part and parcel with the rest of Stanford's mad ranting...or pretended they did, at least. The museum had a long history of ignoring the various eccentricities of its staff, so long as public scandal wasn't involved. As Stanford now resided in a private lunatic asylum, Bradley would find it difficult to damage my reputation in Widdershins.

But certain newspapers in New York would be more than happy to print scandalous rumors about the heir to the Whyborne fortune keeping house with a male lover. Father would crush them, of course, but the suspicion would have been planted.

Griffin swore I'd cost him nothing. His father had been the one to demand too much, to take too much. And I did believe him. But the thought our love might take more from him through some sort of scandal turned my gut to acid.

"Quite well," I said shortly. "Now if you'll excuse me, I have work awaiting me in the library."

Bradley's lip twitched into a sneer, hastily suppressed. "Of course, Percy. I didn't mean to keep you from your dusty tomes. I'm certain your work is quite urgent."

The maelstrom whispered beneath me. The tingle of the power I'd absorbed from the pearl shivered over my nerves.

If I released the magic, with no attempt to shape the result, would it take a similar form as it had in the pearl? Could I curse Bradley, not with death, but something unpleasant?

I took a deep breath. Griffin would never approve of using magic against Bradley, especially for such a trivial reason. "It is," I said, fixing him with a hard look. "But I wouldn't expect you to understand."

There. Let him wonder what I meant.

I walked swiftly away from him. As soon as I came to a window, I looked around, but no one else was in the corridor. Flinging it open, I leaned out. The museum grounds lay below, and I let the arcane power I'd stolen from the curse flow from me in the form of wind. The trees beneath whipped into a frenzy, and the hat of an unfortunate pedestrian tumbled away.

Oh dear. But at least the buzz of power had vanished from beneath my skin.

Thanks to Bradley's delay, Christine caught up with me at the doors to the library. "Done so soon?" I asked in surprise.

"I've no patience for photography," she admitted. "Iskander banished me as soon as we set up the camera and lights."

We stepped into the library. Even as I looked around for a staff member to ask for assistance, a dark figure seemed to materialize at my elbow. "Dr. Whyborne," Mr. Quinn intoned in his sepulchral voice. "How can we assist you today?"

I regarded the head librarian with some unease, but he only stared back with pale eyes, which didn't seem to blink nearly as often as they should. The man had always made me nervous, but the feeling had increased markedly over the last year.

"Er, I need some books," I stammered.

"And in the library, no less," Christine said.

I shot her a glare. "I mean to say, I need some of the books kept under lock."

"Ah." Mr. Quinn's eyes grew even wider. "Excellent. Give me the titles, and I'll bring them to you personally."

What he thought I meant to do with them, I hadn't the slightest guess. Probably unleash some terrible spell on Widdershins, or raise the dead, or something else horrid. I had the awful feeling he would consider such plans an excellent reason to allow me access to the tomes, rather than the reverse. "I, ah, thank you."

"It's our pleasure to serve," Mr. Quinn said, bowing slightly. "Dr. Putnam, have you any requests? Where shall I bring the books? The nook in the southwestern arm of the labyrinth has the most comfortable chairs."

"Er, that will do," I said. Christine told him what she needed, and he glided away a moment later.

"Is it just me, or has he gotten even odder lately?" she asked as we made our way in the direction he'd suggested.

Rumor claimed the convoluted architecture of the library either displayed the final stages of the madness that took the Ladysmith's architect, or had been the driving force behind his insanity. Whatever the case, the librarians were an undeniably odd bunch.

"It isn't just him," I murmured. We passed a group of librarians sorting books for re-shelving. They stopped and bowed to us.

No, to me.

"It seems you've become something of a celebrity," Christine remarked. "Do they do this every time you come in?"

"As of last October, yes. After the fight with Stanford, and the ketoi…" I shook my head. "Everyone else pretends they didn't see anything. I'm not a sorcerer, and there weren't really inhuman monsters from the depths holding them hostage. They all *know,* but they act as if they don't."

A librarian stepped out from the stacks, spotted us, and hurriedly gave way. "Widdershins," he said as I passed. As if it were my name, or a title.

"But here you're practically royalty." Christine grinned. "You should rally them to your banner at the next budget meeting."

"It isn't funny," I muttered.

"Oh, I'm not laughing. Just planning to invoke your name any time I need something found quickly." She rubbed her hands together. "Or —even better—we could tell them to hide any books or journals Bradley needs!"

"Christine, please!"

"Hmm, you're right, he probably doesn't read."

We settled into a nook in the southwestern arm of the labyrinth. Soon enough, Mr. Quinn and two librarians appeared, carrying the books and journals we'd requested. He seemed inclined to hover, so I said, "Thank you. That will be all."

"Of course." Looking disappointed, he retreated. Christine and I exchanged a glance, then went to work.

Ordinarily, I would have resigned myself to a long day of pouring through dusty tomes, as Bradley put it. But with a few hours to contemplate where I might have previously seen such symbols, I was able to narrow down the search considerably.

"Here," I said, keeping my voice low lest I draw the ire of the librarians.

Christine looked up from the journal before her. "What have you found?"

"This is one of the Latin translations of the Pnakotic Manuscripts. What language the translation was made from, and how accurate it might be, is highly questionable." I pushed the heavy book across the table to her. Its iron latch scraped on the wood, and I winced at the sound. "Supposedly this image is a sketch of one of the original scroll fragments. See the writing on it?"

"It certainly looks similar," she agreed. "And it matches the Eltdown Shards. They could still be a hoax…"

"Unlikely." I peered at the etching in the journal in front of her. "The Pnakotic Manuscripts aren't really the sort of thing most people would know about. This is one of the few extant copies—a forger would have had to go to great lengths, when it would have been easier just to make something up."

Excitement gleamed in her eyes. "Then it's real. This stele in Alaska is somehow connected to pottery fragments found in England."

"So it would seem."

She looked up sharply. "You don't sound very excited. What do these manuscripts of yours say?"

"To stay away." I bent over the thick pages, inscribed by some unknown hand centuries ago. "It's impossible to tell how much of this was part of the original scrolls, and how much inserted by the later translator. But it speaks of magically sealing away certain places in order to keep the *umbrae* in check."

"Umbrae?" She frowned. "Shadows? What the devil does that mean?"

I shook my head. "I don't know. From the context, I'm guessing some sort of dangerous creature, but it's impossible to say. Whoever wrote the Pnakotic Manuscripts sealed these *umbrae* away in various places across the earth, never to be disturbed. There is a strong warning against approaching any of these places, especially on *'the night of greatest darkness'* when the seals are at their weakest."

"The winter solstice?" she guessed.

"Yes. And Jack said he's planning to look for more artifacts this winter." I met her gaze. "If this manuscript is right and there is some sort of horror associated with these sites...Griffin's brother is in terrible danger."

CHAPTER 5

Griffin

Even though I felt ill at the news Whyborne had delivered over dinner, I raised my glass of wine. "A toast," I said. "To the happy couple."

We sat in our study, accompanied by Iskander and Christine, whom we'd invited to dinner in part to celebrate of their long-expected engagement, and in part to discuss Jack's artifact. I'd started the meal with a hearty appetite, but by the time we finished, I could barely bring myself to look at the food.

Jack was in imminent danger. Was I to lose my brother so soon after finding him again?

So soon after losing Pa?

"Yes, yes," Christine said, clinking her glass rather brusquely with mine, before downing a good part of its contents. "Kander, tell them what you found in the newspaper archives."

"When Christine told me of the umbrae, I wondered if there had been any..." he paused delicately "...*unusual* deaths connected with the excavation of the Eltdown Shards. I searched through the newspaper archives of the time, to see if I could find something of interest."

I had the terrible feeling I didn't want to know what he'd found. "And?"

"A startling number of local villagers went missing over the same weekend, not long after excavation began. Officials determined they began to celebrate Christmas a bit early and fell through a frozen lake. Their bodies were never recovered, however, and anyone who challenged the findings of the inquest disappeared shortly thereafter."

"The solstice," Whyborne said. "Blast. It seems the Pnakotic Manuscripts were right."

"Jack is in danger." I put aside my wine.

"And anyone else in Hoarfrost." Whyborne absently ran a hand back through his hair. As usual, the dark spikes resisted any attempt to flatten them. "I wonder if the Endicotts did away with the umbra in Eltdown?"

Whyborne's cousins might be dangerous sorcerers, but they were dedicated to the destruction of what they perceived as monsters. Unfortunately, their methods tended to result in the deaths of a great many innocents as well. "They probably did in the villagers too."

"I wouldn't entirely rule it out," Whyborne agreed. "Very well. What are our options?"

"I can't write Jack and warn him. He'd think me—" the word *mad* caught in my throat. Jack had no reason to believe horrors existed beyond the ordinary ones humans perpetrated on each other. A letter would only damage our relationship, and do nothing to dissuade him from disturbing the site further.

"And I can't sit here until spring, knowing there's a valuable archaeological site that might even now be destroyed by overzealous gold miners," Christine added.

"You mean to excavate?" Whyborne exclaimed.

"Why not? An actual globe-spanning civilization, outside of the superstitious ravings about Atlantis, potentially older than any other known culture? Do you think I'd simply sit here and leave it to be torn apart by fools digging for gold? Good gad, man, what sort of scientist are you?"

"The kind who prefers not to be eaten by monsters," he muttered. "But Griffin is right—anyone in Hoarfrost is facing danger, if we can go by the disappearances surrounding the Eltdown excavation. The seals will be at their weakest on the longest night." He stared down at his wine glass as if not really seeing it. "December 21, this year. There isn't a great deal of time to spare."

"I wish we knew what sort of creature this 'umbra' might be," Iskander said. "Did the Pnakotic Manuscripts not give any hints?"

Whyborne shook his head. The firelight caught his dark hair, illuminating the occasional lighter strand, and limned his profile in gold. "Not really. I assume they aren't fond of light, given their name and the fact the longest night of the year seems to favor them. But that describes a great many otherworldly things. Without being certain what we're facing, it might be best to concentrate on learning how to reinforce the magical seals. If we can keep the umbra trapped, wherever it might be, we won't have to fight it."

"Where do you think it would be trapped?" I asked. "Is it something trying to come through from the Outside?"

Not to say I quite understood what the Outside even was. Blackbyrne had tried to summon horrors from the Outside into our world, in the first case I'd worked with Whyborne. And Nitocris, Queen of the Ghūls, somehow withdrew there between her possessions of women throughout the millennia. Possibly the yayhos we'd faced in Threshold had come from there as well, or at least Whyborne had come to believe so.

"It might," Whyborne said. "Or it could be something literally sealed away, in a clay pot or under a stone or...there are a great many possibilities, I'm afraid."

"Well, then." Christine finished her wine. "Our course of action seems clear. I'll go to the director tomorrow. Rather than a full expedition, I'll propose a survey. Just a small team to determine if there's anything worth excavating, stake our claim before any other museums can get there, and leave as quickly as possible. Kander, you can take up your old role and travel ahead. Gather whatever equipment and supplies we need, and act as a liaison with Jack and any other miners who might have a claim to the site."

Iskander's dark brows swooped toward his prominent nose. "But what of our wedding?"

"It can wait," Christine replied impatiently. "We can waste no time —if these seals are truly weakening, we must get to Hoarfrost before December 21."

"I'll go to the director with you, Christine," Whyborne said glumly. "Although I've no idea how to convince him to send me, of all people, on your expedition. Perhaps I can claim a sudden desire to do field work? Do you think he'll believe me?"

"You saved his life last October," Christine said. "And the lives of the board of trustees, the president, and, most importantly, some of the more generous donors."

"And my reward is to tramp about in Alaska. How lovely."

"Oh, do stop complaining." Christine rose to her feet, and the rest of us followed suit automatically. "It's settled. We're off to the Yukon!"

CHAPTER 6

Whyborne

SHORTLY THEREAFTER, I shut the door behind Christine and Iskander. I turned to find Griffin in the hall behind me, one shoulder leaning against the wall, his emerald gaze on me. "Thank you," he said quietly.

"For what?" I asked, puzzled.

Griffin pushed away from the wall as I approached. He tilted his head back to look me in the face. "For accompanying us to the Arctic. I know you hate travel, and we're likely to live even rougher there than in Egypt."

"Do you think so?" I asked in alarm. "I thought there were towns and such near the gold mines. The papers called Dawson the Paris of the North!"

"Somehow I suspect they exaggerated its charms, just a bit." His amused grin told me he thought I was being naïve yet again. "Besides, Dawson and the places like it were boomtowns. Most of them are deserted now the Klondike rush is over."

"Oh." Curse it. "Still, sorcery is involved. What other choice do I have but to grit my teeth and go?"

"That's just it." Griffin caught my lapels and tugged me closer, until we stood pressed together. "You do have a choice. You aren't obligated to travel to the farthest reaches of civilization to save a handful of people you don't even know."

"One of them is your brother," I reminded him. My hands settled at his waist, shaping the line of his hip. "Christine is a brilliant archaeologist, and Iskander's family trained him to fight ghūls, but neither of them are sorcerers." I leaned closer, lips hovering just above his. "And you are my husband. Where you go, I go."

His warm mouth tasted of wine and spice. The kiss began leisurely, then turned more urgent as he nipped lightly at my lower lip with his teeth. When at last we broke apart, he said, "Take me upstairs and make love to me."

I certainly had no desire to refuse such a request. I took his hand and led him to my bedroom on the second floor. We kept two bedchambers, so as to present two sets of used linen to the laundress each week, but never slept apart.

I turned off the lights and lit the night candle with a whisper of power. We kissed, tongues exploring each other's mouths, lips caressing. I pushed his coat from his shoulders and unknotted his tie. We attacked buttons and cuff links, slowly stripping away layers of cloth to reveal skin. My fingers trailed over his body, shaping the familiar planes, finding all the small scars and imperfections.

And a larger one. An ugly scar, left by the caustic touch of the horror beneath Chicago, wrapped about his right thigh. After so long together, I seldom noticed it; it was a part of him, as beloved as the rest.

Of course, I had scars of my own now, tracing the path of lightning from the tips of my fingers to my shoulder. Griffin traced them sometimes, with hands or tongue. Tonight he merely ran his fingers up both arms, the marred and unmarred. His member pushed against my thigh, hard and hot. The pupils of his green eyes went wide with lust, and his breathing turned ragged and eager as he said, "Take me, Ival. Make me *feel* it."

I shoved him onto the bed, climbing in over him. He stretched his hands above his head, wrists loosely crossed in invitation. I pinned them with one hand, and he writhed beneath me. A moan escaped me at the friction of skin on skin. His hard length pressed hot against my belly as I straddled him. I kissed him hungrily, before trailing my lips to his throat. He arched his neck to give me access.

A whimper escaped him when I bit the juncture of neck and shoulder. His hips worked, sliding his cock against my skin, his thigh against my own member. I released his wrists so I could move lower, worrying his nipples with teeth and tongue, then licking down the flat planes of his torso. The scent of bergamot rose from his skin, mingled with sweat and musk.

His cock bobbed against my cheek, as if asking for attention. I licked down to the base, then farther. Shifting my weight, I said, "Spread your legs."

I nuzzled his sac, before dipping lower, drawing a groan from him. In the years since we'd met, I'd learned every inch of his body with an intimacy I'd never imagined having with anyone. And learned a great deal about myself in the process.

We faced months living in God-knew-what conditions in the far north. Would we have our own tent, as we had in Egypt? Or live in a cabin with other men? We always maintained an acceptable fiction as to our relationship in public, but at least we passed our nights in each other's arms. Pretending to have no deeper commitment, with no reprieve day or night, would be agonizing.

Jack could never find out. Griffin's adoptive family had already deserted him because of me. I couldn't bear to cause him even more pain by driving away his blood kin as well.

Anticipating long days of nothing but covert looks, I set myself to pleasuring him with more intent than usual. I traced his puckered ring, teasing and jabbing with my tongue, until he wriggled helplessly.

"I want you," he panted.

I sat back on the bed to look at him. God, I loved seeing him like this: face flushed and breath short, his gaze wild with need. And all for me, *because* of me. "How?" I asked.

He turned, grasped the headboard, and spread himself wide. "Like this. I want you to hold me while you fuck me."

"Yes," I managed to say through a haze of lust. I pulled open the nightstand drawer and retrieved the petroleum jelly.

I took my time preparing him, working his body slowly with my fingers, until he growled, "Damn it, Ival, do you wish me to beg?"

Some nights the answer would be yes, absolutely. But I knew his moods, and this wasn't one of them. "We can't have that, can we?" I asked.

I finally touched my aching member, slicking myself thoroughly. His back arched when I pressed the tip against his fundament, hands tightening on the headboard until his knuckles showed white.

He let out a small cry of pleasure as I worked in, careful not to go too quick. He pushed back against me, asking for more.

I gave it to him, everything I had. Recalling his earlier request, I wrapped my arms around him. The sole advantage of my height was it let me cover him with my body, draping myself protectively over him, while he supported us with his grip on the headboard.

"Yes," he whispered. "Tighter."

I held him close, arms across his chest, hips moving slow and steady. His body gripped my cock, hot and tight, every movement a sweet thrill of pleasure. I slid one hand down to find his erection, wanting him to feel it, too.

He arched his back against me in response. Encouraged, I stroked him in time to my thrusts. "Yes, Ival," he gasped and shuddered. "Faster. Please."

I did as he asked, giving myself over to the blind rhythm of desire. I pressed my face against his neck, inhaling deeply, smelling his sweat and musk. Every shift of skin on skin sent sparks of ecstasy crackling along my nerves. The flame of the candle burned higher, and a breeze born from nowhere ruffled my hair.

Griffin encouraged me with wordless grunts, and I closed my eyes, pleasure cresting like a wave. I cried out against his neck, a night bird echoing me just outside the window. The great vortex of magic turned widdershins beneath us.

Griffin shouted, bucking in my grasp. A moment later, his hot seed slicked my fingers.

I slowed my pace, wringing a last sigh from him before letting go. I remained for a long moment, still wrapped around him, our breathing gradually returning to normal. When I felt steady on my feet again, I pulled free and padded to the washbasin, attending first to myself, then to him.

When I returned to bed, he'd collapsed onto his side. I slid between the sheets, touching his face gently with my hand.

"Do you feel better?" I asked. "And do you want to talk about it?"

CHAPTER 7

Griffin

I OFFERED IVAL a rueful smile. "Was it obvious?"

"To me." Ival linked his hand with mine, gazing into my eyes across a few inches of pillow. "But I like to think I know you a bit."

"Just a bit?" I teased. My body felt limp in the afterglow of pleasure. So much easier to close my eyes and fall asleep beside him than think of these things.

"And now you're trying to derail the conversation."

I turned my gaze from his. The gentle light of the candle sparked off the rings on our joined hands, warming the gold and finding a hidden sheen on the black pearl adorning Whyborne's. "I'm afraid."

It was a hard thing to admit, even to him.

"Of losing Jack?" he guessed.

"In part." There were so many other things to fear. "I only just found him. We've merely exchanged letters, but he seems a good man. A decent man." Like Pa. "But I'm afraid of losing you, too."

Ival's fingers tightened on mine. "What do you mean?"

"We've seen so much horror and death since we met." I finally met his gaze again, needing him to understand. "You came so close to dying in Egypt. And last year, when you went off alone to confront the Endicotts…"

"Persephone went with me," he objected.

"But I didn't." Because his damned brother shot me. Watching Ival walk out the doors of the museum, staying behind while he went to save us all, had been the hardest moment of my life. It gave me the strength to force my bleeding body up, to go after him, to do something, anything, to help.

The sight of him floating in midair over the ruined bridge, blue fire pouring from the scars on his arm, from his eyes, had seared itself into my memory. And then he'd fallen into the river, where he would surely have drowned if Christine hadn't gone in after him. While I stood by and watched helplessly, terrified he was dead, or the maelstrom had burned away his mind, and unable to do anything to save him.

"What if you had died?" My voice cracked on the words. "If Fenton hadn't come back for Christine and me, or if Christine hadn't been there, you would have perished. And I couldn't have done anything to prevent it."

"Oh darling." He pulled me close, tossing his leg over my hip and twining his arms about me. "I didn't know it weighed on you so."

I clung to him, hiding my face in his neck. Breathing his scent of salt and ambergris, of the ocean wind. "Things have been so much better this last year. Quiet. I thought perhaps our lives would be normal now, or as normal as they can be in this town." I swallowed against the tightness in my throat. "And now this, with Jack, and Pa, and everything. I'm dragging you back into danger again, and if anything happened to you..."

I felt like a raw nerve, like a clam with its shell pried open and its soft body exposed. His hands stroked my back soothingly, and his lips pressed against my hair. "Shh. It's all right. Is that what you've been having nightmares about?"

"No." I felt wretched putting this on him. "Or yes, occasionally. But most of my nightmares have been about Egypt, except *I'm* the daemon chasing us. And this morning, for a moment I was so sure I recognized the stele fragment, but I didn't, I couldn't. I'm afraid...what if the doctors at the asylum weren't completely wrong? What if I do have some seed of madness in me?"

"Griffin, listen to me." He propped himself up on his elbow, gripping my shoulder with his other hand. "You aren't mad. There was no justice to your confinement."

I avoided his gaze. I'd told him how I'd shrieked at the other Pinkertons about the monster beneath Chicago, but he didn't really understand. They'd thought me mad, yes, but I'd *felt* mad. My mind had been full of screams and pain, of the sight of Glenn's bare skull and the gelatinous thing slowly dissolving him alive.

He caught my chin and turned my head, so I had to look at him. "As for the stele, there's a perfectly reasonable explanation. The shards were discovered in 1882. You would have been, what, thirteen at the time? You probably saw a newspaper article, then forgot all about it."

The explanation was so sensible I was shamed not to have thought of it myself. "You're probably right."

"Of course I am. And as for the dreams, I'm sure they're just some trick of the mind. Strange, but not aberrant." He ran his thumb tenderly over my jaw. "You've been under a great deal of stress, and this discovery of your brother's has only made it worse. But you'll be all right. You're a good man, Griffin Flaherty, and I love you more than I can possibly say."

I held him tight. "I love you, too, Ival." And hoped he was right.

CHAPTER 8

Whyborne

TRUE TO HER word, Christine dragged me into the director's office first thing the next morning. She began with demanding funds to make a survey, and ended cataloging the list of horrors that might be visited on an invaluable archaeological site should we not arrive quickly enough.

The director seemed a bit taken aback. On the one hand, he'd dealt with Christine before and was well prepared for her tendency to simply bully everyone into submission. On the other, her record spoke for itself. The discovery of the tomb of Pharaoh Nephren-ka had catapulted the Ladysmith into the international spotlight, not to mention brought in a great deal of revenue.

When she finally ran out of steam, I leaned forward in my chair. "I've examined the fragment in question," I said. "The markings on it match those of the Eltdown Shards. If some unknown civilization lies buried beneath the permafrost and is destroyed in a stampede, the loss to science could be incalculable."

The implication, that the loss of revenue would be equally incalculable, wasn't lost on Dr. Hart. Less than an hour later, we left his office with orders to make our way to Alaska and secure the find as quickly as possible.

Furious activity filled the next two weeks. Iskander left within a few days, bound for St. Michael to meet Jack and secure whatever we'd need to survive a winter in Alaska. Most of the supplies would be shipped immediately from St. Michael to Hoarfrost, before the Yukon River froze in mid November. Although far more expensive than purchasing supplies in the states and bringing them with us to the territory, it would allow us to travel light when we arrived.

The director might have rethought his permission given the expense, but a quiet note to Father ensured Whyborne Railroad and Industries helped underwrite the expedition. What he'd want from me in exchange for the favor I didn't wish to contemplate. At least I wouldn't have to worry about it until we returned a few months hence.

On the final day prior to our departure, I left my office a bit before closing. Miss Parkhurst rose to her feet on seeing me. "You're leaving, Dr. Whyborne?"

"I'm afraid so," I said glumly. I disliked travel of any sort, and this trip promised to be even more taxing than our journey to Egypt. How was poor Iskander faring in St. Michael? Had the cold been a terrible shock to him, after spending his life in England and Egypt?

"I'll—I mean, we'll—miss you." A light flush spread across her cheeks.

I winced. "I'm sorry you have to return to the general secretarial pool while I'm gone. With any luck I'll be back by spring."

"Oh, no, it's not...never mind." Her color deepened. "I-I have something for you." She opened a drawer. "The papers all say it's terribly cold in Alaska, and I thought you'd need a scarf."

Now truly crimson, she thrust out what was possibly the ugliest scarf I'd ever seen. Its color could only be described as puce, and it appeared to have been knitted by a drunken spider.

"Er, thank you?" I took it from her, trying to look as though I enjoyed the ghastly color.

"Do you like it?" she asked anxiously. "I made it myself. For luck."

"It's lovely," I said, although I meant the gesture rather than the scarf. I pulled off the much more somber scarf I wore and replaced it with the puce. A light floral scent rose from the folds, and I recognized it as the perfume she ordinarily wore. Had she accidentally spilled some while knitting? "Thank you, Miss Parkhurst. You've always been very kind to me, and...well. I appreciate it."

A tremulous smile touched her mouth. "I'm glad you like it. Safe travels, Dr. Whyborne. I'll...I'll be here waiting when you get back."

It seemed an odd thing to say. Had one of my colleagues, dissatisfied with his secretary, tried to steal away mine? Just the thought of having to work with a stranger, perhaps one less agreeable than Miss Parkhurst, put my nerves on edge. "Thank you," I said fervently. "Your loyalty means a great deal to me."

I left the museum, pausing on the bottom of the steps leading down to the sidewalk. The sounds and sights of Widdershins spread out around me: rushing hansoms, the occasional motor car, the newly installed electric trolley making its way toward River Street. I breathed deep, smelling the scent of fish and salt permeating every corner of the town.

Instead of making straight for home, I wandered. My feet took me almost of their own accord to the Front Street Bridge over the Cranch River. The eye of the maelstrom.

The bridge had been rebuilt last summer. I paced to the center of the span, standing against the low railing while traffic of every sort clattered behind me. Beneath my feet turned the magical vortex that gave Widdershins its name. Lines of arcane energy poured down from the land and spiraled up from the sea to meet here, in a single point of titanic power.

I'd touched that power last year. It had filled me, burning through my blood, leaking through the scars on my arm until my shirtsleeve turned to ash. And for a moment I'd felt every living thing in the city—every heartbeat, every footstep, every quavering breath.

Some believed Widdershins possessed a will of its own. It collected people to it, for unknown reasons. And once it claimed a person, or a family, or a bloodline, they would never be able to leave for very long. I'd always hated travel, had taken a job at the museum here, instead of leaving this place and my family behind. Mother had remained, even when she might have taken up residence at a sanitarium for her long illness.

I'd left before, for months at a time while at university. And later during our trip to Egypt. But at the time, Widdershins hadn't awakened to my hand. And though it slept now, like an uneasy beast, I couldn't deny I'd grown used to feeling the whisper of power beneath my feet. What would happen when I left?

Nothing, hopefully. Perhaps it would even be for the best. Maybe whatever I'd roused would return to deeper dreams without my presence, and when we came back everything would be ordinary again. Or as ordinary as Widdershins had ever been, at least.

Perhaps. But some doors once opened could never be shut again.

CHAPTER 9

Whyborne

By the time we put into port in Alaska a month later, I was heartily sick of the steamer that had brought us to these wild shores. And yet my first glimpse of land over the rails quelled whatever desire I had to leave the ship.

The journey began auspiciously enough. We'd traversed the country in comfort, thanks to Whyborne Railroad and Industries. I'd felt a bit odd once we'd left Widdershins, as though I were slightly off balance, but the luxuries of our private car softened any sensations of discomfort.

The steamer awaiting us in San Francisco, however, provided no such amenities. The thing was more scow than passenger ship, and packed to the rafters with exactly what Christine most feared: a hundred men and women who, having missed the great stampede to the Klondike two years ago, now rushed to the new finds in Nome and Hoarfrost.

The sight of so many people who, as she put it, wanted to destroy her dig site, sent her wild with indignation. Griffin tried to calmly point out they would likely be stuck in St. Michael for the winter, until the spring thaw allowed them and their goods to be transported up the Yukon. It did little to improve her mood.

I hid in the cramped berth I shared with Griffin and tried to avoid everyone for the duration of the voyage. My sensation of being slightly off, as though some mild illness weakened me, persisted. Combined with my intense dislike of traveling on the water, it left me miserable and short tempered. When not complaining of our fellow passengers, Christine teased me for being a fish-man afraid of water. I quickly tired of her sport, and our barbed exchange ended with us thoroughly out of sorts with one another.

As a result, I'd been desperate with longing to leave the blasted steamer and have dry land beneath my feet again. Now I viewed the wharf, such as it was, and wondered if I hadn't appreciated the confines of the ship quite as much as I should. The thin sunlight, which lasted only a few hours at this latitude, revealed a chaotic scene of ships, cargo, people, and animals. Stevedores cursed in French, English, and Russian, horses whinnied in alarm as they were hoisted off the deck of a nearby ship, and dogs barked incessantly. Unlike the old quays of Widdershins, these docks were hastily built from raw lumber and looked as if they might collapse at any moment. The solid land beyond was nothing but a churned mess of half-frozen mud, snow, ice, and dog waste.

I'd expected to see a town much like Widdershins—not as venerable, of course, but consisting of orderly streets lined with shops and homes. Instead, the place was a ramshackle sprawl of tents, shacks, and rough buildings, its roads nothing more than raw muck.

"This is St. Michael?" I asked faintly, in the desperate hope the steamer had put into the wrong port. The bitterly cold, dry air stung exposed skin and savaged my nose and throat with each breath. I tugged the hideous puce scarf up over the lower half of my face, grateful when it blunted the cold.

"I'd advise against that," Griffin said, pulling the scarf back down. "The humidity from your breath will soak it, and the whole thing will end up frozen to your face."

Wonderful. "And the town? I expected something a bit more... established? I thought the Russians founded it seventy years ago."

"It's still a frontier town." Griffin noticed the expression on my face and grinned. "I suspect by the time we reach Hoarfrost, you'll look back on St. Michael with great fondness as a bastion of civilization."

Clapping me on the shoulder, he turned away to retrieve our baggage. I stared at the filthy collection of buildings—I could hardly term it a city—with mounting horror. What had I gotten myself into?

Iskander awaited us on the dock, heavily bundled in a fur-lined parka. Had his Egyptian blood adapted to the cold, or had he spent the weeks cursing Griffin's brother for drawing us here?

A smile spread across his face when he spotted us—or, rather, Christine—coming down the gangplank. He hurried over, and, ignoring the curses of the dockworkers trying to unload the ship, took her thickly gloved hands in his. "Christine," he said. "It's good to see you again."

She flushed, but didn't look away from his eyes. "And you."

Griffin cleared his throat politely. "Perhaps we should get our baggage unloaded?"

Iskander released Christine and took a hasty step back, folding his hands behind him as if to restrain himself from touching her. "Yes. You brought everything on the list?"

Although most of our supplies already awaited us in Hoarfrost—assuming they hadn't met with some disaster on the way, at least—we'd brought a few things with us.

"Of course we did," Christine replied. "Food for the trail, clothing, and medicine for each of us."

"And lime juice and tomatoes to ward off scurvy?"

"Scurvy!" I exclaimed. "No one said anything about scurvy to me."

"It's quite the problem, I understand," Iskander said. "As you can imagine, there is little opportunity for fresh food in the hinterlands once winter sets in."

"Jack didn't come with you?" Griffin peered around at the crowd. A little frown line sprang up between his brows.

"He needed a few moments to attend to some business, as we'll be leaving in the morning," Iskander replied. "I'm sure he'll be along shortly."

"Well, come along, let's see to our things, before the captain decides to fling everything overboard," Christine said.

As Iskander called to some of the dockworkers, I turned to Griffin. "Did anyone mention scurvy to you?"

"Jack spoke of it in his letters." Griffin rubbed at the stubble on his chin, not looking me in the eye. "I didn't think it worth mentioning."

"Is there anything else you haven't bothered to mention?"

"I'm going to see if Iskander needs any help." Griffin patted me on the arm. "Why don't you wait for us over by those crates?"

Curse the man. I glared at his back as he beat a hasty retreat.

As Griffin had suggested, I found a quiet—well, quieter—spot to wait, well out of the way. Nearby, a troop of women greeted the newcomers from the steamer. Their clothing, revealing even in these frigid temperatures, left little doubt as to their profession. They smiled and flirted, but I caught sight of a few shivering. Should I offer one of them my coat?

Before I could determine the polite course of action, two men strolled past, deep in conversation. One I recognized from the steamer: a strapping young fellow with a strong Iowa accent, chasing the prospect of gold. The other was much more finely dressed than anyone else I'd yet seen on the docks.

"I've made my fortune," the well-dressed man said. "But I still have an unworked claim, right beside the one I pulled a million dollars out of. Now, I'm ready to get back to civilization, so it's no good to me. I don't suppose you'd be interested in buying me out?"

The young man's eyes widened. "For how much, sir?"

"Why, if I asked for what it's worth, thousands of dollars, at least." The older man smiled genially. "But as I said, I've plenty of money already. And, just between us, you remind me of myself, when I first arrived. I'd like to give you a break, the way I would have wanted someone to give me a break."

"Someone ought to give you a broken leg, Callahan," said a new voice.

The newcomer ambled up, his easy gait belying the hard look in his emerald green eyes. His animal hide coat more closely resembled what an Eskimo might wear than the mackinaws sported by most of the others on the dock. A fur hat crowned his chestnut locks, and his cocky grin added to devilish good looks.

Callahan's own smile slipped. "I don't know what you mean."

"Oh, course you do." The newcomer clapped Callahan on the shoulder. "Have you introduced yourself properly to the cheechako?" Turning to the young man, he bowed slightly. "This here is Bill Callahan, the town's biggest swindler. Picks a likely fool off every boat and offers to sell a rich claim at a bargain price. Of course, the claim doesn't exist."

The young man's eyes went wide with alarm. "Er, excuse me," he said, and hurried away.

Callahan pulled free, his face dark with anger. "Devil take you, Hogue. I don't know what you're playing at these days, but you'd better watch your back. Someone might put a bullet in it."

Hogue?

As Callahan stormed away, I called, "Jack Hogue?"

"That's me," Hogue said brightly. "What can I do for you, sir?"

"Please, allow me to introduce myself," I said, extending my hand. "I'm Dr. Percival Endicott Whyborne, with the Ladysmith Expedition."

Surprise widened his eyes, although I couldn't imagine why. What on earth had Griffin said about me in his letters? Then Hogue's smile returned to its previous brilliance. "A pleasure to meet you, Dr. Whyborne." Up close, his resemblance to Griffin became obvious.

They had the same eyes, the same hair, even the same grin. A spray of freckles decorated Hogue's nose and cheeks, just as they did Griffin's.

Although he would never know it, this man was in a way my brother-in-law. "Please, it's just Whyborne," I said. "We might not have corresponded, but any brother of Griffin's is a friend of mine."

He grinned, a devilish smile I knew well from seeing it on Griffin's lips. "Jack, then."

"Whyborne!"

For once, my height gave me an advantage, and I spotted Griffin quickly. "Griffin! Over here!" I called back. A moment later, he'd pushed through the crowd to join us.

"Griffin?" Jack asked. His voice sounded oddly hopeful.

Griffin's eyes widened at the sight of his brother. His tremulous smile made my heart ache. "Jack? Brother?"

Jack laughed and pulled Griffin into an embrace, their first in over a quarter century. I shuffled back a few paces, wishing I could have given them more privacy for their reunion.

"I can hardly believe it," Griffin said.

"Here, let me look at you." Jack held Griffin at arm's length, still clasping his shoulders in his hands. He stood slightly taller than Griffin, and his nose had a crook to it where an old break hadn't set properly. Otherwise, they looked remarkably alike. "My baby brother, all grown up."

Griffin blinked rapidly. "Yes." He swallowed. "We have so much to talk about. Our whole lives to catch up on."

"Quite," Jack said. "But there will be plenty of time on the trail. For now we need to get your things off the ship and packed onto the sleds. I've hired some fellows to help out, but even so, there's not much daylight left."

"Of course." Griffin nodded, but couldn't keep the smile from his face. "Let's get to work."

Chapter 10

Griffin

"How many to a bed, did you say?" Whyborne asked, sounding a bit faint.

I put an expression of mild concern on my face, although in truth I wasn't surprised in the slightest. Having been to many a frontier town—albeit never one so damnably cold—I'd guessed our accommodations would be a far cry from our hotel in Threshold, let alone Shepheard's in Cairo. But, as with the scurvy, I'd neglected to mention the details when discussing it with Whyborne.

Not to suggest I'd truly wished to deceive him. Nor had I omitted things because I feared he would otherwise refuse to come. But Christine and I quietly agreed that this way, we would only have to listen to Whyborne's complaints once we actually arrived, as opposed to the entire trip here.

"Four," Iskander replied, rather apologetically. We stood in the cramped front room of the hotel, which doubled as a saloon and restaurant. Men sat at rough-hewn tables, and a few of the town's women circulated among them. The air stank of wet wool, raw lumber, and unwashed bodies.

"Four," Whyborne repeated.

"The beds aren't narrow—they're made extra wide," Iskander offered. "They aren't what one would call comfortable, and of course there's the danger of lice, but they're quite warm at least."

Whyborne paled at the mention of lice. The color looked particularly bad when paired with the puce scarf.

"We've roughed it before," I said, patting his arm. "Egypt was hardly a pleasure jaunt. And it is only for one night."

My reminder didn't serve to cheer him. "Not that I'll sleep a moment of it. I don't mind living rough, but..."

"Don't you worry," Jack said. He gave Whyborne a bright grin. "St. Michael might be rough, but it's no Skagway. None of these fellows will try to rob you in your sleep, I promise."

Ival's look of alarm confirmed my guess he hadn't even considered the possibility until now. "Oh, do stop complaining, Whyborne," Christine said. "We're all exhausted, and standing about isn't going to change things."

"Easy for you to say," he muttered. Christine would of course be bunking with the two or three other respectable—or mostly respectable—ladies who had come on the steamer with us. I suspected their small room in the back of the hotel would be far more comfortable than ours, if only because it wouldn't be packed to the rafters with snoring men.

"Perhaps we should turn in," Iskander suggested. "An early start and all that."

"Yes, quite." Christine looked as if she wished to say something further to him, but felt constrained by our presence. It must have been difficult, having been separated for so long, but unable to touch or speak openly without inviting scandal. At least Whyborne and I could slip away alone without causing comment.

Of course, once they married, Christine and Iskander would be expected to sleep in the same bed, and do so openly. I pressed my thumb against the heavy band on my left hand, the gold warm from the heat of my body. There was no reason to resent Christine; it was hardly her fault, and she'd been nothing if not staunchly loyal.

Still, it meant this trip would probably include an extended interlude of celibacy, unless we were exceedingly quick and discreet about things. Another fact I hadn't mentioned to Whyborne.

Jack turned to me. "Would you care to get a drink before turning in?"

"Of course." I tried to tamp down on a mix of both excitement and trepidation. I'd searched for my brother for so long...but there were so many things I could never share with him.

"Good night," Whyborne said. He didn't look any more pleased than before.

I longed to touch his hand, but such a fond gesture was impossible in front of Jack. I only said, "Sleep well."

He shot me a glare, before following Iskander to the rickety stairs leading to the second floor.

"He's a bit grumpy, isn't he?" Jack observed when we were alone.

I chuckled. "A bit."

"And the scarf is...interesting."

"A gift from an admirer," I said, although Whyborne would never have agreed with my assessment. Poor Miss Parkhurst.

Jack led the way to a pair of empty seats at the end of one of the long tables. A Yukon stove lent a pleasant warmth to the air. "Two whiskies, Madge," Jack called to one of the girls. Judging by her dress, buttoned up to her chin, she was there to serve drinks and food and nothing else. Even so, I found her more attractive than the prostitutes; she had a stern set to her chin and a gleam in her eye.

I preferred the company of men, but women appealed to me as well. I'd slept with more than a few, usually in service to one of my cases when I'd been a Pinkerton, and enjoyed the experience. Still, I'd never really considered marrying and having a family, like many of the men I'd met in the bathhouses did.

"Do you play poker?" Jack asked, reaching into his coat for a pack of cards.

"I'm a fair hand," I replied. "Shall we play for pennies?"

Jack laughed. "Gold dust is the currency of the North, brother. But I have a few pennies left in my pocket."

The serving woman brought our drinks. I lifted mine in salute. "To family," I said.

Jack grinned and clinked his against mine. "To family," he agreed.

The whiskey burned going down, but it wasn't as bad as some of the rotgut I'd imbibed over the years. Jack only sipped his, then set it aside, rather than drinking the entire shot at a go as most would have done. Was he the sort of man who liked to keep his wits about him?

As Jack considered his hand, he said, "How well do you know Dr. Whyborne?"

I hadn't expected the conversation to enter dangerous territory so quickly. Keeping my face neutral, I shrugged easily. "Well enough," I said. "As I mentioned in my letters, we're close friends. Why do you ask?"

Jack studied his cards, then raised the bet by a penny. "I noticed your rings during dinner."

Damn it. Should I have taken mine off? Or asked Ival to remove his?

Shame washed through me on the heels of the thought. How could I even consider such a thing? I'd chosen him, and I'd never regretted it for a moment. I only regretted the split with Pa.

"We belong to the same society," I replied, drawing three cards. "Widdershins is full of clubs and secret societies. Some of the more powerful families are members, which means most of the cases that come my way have a certain monetary benefit to them."

"I see." Jack discarded a single card. "I assume the different colors of the pearls indicate a different rank in the society?"

"Astute." I needed to turn this conversation from my fabricated life. "You should have been a detective yourself, instead of mining for gold."

Jack finished his drink and beckoned for another round. "I've done well enough."

"And now you find yourself in possession of an archaeological find instead of gold."

"Oh, there's gold in the claim, too. But Nicholas thought the stele might be more valuable." Jack settled back.

"I'm glad you decided to send it my way." I upped the ante by another penny.

"As am I." For a moment, Jack's smile faltered. Then he shook his head and smiled again. "I imagine Dr. Whyborne showed quite the interest in it from the beginning."

"He is a scholar," I said cautiously. What did he mean to get at? Or did I read too much into harmless remarks? "An unknown, possibly ancient, system of writing was impossible for him to resist."

"I expect it was." Jack frowned slightly and discarded another card. "Still, he isn't of the usual...type...one tends to find in the gold fields."

The men seated at the tables around us were lean and tough as whips, their skin rough and features hardened from the demands of frontier life. Whyborne, to be charitable, was not the most athletic of men. I looked at him and saw the brave man I'd fallen in love with, not to mention a powerful sorcerer. But a stranger likely wouldn't see anything beyond his bookish appearance.

I smiled ruefully. "I can't argue with your assessment. But don't worry. I won't say I think he'll enjoy our expedition, but he'll endure it well enough."

"I'll take your word for it." Jack laid down his cards. "Straight flush."

"Curse it," I said good-naturedly. "Four of a kind. Shall we play again?"

Chapter 11

Whyborne

I lay rigidly on my back in the bed. To my left, a bony man twitched and muttered in his sleep. To my right, an enormous fellow let out snores that could probably be heard in Canada. The bunk above us sagged alarmingly, and the entire room echoed to a chorus of snores, wheezing, and other, even more indelicate sounds. I doubted most of the men had bathed this week, and those who didn't reek of sweat were pickled in alcohol.

At least it was warm. That had to count for something. Didn't it?

The squirmer on my left flung a loose arm over my chest. "Mabel," he mumbled.

Enough. I could take no more. I didn't know who Mabel might be, but I certainly had no desire to take on her role. Given his breath, the real Mabel probably wouldn't have either.

I slid out of the covers and climbed rather awkwardly over the large man on my right. "Sorry, sorry," I whispered, and hoped he didn't take my inadvertent groping the wrong way. I rather liked my teeth where they were. Fortunately, he only snorted sleepily and rolled over. Freed at last, I found my sealskin boots, scarf, moose hide mittens, and twill parka amidst the other jumble of clothing.

Where I meant to go, I didn't know, exactly. Perhaps I could order a drink at the saloon downstairs and pretend to pass out. Would they leave me there unmolested as I'd already paid for a bed? Or perhaps one of the prostitutes would let me sleep in her tent if I offered her ordinary rate. Did they charge by the hour or the customer?

I imagined someone spotting me emerging from a prostitute's tent and felt faint. Perhaps not.

The crowd at the saloon had thinned considerably. Griffin and Jack sat not far from the stove, playing cards. I started toward them, then caught myself. Griffin surely wanted time to get to know Jack on his own, without my hovering.

I hadn't imagined it would bother me for Jack not to know of our relationship. And yet I couldn't help but think how different the situation would have been, had I been Griffin's wife instead of his husband. All other things aside, Jack would have looked on me as part of his family, someone who had a right to Griffin's affection and something of a claim on his.

For all the terrible things I could say about Father—and heavens knew I had plenty—he'd made Griffin a part of family gatherings even before Mother went to the sea. True, most of his acceptance stemmed from the fact he viewed me as illogically obstinate on all points, and thus knew he might as well resign himself to my male lover, as I wouldn't change to please him or anyone else.

And of course Mother adored Griffin from the first. Persephone appeared fond of him, but the ketoi didn't seem remotely interested whether or not the sex of one's spouse matched one's own. In truth, I had far more family—and friends—who understood our relationship than I had any right to expect. How could I complain when Griffin's family, adoptive or otherwise, didn't number among them?

Perhaps a walk outside would clear my head. I pulled up my fur-lined hood, tugged on my mittens, and slipped out through the door.

And instantly regretted it. Dear heavens, it was cold. Not nearly as cold as it would be in the interior, but enough to steal my breath and nip at the skin of my cheeks.

Still, turning around and immediately rushing back into the saloon would attract attention and make me look a fool in front of Jack. I didn't want to embarrass either Griffin or myself, so I huddled as deeply as possible into my parka and started off at a brisk walk. I'd go a short distance, then return to the hotel. Perhaps the relief at being warm again would overcome the awfulness of my surroundings, and I'd drift happily off to sleep without caring if my bedmate called me "Mabel."

I found myself grateful for the fur lining my parka and for the sealskin boots. Few lights showed—I hadn't taken into account such a place wouldn't have any street lamps—and only the stars and fat, full moon illuminated the frozen mud of the roadway.

Not to suggest the town slept peacefully—far from it. Dogs howled in their multitudes, a maddening chorus of barks and yips. The gambling halls and brothels did an excellent business despite the hour. The sound of a badly tuned piano drifted out from one as I ventured past. Burly men in mackinaws went from one tent to the next, swearing and shouting.

Hadn't I read something earlier in the year about Congress providing funds to the District of Alaska to curb lawlessness? Or was I misremembering things? I certainly hoped a cry for help would bring a policeman of some sort, and yet I began to doubt it.

I really should go back to the hotel. My bed partners might not be pleasant, but at least they weren't dangerous.

Decided, I turned around and found myself face-to-face with a man.

I couldn't make out his features—his hood was drawn far forward, throwing them in deep shadow, and he wore a scarf wrapped around the lower part of his face. He stood rather closer to me than I would have liked. How had I missed the sound of his footsteps behind me?

"Excuse me," I said automatically.

"You wish to break open the mountains and release the great worm," he growled in a low, threatening voice.

The devil. Was the man drunk? I stepped back hastily and held up my hands. "I assure you, I have no intention of breaking anything," I said.

Apparently he didn't believe me, because he raised his arm. A long dagger flashed in the moonlight.

I let out a startled shout and scrambled back from him. My foot caught in a rut, and I fell, tailbone impacting painfully with mud frozen into the consistency of concrete. He lunged at me, blade swinging down, and I shouted the secret name of fire.

Fortunately, I rolled to the side even as I did so, because the spell did not a damned bit of good. The blade flashed red with heat, and the smell of scorched leather filled the air, but his heavy mitten prevented a burn as surely as it held back frostbite.

Blast.

I made it to my feet and ran. Boots pounded after me, and I stretched my long legs to their fullest. My assailant was quite a bit shorter, but didn't seem to have any trouble keeping up with me. The cold air burned my lungs and stripped moisture from my throat.

My steps turned instinctively in the direction of the sea. The waves pounded against the shore, the occasional gleam of white marking where a small floe of ice had been tossed onto the strand. If I could only make it...

He tackled me from behind, and I fell heavily. His body landed atop me, and I snapped my head back hard. My skull impacted with his jaw, and his teeth cracked loudly together. He fell heavily to the side, and I gathered my limbs beneath me.

There. A net, hanging from the nearby dock.

I tore off my mittens so I could grasp the thick cords. Even as I hauled myself up, the net began to shake under another's weight.

Still. I was close enough.

The maelstrom of Widdershins might not turn beneath me, but I had the blood of the sea in my veins. There came an angry roar, the cold water ripping across the sand. The man below me let out a startled cry as the tide suddenly rushed in, lapping about his waist.

I didn't wait to see if he washed out to sea. Hauling myself onto the dock, I ran in the direction of the hotel without looking back.

By the time I reached the door, I was half frozen and completely out of breath. The bar had closed for the night, the saloon empty save for Griffin, who still sat at one of the tables. As I entered, he shot to his feet. "I was about to come looking for you," he said. "Where on earth have you been?"

My teeth chattered. "I couldn't sleep, so I went for a walk." God, it sounded stupid even to me.

Griffin's expression suggested he agreed with my assessment. "You went for a walk? Whyborne, this isn't Widdershins. St. Michael is no Skagway, as Jack said, but it's not the sort of place to go wandering about alone!"

"Well...yes. I couldn't sleep, and you were busy talking to Jack, and it seemed the thing to do." I didn't want to admit to the extent of my foolishness, but had no real choice. "Except I was set upon."

"Set upon?" He started to reach for me, then seemed to recall we weren't in private surroundings. "Are you hurt?"

"Only my pride." I sighed. "Less than twenty-four hours in Alaska, and already someone has tried to kill me."

CHAPTER 12

Griffin

I managed to coax Ival into bed, securing us spaces beside each other by whispering to one man that my friend had gotten terribly drunk and might vomit at any moment. It convinced him to stagger to another berth, and allowed poor Ival to sleep on the outside edge of the bunk, with me as a barrier between him and the next man.

Still, sleep came slowly for us both. Who had attacked him? And why? The words he'd related sounded like the ravings of a drunkard or a lunatic.

"Could it have anything to do with the umbra?" I whispered in Whyborne's ear, as we lay together in the crowded bed. "This 'worm' he mentioned."

"I've no idea," he whispered back. His breath stirred the small hairs of my ear, and sent blood rushing to my cock. I wasn't at all looking forward to the upcoming days of enforced celibacy. "And 'break open the mountains?' None of it makes sense. The Eltdown Shards were found nowhere near a mountain, or what passes for a mountain in England, anyway."

"Still, a random lunatic seems unlikely."

"Agreed." Whyborne sighed.

Well, with any luck the fellow had been swept out to ocean and frozen amidst the ice floes. A callus way of thinking, perhaps, but as he'd tried to kill Ival, I couldn't find any pity in my heart for him.

The next morning, we gathered around the breakfast table. Iskander declared his desire to take a photograph of the entire expedition. Crowding in so he could capture everyone gave me an excuse to fling a comradely arm around Ival's shoulders. I'd have to remember to ask Iskander if he would consent to taking a private portrait when we returned to Widdershins.

There was no sign of the sun when we left our hotel. The stars blazed above, shockingly bright in the cold, clear air. Our guides already waited with the sleds, busy strapping the howling, barking dogs into their harness. One man coaxed leather moccasins onto the dogs' feet. Presumably the dogs were used to such footgear, as they wore them with good humor.

"Ordinarily most of our guides would be Tagish," Jack said. "Or Russian creoles like Vanya. But the measles outbreak this summer...it was an awful thing to see. Whole towns left abandoned, and at least half the aboriginal population of St. Michael carried off. The Russian creoles died in droves as well. At least I could bring men from Hoarfrost with me, and I'm an old hand at mushing myself. Otherwise we might have been in trouble."

"I wouldn't mind learning how to drive a sled myself," I said, stopping to pet one of the enthusiastic dogs. Whyborne stayed well back, regarding them with great uncertainty.

"I'd love to teach you." Jack looked around. "Speaking of Vanya, where is he? We need to get started."

One of the other guides shrugged. "I haven't seen him, Mr. Hogue."

In the end, the search for the missing Vanya severely delayed our departure. The wait wore on Christine's nerves, and she cursed the missing man roundly in Arabic as the day—such as it was, given the lack of sunlight—stretched on. As usual in the field, she wore a pair of men's trousers in lieu of a skirt. The guides stared at her openly, although to be fair they gave Whyborne some rather dubious looks as well.

At last, Jack returned alone. "I've no idea," he said. "Vanya seemed a solid fellow. I wouldn't have thought him likely to desert us."

"Probably drunk somewhere," one of the men opined. "Dirty creole. Lazy drunkards to the last man."

"What else would you expect from someone whose father was a squawman?" another guide put in. There came a general round of nodding, as if the statement were too obvious to contradict.

I glanced at Iskander, who wore a rather fixed expression on his face. I doubted the guides held any better opinion of Arabs than they did Indians, although presumably the fact Iskander was in charge of their pay might curb their tongues. In his hearing, anyway.

"We should go," Jack said brusquely, cutting off any further abuse of the missing Vanya's parentage and habits. "Haswell, take over Vanya's team. Dr. Whyborne, Dr. Putnam, Mr. Barnett, Griffin, if you'll come with me?"

We followed him to the sleds. Most were piled high with our supplies, which would have to last us until we arrived in Hoarfrost. Two bore lighter loads, however, and I guessed Whyborne, Christine, Iskander and myself would be expected to ride on them.

"This is my sled—do you trust to ride with me?" Jack asked me with a grin.

"Of course," I replied immediately.

"You say that now, but we've time to make up. Wait until I've delivered us to camp without sending the sled over on a boulder." He clapped me on the arm. "Be sure you bundle up well in the furs."

Looking rather uncertain, Whyborne settled himself in the sled. I arranged myself between his long legs and covered us both with the fur robes. As I tucked them in about us, I murmured, "It seems likely this Vanya was the man who attacked you last night."

"Possibly. Although I suppose there might be other reasons for him to vanish," Whyborne whispered back.

I glanced at him over my shoulder. "Do you really believe that?"

He sighed, and a rueful smile curled one corner of his mouth. "No. I'm afraid I don't."

Chapter 13

Whyborne

Our journey took us upriver from the Yukon delta, using the frozen river as a road. The sun glowered from low in the south for a brief time, long after we'd set out. By the end of the first day, I found myself torn between misery and wonder, two sensations that only increased the farther we traveled.

When on smooth ice, the sled hissed across it without trouble, but any little bump or irregularity jolted me to the bone. The wind turned the cold from tolerable to brutal.

Fortunately, we had fur robes to spread over us. Griffin and I cocooned ourselves within them in order to share the heat of our bodies, so wrapped only our eyes showed. Jack's long whip cracked past us on occasion, and he shouted commands at the dogs in one of the native tongues. Within an hour, the muscles of my legs ached, but the narrow sled gave me little room to move, especially with Griffin tucked in front of me.

But the astonishing beauty of the landscape almost made up for the discomfort. Forests of spruce stood tall beneath their winter burden of snow. Occasionally, a loud crack like a gunshot would sound from within the trees as frost shattered a limb. Eagles and ravens milled overhead, and white clad mountains reached ponderously toward the sky. Each twist and turn of the river revealed some new vista of startling majesty.

When we stopped to camp the first night, just after sunset, I found myself so stiff I could barely crawl out of the sled. Jack noticed and levered me to my feet with one of his cheerful grins. "What do you think of Alaska, Dr. Whyborne?"

"It's beautiful," I confessed. "Although I'd preferred to have visited in summer."

"Don't be certain." The blaze of the campfire coming to life painted the side of his face in gold and gleamed from the pale fur lining his hood. "During the summer, the mosquitos are so bad your eyes will swell almost closed from the bites."

"Surely not." He must be having a joke at my expense.

"I swear it's true. They can kill a caribou calf in particularly bad years." His expression shifted into something more wistful. "This is a harsh land, and the hard men filling it are the least of its dangers. Grizzly bears, cold, starvation, scurvy, disease, a fall through the ice into freezing water...there are a thousand ways to die here."

"So why come?" I asked.

He shrugged. "The same reason anyone else comes here. The promise of a better life."

"By which you mean gold."

"Of course."

"But you stayed," I pressed. "Griffin said you came here as part of the Klondike stampede in '98. You've had plenty of opportunity to leave since, if it isn't to your liking."

"But there are so many reasons to stay," he said, his voice taking on a lighter air. "I'd miss the hospitable climate, the beautiful women, and the abundant supply of moose. I'm afraid I've quite grown fond of the taste, you see."

I recognized his tactic only because it was one Griffin used, deflecting my questions with some foolish answer. But I could hardly demand answers from Jack as I could Griffin, so I only responded with a laugh and let the subject drop.

We gathered for dinner around the fire shortly thereafter. Like lunch, it consisted of bacon and beans, with some tinned tomatoes to prevent scurvy. Even if I hadn't been ravenous, I would have made certain to clean my plate of my portion of the latter. I'd heard of the horrors of the disease, although I'd always associated it with long ship voyages, and had no wish to encounter them first hand.

As we ate, green light flashed across the sky. The flashes grew stronger, and soon a curtain of brilliant illumination waved above us, obscuring the stars.

"The Northern Lights," Christine observed. The greenish light gave her skin a sickly tint.

"They are rather beautiful," Iskander said.

"How are you adjusting to this cold climate, if I might ask?" I said.

His Egyptian features looked rather odd juxtaposed with the fur-lined hood, the heavy parka, and the thick mittens he'd pulled back on as soon as he set his fork aside. "It's been a challenge," he admitted. "But the scientific knowledge at stake gives me purpose."

"Well said," Christine agreed, giving him a fond look. No doubt she thought his declaration the height of romance. Jack looked somewhat taken aback, and Griffin hid his grin behind his coffee.

Due to the snowy ground, the fire had to be built on top of a platform of green logs. The heat gradually melted the snow beneath, causing the logs to sink. The flames began to hiss and die away. "We should get to bed," Jack said. The guides had pitched tents, one for themselves, one for Christine, and a third for the rest of our party. "Make certain not to leave anything leather where the dogs can get to it. They'll eat your coat, your boots, their own traces, and anything else they can get their teeth into."

I stared at the milling dogs in alarm. They'd devoured their dinner of dried fish, and seemed to be settling in for the night, a process conducted with a great deal of snapping and snarling. I'd never interacted much with dogs—not to say I bore any dislike for them, only that they were so large and noisy, always jumping about and barking. I preferred the companionship of quieter creatures. "Will they? Why?"

He shrugged. "It's in their nature. I've seen them ignore a lovely dinner of fish in favor of tearing apart an old rawhide coat some poor cheechako left in their reach."

"Cheechako?"

"Tenderfeet. Newcomers." Jack grinned at me. "Stay long enough, and you'll transform into an old sourdough like me."

"No thank you," I said with a shudder. I'd no desire to linger in this place any longer than necessary. As I glanced away, I noticed the guides exchanging grins and rolling their eyes. At my expense, no doubt.

Exhausted as I was, the thought of sharing a tiny tent with four other men barely troubled me. Before I could stumble in its direction, however, Griffin said, "I wish to observe the aurora a bit longer. Walk with me, Whyborne?"

"You'll see it plenty," Jack said from the entrance to the tent. "Soon enough you'll barely even notice it anymore."

"Then I should appreciate it while the phenomenon is still of interest," Griffin replied with a smile. "Don't worry—we won't go far."

Griffin led the way from the dying fire. The dogs had settled in the snow, tails tucked over their noses. As we passed, one of them raised her head and let out a soft whine.

"Shh." Griffin scratched her behind the ears. Her tail thumped once, before she settled in again.

We pushed through the heavy snow for a short distance, until Griffin stopped at the edge of the frozen expanse of the river. I shivered in my parka, missing the fire and our fur robes already.

Still...perhaps I might do something about the cold. "Hold up a moment," I said, and crouched down. I dug through the snow awkwardly with my mittened hands, until I came to the frozen ground. An old flood had left a number of smooth, round river rocks exposed on the bank.

"What on earth are you doing?" Griffin asked in amusement. "Or has the snow already left you desperate to see bare earth?"

"Not quite. I'm going to try to warm us up a bit." I stripped off my mittens and winced at the instant bite of freezing air against skin. Laying my hands against the iron-hard ground was even worse, but I ignored the pain. Focusing my will, I whispered the secret name of fire.

A moment later, I snatched my hands back with a startled curse. "Ah! I think I burned myself."

Griffin caught my hand and inspected my palm. "No. It just seemed like it from the difference in temperature." He reached down and pulled a stone free from the now-thawed earth. "Brilliant!" He handed it to me. This time it only felt wonderfully warm against my skin.

We tucked the heated stones inside our coats, alongside the canteens our bodies kept from freezing. "We'll have to find some way of comfortably wearing them in our boots," Griffin said with a grin. "A shame we can't share them with the rest of the company."

"Indeed." And finding a private moment to heat them again would likely prove difficult. Still, at the moment I felt warmer than I had all day.

Griffin leaned against me, his head tilted back to stare at the aurora. "It's beautiful, isn't it?"

I looked down at him. The ethereal light reflected in his eyes, green on green. "Yes."

His lips curved in a smile that told me he knew I hadn't referred to the aurora. I leaned down and kissed him gently, his mouth hot as a brand after the cold air.

"This isn't going to be easy," he whispered against my lips. "Being in such close proximity, unable to touch or hold you..."

"A good reason to get this business wrapped up as quickly as possible," I agreed as I drew back.

"Indeed." He regarded me carefully. "How are you feeling?"

"I miss the sea already," I confessed.

"And your sensation of weakness?"

I tilted my head back. The aurora flickered and danced madly, hints of red and white creeping into the green. I didn't want to admit it—hadn't wanted to admit it to begin with—but I owed him my honesty. "Still there. As though I'm on the verge of coming down with some mild illness. But I think I'm adapting—it's not as noticeable as before."

Griffin caught my mittened hand in his. "I'm sorry, my dear."

"It isn't your fault. If the accursed Endicotts hadn't forced me to touch the maelstrom...but they did, and there's no complaining about it now." I leaned against him. "May I ask...how have your nightmares been as of late?"

He'd waked me once or twice on our voyage, but no more than usual. Still, I couldn't help but worry for him. Given the shame he seemed to feel over his fits, I feared he wouldn't confess even this lesser form of disturbance if I didn't ask about it directly.

"Unchanged," he said with a shrug. "Hopefully I won't wake anyone in the tent with my thrashing about."

And with Jack in the tent with us, I wouldn't be able to hold Griffin and calm him, should some worse fit strike. "I'm sure you won't," I said firmly. "Did you manage to tell Iskander about the attack on me?"

"I whispered the details and our suspicions in his ear while we unpacked the tinned tomatoes," he said. "He'll tell Christine tomorrow. With any luck, we'll have no further trouble, but..."

"When have we ever had luck?" I finished wryly. "But for now, there's no point worrying. I think we're as safe as it's possible to be, out here in the wilderness."

Griffin turned back the way we'd come, then paused. "May I ask what you think of Jack?"

"I haven't spoken with him much, but he seems kind. A bit rough around the edges, but less so than our guides, certainly." I related the scene I'd witnessed on the docks, when Jack had prevented the swindler from taking advantage of the young prospector. When I finished, Griffin stood in silence for a moment.

"Yes," he said slowly. He looked up at me, and his smile returned. "Thank you for telling me."

"You're welcome. It seemed very much like something you would have done, in his place. Perhaps you have more in common than looks."

Griffin's smile turned sly. "Oh? Do you mean to say you find him handsome?"

Thank heavens the hood hid the reddening tips of my ears from him. "No, of course not."

His snort turned to ice in the air. "You're a terrible liar, my dear." He stepped away from me, the snow groaning beneath his weight. "We should return to camp. Tomorrow will be another long day, and more to come after, until we reach Hoarfrost."

"Wonderful," I muttered, and followed him to our tent.

Chapter 14

Griffin

At one time, I'd spent many a night sleeping beneath the stars. With the Pinkertons, I'd played at being a cowpuncher, chased outlaws across the desert of Arizona, and hunted for fugitives amidst the wilds of the Sierras. But aside from our Egyptian expedition, I'd spent the last several years sleeping in beds with firm walls around me.

Still, my heart thrilled at the prospect of once again testing myself against the wilderness. The howls of wolves, echoed by the howls of our sled dogs, formed a familiar music. The fresh-cut spruce boughs beneath my sleeping bag released a raw scent, which beckoned to some primitive part of my brain. When I awoke the next morning, I found the condensation from my breath had frozen in the fur lining of the bag, despite the warmth of my body and several others in the tent.

The guides were already seeing to breakfast, and Jack had slipped from the tent. His movement must have awakened me. Close to the tent flap, Iskander sleepily pulled on his boots.

I sat up and reached over to shake Whyborne's shoulder. "Time for breakfast."

"Bring it in here," he mumbled from the depths of his sleeping bag.

I grinned and prodded him. "Not likely, lazybones. If you're not up in five minutes, I'll come back and tip you into a snow bank."

"You're a terrible person and I hate you," he muttered. And didn't move.

I shook my head and pulled on my boots, which had remained in my bag with me to keep them warm and safe from the dogs. I slithered out of the tent to find Jack crouched by the rebuilt fire, boiling water for coffee. My brother glanced at me. "Dr. Whyborne doesn't seem impressed by Alaska," he remarked.

"As I said our first night here, Whyborne isn't one for roughing it." I set about opening the cans of beans for our breakfast, and got a nod of thanks from him.

"But you are?" he guessed.

"It can be...enlightening, I suppose. To test oneself on such a journey."

"I think that's what brought me here." Jack set the opened cans in the coals to thaw. "Staying in one place, putting down roots...well, I would have remained in Missouri, if that's what I wanted."

"You gave me your coat," I said. Jack shot me puzzled look, and I clarified. "When you were adopted off the train in Missouri. You wrapped it around my shoulders and told me to be good." The coat had been the last thing I'd possessed of my birth family, when I stood shivering and alone on the railroad platform.

Jack laughed. "I'd forgotten. My new mam was angry about it, when the old man brought me home. Said he might at least have picked one they wouldn't have to spend money on."

I was all too aware of how fortunate I'd been. Before they'd turned their backs on me for the crime of loving Whyborne, my adoptive parents treated me as their own child. But I'd heard stories, rumors, and knew not all of the children from the orphan trains had been so lucky. "I'm sorry."

"Water over the dam and all that." Jack poked at the beans. "The Hogues had seven children of their own already, and the biggest farm in the county. Adopting me was cheaper than hiring another hand. I could have stayed, though. Grown up, married a local girl, had children of my own."

Such a life had almost been mine. Would have been, if I'd not given into temptation. Or, rather, not been caught doing so. Bending over the milking stool in the neighbor's barn while their eldest son fucked me hadn't been the wisest decision I could have made.

Or perhaps it had. Could I really have been happy as a farmer, married to cousin Ruth or some other woman? I would have liked to have children, but it was hard to imagine I'd ever have been truly content.

And I'd never have met Ival, of course. Certainly I couldn't regret that.

"Why did you leave?" I asked.

Jack snorted. "What, live my whole life ten miles from where the train left me? Break my back farming, always at the mercy of the next hailstorm or drought? See the same faces every day for years on end? I knew early on it wasn't for me." His eyes warmed with memory. "A circus came by one spring. Half the town was ecstatic for some entertainment, and the other half thought they were the devil's own come to tempt us. As for me, I loved it—the color, the sounds, the people. When they left, I went with them."

"You never mentioned this in your letters." I poured coffee for us both. "Only that you'd traveled a great deal."

"I did. I left the circus eventually. Wandered around the west for a time. I'd stay in a town for a year, or six months, then find myself on the move again. When word came of the strike on the Klondike, I thought, 'why not?'" Jack shifted one of the cans of beans about in the coals. "I worked in Skagway for a while, until I managed to run afoul of Soapy Smith. I won't say I was sorry to hear when he was gunned down. From there, I went to Dawson, and then to St. Michael. I'd been thinking about leaving Alaska altogether when I met Nicholas. He wanted to look for gold farther north, so I joined him." Jack bit his lip, staring for a moment at the coals. "He has a way of making a man believe in himself. Believe he's meant for more in this world than just drifting through it."

"I look forward to meeting him," I said.

"I can't wait to introduce you." Jack's expression remained melancholy, though. "Maybe you'll see things differently, after talking to him."

I wanted to ask what things, but something about his look made me think I wouldn't get a straight answer. I only said, "He'll make a sourdough out of me, will he?"

"Dear heavens, don't even joke about such a thing," Whyborne said. He slumped down on the rough-hewn log between us. The bright green light of the aurora emphasized the dark shadows beneath his eyes, and made the puce scarf about his neck look even more horrid, if possible. "Even Egypt was preferable to this wretched place."

Jack's mouth tightened. "Don't worry, Dr. Whyborne. I'm sure it will be worth it in the end."

Jack rose to his feet and left to check on the dogs. "I wish I was so certain," Whyborne muttered. "Is the coffee ready?"

I passed a cup to him, but my attention remained on my brother. Why did he seem upset at Whyborne's comment? Did he feel Whyborne insulted his home? Or did he simply look at Whyborne and see a soft scholar, the pampered son of a rich man? A complainer who moped about while everyone else did the hard work?

    I hoped not. I wanted them to like one another. And perhaps our time on the trail would give Jack the chance to see past any superficial assumptions he might have made.

CHAPTER 15

Whyborne

ALASKA STRUCK ME as almost as lonely as the desert wastes we'd crossed in Egypt. In part this was due to the measles epidemic; many of the native settlements we passed were either severely depopulated or utterly deserted. The only real habitation we came to was the town of Nulato, an old trading post that had blossomed somewhat with the influx of miners making their way from the Klondike to Nome. We didn't stay the night, however, only paused long enough to replenish our stores of dried fish for the dogs. Not long after, we turned north along one of the Yukon's many tributaries. The land grew ever more rugged away from the great river. We saw caribou and eagles, and once an entire wolf pack watched us lazily from the hillside.

Griffin adapted to the rigors of our journey with an enthusiasm that took me aback. He exchanged crude jokes with the guides, all of whom seemed to have manly nicknames like "Grizzly" or "Buckeye." He learned the routine of the camp and pitched in with gusto, chopping firewood or the spruce boughs for our beds, feeding the dogs, even mushing short distances under Jack's watchful eye.

I'd never really seen this side of him before. Oh, I knew he'd worked in some dubious places out west as a Pinkerton. Disguising himself as a cowpuncher in order to track down a criminal, or running down train robbers on horseback, that sort of thing. But it had all seemed so distant from the Griffin I'd known, living in a modern house in a modern city.

It was easy to forget he'd learned manners and proper speech in Chicago, and his only real education came via a few years in a one-room schoolhouse on the prairie. His life chasing outlaws in the west was only a few years behind him, and not just a story he related on occasion to entertain others.

He'd chosen me, I reminded myself as I watched him split green logs to form the base for the evening fire. My sole offer to help had been rejected more or less politely, which was probably just as well, considering I'd never handled an ax in my life. Griffin fell in love with me, not one of these muscular frontiersmen who went about chopping wood and mining gold. Or wrestling bears, for all I knew.

And it wasn't as if I was unaware of my own shortcomings in certain areas. My brother spent a great deal of my childhood mocking me for being slender and sickly. But it had been some years since I'd felt my lack of athleticism quite so keenly.

The terrain became rougher as we passed into the mountains, even as the daylight hours grew shorter and the weather colder. Often we had to leave the river, as an increasing series of rapids made passage difficult even when frozen, and find our way around them along the steep slopes.

Our progress slowed to a crawl, and I began to wonder if we would in fact arrive in Hoarfrost before the solstice. Back in St. Michael I'd thought we had plenty of time, but I hadn't appreciated just how difficult it would prove to actually get there. Griffin also appeared to anxiously note the days. If we didn't arrive in time, what might happen? Would we find the town destroyed by some unleashed creature? Surely the hardy prospectors were more able to defend themselves than the Eltdown villagers, since as far as I knew no grizzly bears prowled the English countryside. But would such ordinary defenses suffice against an otherworldly threat?

Perhaps. Bullets worked quite well against ghūls and ketoi. On the other hand, it took a magical lightning blast to destroy the daemon of the night in Egypt.

The trail, such as it was, brought us at last to a place where the river became a frozen waterfall cascading down from the heights. "We're not getting the dogs up that," Griffin commented.

"No," Jack agreed. He pointed to the sheer slope of the ravine cut by the waterfall. "Fortunately there's a trail we can use."

"A trail?" I exclaimed. "For what—mountain goats?"

"It is a bit narrow," he admitted. "And a few horses have been lost on it. I propose the four of you go on foot, while we redistribute weight more evenly among the sleds, just to be safe."

It was a cold, miserable hike. The trail started out wide enough, but quickly grew far narrower than I would have liked. I soon found myself plodding along at the very end of the line, gasping in the thin air and silently cursing Seward for buying this accursed wilderness from the Russians.

Jack's sled was directly ahead of me, and his occasional calls to the dogs echoed back. I tried to distract myself from the unending climb by studying the frozen waterfall. The sun crawled over the horizon, although it never got very high now before descending again, and its reddish light reflected in the cascade of ice. If I'd been sitting beside a warm fire with a cup of cocoa in my hands, I would have called it glorious.

As it was, my aching legs and cold feet somewhat detracted from the scene. With a sigh, I turned my attention back to the trail, just in time to see the outermost runner of Jack's sled slip off the edge.

Everything happened very fast. The sled tilted, shifting it even further toward the precipitous drop. Jack yelped and flung his weight to the inside, but it was too little too late. The sled began to pivot off, sliding off the trail, the poor dogs barking frantically as they dug in.

"Cut the dogs loose!" Jack shouted, and jumped for the trail himself.

The sled slid farther just as he leapt. His foot missed the edge of the trail, and he slammed into the snow and rock of the slope. He flung his arms out, scrabbling wildly, but finding no purchase. He slid toward a drop that would end with his body lying broken at the bottom of the waterfall.

I didn't think, just hurled myself to lie on my belly, hands reaching over the edge for him. I managed to grip one of his wrists, and he got my other wrist with his own hand. His green eyes went round with terror.

"I've got you!" I said.

We began to slide toward the edge.

I swore furiously, tried digging in with the edge of my snowshoes, but it did no good. Jack's weight dragged us both inexorably toward the abyss.

I tightened my grip on him. "Help!" I shouted. "Someone help!"

There came a terrifying crunch, and the sled plummeted past Jack —thank God with no dogs attached. The edge of a runner struck his shoulder, yanking us both forward.

A heavy weight landed on my legs.

CHAPTER 16

Griffin

THE WORLD SOMEHOW moved both very fast and very slow.

Jack's cry of fear rang out, echoing against the heights. Then the sled was sliding over the edge, and Jack clinging to it, and the dogs howling their terror as they fought against the sled dragging them to their deaths.

The guide Haswell drew a sharp knife and ran forward, shoving his way past me. The dogs blocked us from getting to Jack, so he began to saw on the harness holding them to the sled. "Grab hold!" Haswell shouted at me.

I latched my fingers into the harness of the lead dog and threw my weight backward, struggling to keep them from slipping any farther. Where was Jack? Had he—

Whyborne hung over the edge of the slope, clutching Jack. His eyes were wild, teeth gritted, as his body inched slowly closer and closer to the point where gravity would take over completely, and suck them both down into the void.

My heart stopped. Haswell shouted something I couldn't make out, and the dogs suddenly surged forward. I let go of the harness and ran, even as the tumbling sled caught Jack's shoulder and jerked them those last, few fatal inches.

Then time snapped back into place, and I lay on Whyborne's legs, my arms latched around his thighs. My throat felt raw—I'd screamed his name, although I didn't remember doing so. Haswell joined me, followed by Iskander and Christine.

"We've got you!" Christine shouted encouragingly. "Don't let go!"

Inch by inch, we dragged them back up. As soon as Jack came into reach, Christine and Iskander seized his arms, and between us all we managed to easily haul them both onto the trail.

Whyborne collapsed against the sheer wall behind us, gasping for breath. "Ival?" I grabbed his arms. "Are you all right, my dear? Friend," I added hastily, remembering Jack and the guides.

"My arms hurt," he said. "And I rather think I could use a stiff drink. But otherwise, I'm fine."

"You'll have that stiff drink, if I've anything to say about it," Jack said fervently. "Thank God the whiskey wasn't on my sled, eh?"

"Unfortunately, food and lamp oil were on it," Iskander said. "I fear we'll be on short rations these next few days. But at least no one was hurt."

Jack ruffled the fur of the lead dog, who pressed close against him as if looking for comfort. "And we didn't lose the dogs—good work, Haswell."

The guide nodded. "We'll just distribute them among the other teams and continue on once they're settled."

He led the dogs away, and there followed the usual minor commotion as the harnesses of the teams were adjusted. Christine and Iskander went to offer assistance, but I hovered, unwilling to leave my husband or my brother. The moment when I'd thought they would fall to their doom kept replaying in my mind. More than anything, I wanted to sweep Whyborne up in my arms and plant kisses in his hair, on his face. I wanted to find somewhere warm and private, where I could inspect every inch of his skin and make certain for myself he was unharmed.

But I couldn't. I contented myself by saying, "Can I get either of you anything? Are your canteens full enough? Or…"

"I'm fine," Whyborne said. "But you're right—water would probably be wise after such a fright."

I hadn't meant it thus, but he was correct. Ironically enough, one of the dangers we'd been warned against in this land of snow and ice was dehydration, as cold apparently suppressed a man's desire for water. Whyborne and Jack both took long drinks from their canteens, and I had a smaller sip from mine.

"Not quite as good as the whiskey, but bracing enough," Jack said, tucking his back into his coat and refastening the bone buttons. He hesitated, glanced at me, then at Whyborne. "Dr. Whyborne…you saved my life."

Whyborne blinked back him. "You were about to fall off the trail."

"And you kept me from doing so. At great risk to your own life." Jack's brows drew slightly together, as though he wasn't certain what to make of Whyborne.

"Of course," Whyborne said, baffled. "You would have fallen to your death, otherwise."

"When I started dragging you down with me, you could have let go," Jack persisted. "But you didn't. You held on tighter."

Whyborne stiffened. His face went pale, save for two spots of color high on his cheeks. "I know I may not be as athletic as most of the men you encounter here in Alaska, but it doesn't make me a coward."

Jack's eyes widened. "No! No, I'm sorry, I didn't mean...well. I was only surprised."

I found myself becoming annoyed as well. My earlier worry appeared correct—Jack judged Whyborne a useless fop simply because he wasn't used to rough living. "I assure you, Jack, Whyborne is one of the bravest men it's ever been my honor to meet."

Whyborne looked away, no doubt to hide a blush. Jack held up his hands for peace. "No—I'm terribly sorry. I'm saying this all wrong." He glanced from me to Whyborne. "Please. Forgive me. I never meant to cast aspersions on your courage. The whole incident has shaken my nerves, and I don't know half of what I'm saying."

For a moment, Whyborne wavered. Then he nodded. "Of course. Despite Griffin's kind words, the truth is I was absolutely terrified the entire time. The experience has put me off as well, and I'm too quick to take offense." He took a deep breath, then held out his hand to Jack.

Uncertainly flickered across Jack's face, there and gone so quick I wasn't certain I'd really seen it. He shook Whyborne's hand heartily. "The fault is mine, and I thank you for being good enough to indulge me." He looked to the guides, then climbed heavily to his feet. "I should oversee the work, if we're to cross to the other side of this damnable portage before nightfall. But...I owe you, Dr. Whyborne."

Whyborne waved tiredly at him. "You don't owe me anything. Anyone else would have done the same."

Jack didn't look as if he accepted it. But he nodded before hastening away, back toward the head of the column. I rose to my feet and held out my hand to help Whyborne up.

He rose with a groan. Under the pretext of hauling him to his feet, I pulled him close. "You're wrong," I whispered. "Many men wouldn't have done what you did. I love you."

Ival leaned in, his forehead close to mine, but not quite touching.

"I love you, too," he whispered, the steam of his breath brushing my face like a kiss. Then he pulled away, and we resumed our places on the trail.

CHAPTER 17

Whyborne

"No," Christine said, sounding numb. "We're too late."

Griffin frowned. "I don't understand what you mean," he said looking down the slope to Hoarfrost. "Everything seems ordinary to me. There are people moving about, and we still have almost a week until the solstice. Surely the town can be saved."

"Not the town," she snapped. "My site! Look at it, man!"

It was, I had to admit, a depressing sight. The low, reddish sun was already on the wane. Even so, it gave more than enough light to see the extent of the destruction.

The forest had been cleared for hundreds of yards to either side of the river, nothing left but hewn stumps and broken branches. Deep holes pitted the riverbanks, accompanied by piles of raw earth waiting to be sluiced for gold once the spring thaw came. Scaffolding and sluices crisscrossed the landscape, ready for use once the water flowed free once more. Ramshackle cabins stood near the pits, built on the same claims the miners worked. Other buildings sprang up away from the diggings themselves, although many of them were nothing more than wooden fronts with large tents behind them.

Even in the cold, Hoarfrost was a hive of activity, with curses and shouts, the hiss of saw blades on downed trees, and the omnipresent bark of dogs. The scent of smoke hung heavy on the air, too thick to be accounted for by the stovepipes projecting from the cabin roofs.

Beyond the camp, the mountains rose sharply up, their flanks of bare rock mantled with snow. The great mass of a huge glacier wended down the valley toward us, a river of ice creeping inexorably onward.

I patted Christine's shoulder, glancing back to see if anyone overheard Griffin. Certainly it would lead to awkward questions. No one seemed to have, however, over the wild barking of our dogs in response to those howling from the camp.

"Perhaps something might yet be salvaged?" I suggested weakly.

"Salvaged? Look at that!" She gestured rudely in the direction of the gold camp. "The site is completely disturbed."

Jack joined us. "The broken stele has been preserved," he assured her. His attitude toward me had altered strangely since the incident at the waterfall. Where before he'd been confident in speaking to me, now he seemed uncertain, and I'd caught him watching me thoughtfully several times.

"There will have been more to the site than the damned stele," Christine bit out. "Even if it was the only monument, people can't go anywhere without leaving some sort of detritus. Broken projectile points. Bones from dinner. Beads spilled from a necklace. Pottery like the Eltdown Shards. All of which was desperately important in understanding who they might have been, and is now gone. Gone! And for what? Most of these men will leave here no richer than when they came."

"There's nothing to be done now, dear heart," Iskander said soothingly. He took one of her hands in his. "Let's proceed into the camp and see what awaits us."

The corners of her mouth had gone white, but she took a deep breath and nodded. "Yes. You're quite right, Kander. We've experienced setbacks before, and we've overcome them, just as we will now."

Work stopped as we drew close; no doubt word of our coming preceded us. Men filthy with mud climbed out of the pits, or else stared at us from the rope and pulley system used to winch the pay dirt up from the bottom of the shafts. A second look showed not all were men; women worked the claims as well, alongside husbands or each other.

Our journey ended in what passed for the town here in the wilderness. We trudged past the low row of mixed tents and buildings. A post office rubbed shoulders with a gambling hall, which sat immediately beside a hovel carved out of the hillside and advertising itself as a hotel.

Dear lord, if that were to be our lodgings, I'd burrow into a snow bank with the dogs."

"Twenty-five cents for waffles and coffee!" Christine exclaimed. "Robbery!"

"A good meal can be hard to come by out here," Jack replied with a shrug. "A lot harder than gold dust. When you can dig money out of the ground, it begins to have less value to these men than a hot meal or a tin of tomatoes."

"Hmph." Christine's dark brows lowered in disapproval. "I hope at least the working ladies are getting paid well for their time."

Jack looked shocked at her comment, but I rather thought she had the right idea.

"Which claim is yours?" Griffin asked.

Jack pointed. "The one with the tent over it. We put it up to protect the find."

"At least there's that," Christine muttered.

Griffin frowned. "And you said Nicholas took up running the saloon while awaiting our arrival?"

"Yes—there it is." Jack indicated a ramshackle building with THE NUGGET SALOON on a crude sign out front. "He realized pretty quick we could make more money selling whiskey and running gambling tables than we could hope to haul out of the ground. We'd already intended to hire a few men to work our claims in our place. The stele changed our plans, of course. Come on—he should be inside."

The saloon was murky after the brightness of the snow, even given the dim light of a short winter day. An iron stove heated the building's interior, at least in its immediate surroundings. Two men sat at one of the crude log tables, and a third behind a rough-cut counter, but otherwise it seemed deserted at the moment. Parkas, fur pants, and moose hide gloves hung from the rafters near the stove to dry, and the air smelled strongly of wet wool and sweat.

"Nicholas!" Jack called as he knocked the snow off his boots. "I'm back, and I've brought the Ladysmith expedition with me."

The man behind the counter looked up. He was older than Jack, perhaps in his late thirties, the sandy hair beneath his bowler hat touched with gray. But his body remained sturdy, shoulders straining at his coat.

A bright smile immediately creased his weather-seamed face. "Jack! Well done, well done." He emerged from behind the counter to shake hands with his partner.

Jack introduced each of us, and Nicholas Turner shook our hands with great enthusiasm. "I'm so glad you've come," he said. "I'd wager few camps in Alaska have entertained such eminent guests, Dr.

Putnam, Dr. Whyborne."

Christine looked somewhat mollified. Why Turner thought me eminent, I didn't know, unless he was unusually familiar with philology. Or perhaps Jack had told him my father ran one of the biggest railroads in America. That seemed more likely, although somewhat depressing personally.

"You must all be exhausted after your long journey," Turner went on. "I'll show you to your cabins."

"I'd like to see the stele," Christine said.

"First thing tomorrow," Turner agreed with a nod. "For now, even though most of our work takes place in the dark, Hoarfrost still marks the end of the day with sunset. The saloon will fill up soon, and I won't be able to get away. I confess I'd like to be on hand when you first see the stele."

Blast. We didn't have much time left—only six days until the seals became their weakest, and we still had no idea what the umbra might be. Let alone from where we could expect it to emerge—through a tear in the veil to the Outside, from beneath the stele itself, or from somewhere else. I exchanged a glance with Griffin, but what could we do? Hopefully a few hours wouldn't make much difference.

Christine seemed no happier than us, but she conceded with a nod. "Very well, Mr. Turner. We shall do things your way."

Chapter 18

Griffin

Our cabin was small but well built, the windowless walls of thick logs sealed against the cold outside. The only furniture consisted of a bunk, both upper and lower bed wide enough to accommodate two men; four chairs whose seats were made from logs split in half and sanded, and a rough table.

Whyborne lit the Yukon stove with magic while Iskander and I transported our belongings from the sleds to this tiny building. By the time we finished, the little cabin had warmed nicely. Whyborne took out his river stones and heated them with his hands, before tucking them into the sleeping bags and fur robes we'd spread on the beds.

Iskander glanced at the door, then at us. His white teeth flashed as he bit his lip. "I'm, ah, going to find Christine," he said. "I imagine we'll dine at the restaurant. She'll complain of the expense, but a hot meal of something other than beans and bacon will do wonders for us all."

"Should we help you look for Christine?" Whyborne asked innocently.

I restrained the urge to kick his ankle. Iskander's bronze face flushed darker, and he shook his head. "No, it's…no. I'll be back later. *Much* later."

He fled. I shook my head with a chuckle. "A good fellow," I

remarked, as I finished making our bed. "Not entirely comfortable with us yet, I think, but I won't fault him for his thoughtfulness."

Whyborne blinked at me. "What do you mean?"

I turned from the window and stalked toward him. "Iskander went out of his way to let us know he wouldn't be back for some time. Freeing us for...other things."

Whyborne's eyes widened, and his cheeks went scarlet. "I...you mean...if we...he'll know?"

"*Assume* is the word I'd use." I laughed at his horrified expression. "Really, my dear, I'm fairly certain neither he nor Christine are under the impression our relationship is celibate."

"Well, no, but that's in general." Whyborne flapped his hand vaguely. "This is...specific."

He sat near the stove, on one of the log chairs. I dropped to my knees in front of him, and rested my hands on his wool trousers. He'd already stripped off his parka, sealskin boots, and fur stockings, and hung them to dry. "And?" I prodded. "Does it matter so very much? Shall we leave the cabin and follow along behind Iskander, when we could be doing something far more entertaining?"

His gaze went to my lips, and he licked his own. "No," he said, and lunged forward to kiss me.

I returned his passion. The long days and nights in close proximity, without so much as a caress, left us both wild with longing. He bit at my lips, and I shoved him back, plundering his mouth with my tongue as I straddled his lap. I sank my fingers into his spiky hair, which hadn't fared well trapped beneath the fur-lined hood.

"God," he mumbled when I let him have the breath and space to speak. "Let's get out of these clothes."

We stripped hastily. Although the inside of the little cabin was warm compared to the air without, the chill still stung my exposed skin. But it was worth it to see him, pale and long and beautiful. The scars running from the fingers of his right hand all the way to the back of his shoulder had faded slightly over the course of the year, but still traced patterns of pink frost on his skin.

I'd been with men and women whom society would consider more attractive. But I'd wanted him from the moment I'd first seen him, and his gangly limbs, slender build, and absurd hair never failed to move me.

I scrambled up the short ladder to the top bunk. As Iskander had been polite enough to offer us some time alone, it only seemed right to leave him the more convenient of the two. Whyborne climbed eagerly after me, ducking beneath fur covers heated with stones.

The feel of his skin on mine again after so long drew a moan from me. He pressed tight, flinging one leg over my hip, sliding his arms about me. His cock pushed against my belly, hard and hot.

"I missed this," I murmured to him.

"As did I." He kissed me deep, and I clung to him, our bodies rubbing together.

I slid my hand down his back to clasp one buttock, pulling him even tighter. We both stank of the trail, but I breathed deep, letting the scent of salt and ambergris fill my lungs. I'd never understood why he always smelled of the ocean, until I'd learned of the inhuman blood in his veins.

I loved his scent. The feel of his skin. How he gasped and shuddered when I put a hand to his cock.

I loved him.

It had been too long for either of us to want something slow. We rutted against one another, kissing and caressing, drinking in one another's feel and taste and scent. His fingers threaded through my hair, gripping gently, and he kissed me hard. I parted my lips, let him fuck my mouth with his tongue, even as his hips ground his cock into my belly. He was heat and passion and magic-scarred skin, my lover, my husband, and the world narrowed to only the two of us here in this bed. All of my worry and grief, that Jack would discover us, that the umbra might prove to be something too powerful for us to face, vanished. There existed only this moment, and us.

I bit back a shout as I spilled, all of it too much. His grasp tightened on my hair, forcing me to look at him as I spent between us. The intimacy of the act wrung a second, smaller burst of pleasure out of me. His kiss-swollen lips parted, and for a moment I thought he'd speak. Then he hauled me close, teeth biting hard into my shoulder to muffle his cry as he gave himself over to his own climax.

We lay in each other's arms for a long time, just breathing and drinking in the sensation of being together. But gradually the heat faded and the punishing cold threatened to slip in again.

"We should clean up and join the others for dinner," I said. My head rested on his shoulder, and I pressed a kiss to the skin in easy reach.

"Probably." He didn't sound happy about the prospect. A moment later, his lips brushed my forehead. "I love you. You...you know I do, don't you? This was wonderful, but it's not the only thing binding me to you."

Sometimes I truly wondered what thoughts moved through that brilliant mind of his. "Of course—you're being absurd." I propped myself up on my elbow and took his left hand in mine, so our rings gleamed in the dim light of the oil lamp. "Why do you say such things?"

He looked vulnerable, in a way he never allowed anyone else to see. "I just...we've never gone this long without making love, and I didn't want you to think it had any bearing on my affection."

I snorted. "I don't know...wasn't one of your vows to love and cherish me, so long as I satisfied you sexually on a regular basis?"

"Beast." He thumped me lightly on the shoulder. But I'd gotten him to smile. "As you said, we should find dinner."

"In a moment." I rolled over to straddle his body, then pressed a tender kiss to his mouth. "I love you, Ival. And I'm thankful to have you here with me."

He returned the kiss. It edged toward passion, and after a moment, we pulled apart again with dual sighs. "Let's go," he said. "If Iskander returned and found us...well. I don't think I could ever look the man in the eye again."

CHAPTER 19

Whyborne

THE BITTERLY COLD air stung the skin of my face the moment we stepped out of the comparative warmth of the cabin. Night had fallen, and a gasp escaped me as I took in the landscape around us.

Fires blazed everywhere, their low, angry glow lighting up the bellies of great plumes of smoke rising toward the sky. For a moment, I thought the mining camp itself to be on fire. But no, the flames appeared to come from the shafts dug into the banks of the creek.

"What the devil?" I asked aloud.

Griffin followed my shocked gaze. "The fires? Jack spoke to me of them, when I asked him about mining. The permafrost is too hard to dig through. Prospectors burn fires throughout the night, then excavate the thawed ground the next day. Or what passes for day here, at least."

"Oh." It sounded unpleasant, backbreaking work.

"Most won't even know if they've uncovered anything of value until spring," Griffin went on. "Until the river runs free of ice, they can't sluice any gold from the pay dirt. Imagine an entire winter of such labor, only to find you're no better off than when you started."

"It sounds abominable," I agreed. "To travel to such a forsaken place, unsure if there's any profit to be had in the trip. Why would anyone do such a thing?"

"Desperation for some. Gold fever for others." Griffin shrugged. "Men do strange things in pursuit of wealth."

I couldn't argue. My own family had practiced everything from sorcery to mating with creatures from beneath the sea in such pursuit. Compared to that, traveling to this wilderness seemed rather tame after all.

We walked over the expanse of frozen black mud and snow to the restaurant. Long tables sat beneath a canvas tent, packed with bodies. Apparently, this was a popular place to find a hot meal after a day of digging half-frozen gravel out of the ground. A prominent sign warned there was to be no swearing, spitting, or dogs allowed inside.

"Whyborne!" Christine called. "There you are."

My face grew hotter within the protection of my hood. Had Iskander indicated anything to her? Probably not, but no doubt she'd guessed we'd taken the opportunity to be intimate.

Griffin, of course, looked as if we'd merely lingered in the cabin to organize our belongings. "Christine," he greeted her. "Iskander."

"Have fun, gentlemen?" Christine asked slyly.

God. I'd never survive this trip.

"Indeed," Griffin agreed, swinging a leg over the bench and settling opposite them.

"Do sit down, Whyborne," Christine ordered. She gestured to the figures sitting beside her. "This is Matilda and Sarah. I'm sharing their cabin while we're in the camp."

The heavy coats and hoods had fooled my eyes. "Ladies," I said, touching my hood in lieu of tipping a hat.

"Matilda and Sarah are miners," Christine added.

Dear Lord, even the women here were manlier than me. Both looked as if they could snap me in half, and I had no doubts as to their ability to dig through the permafrost. "Dr. Putnam says she will tell us of science," one said in a thick Scandinavian accent.

"I'm sure she will," I muttered.

"Excuse me," said a new voice. "May I join your table?"

A tall, thin man stood beside an empty spot on our bench, a polite smile on his face. "Reverend Scarrow, please sit," Matilda said.

My heart sank slightly. I had nothing against men of the cloth per se, but in my limited experience they seemed to talk of nothing but God, and wished me to do the same. "Felix Scarrow," he introduced himself. His handshake was strong, the skin of his palm more callused than I would have expected.

As we introduced ourselves, our dinners were served: moose steak, beans, and applesauce. I tucked in immediately, not wishing it to get cold. Griffin however waited with an expectant air.

"We thank you for this food, O Lord," Scarrow intoned, bowing his head over his meal. Griffin did the same.

I paused in eating, feeling horribly uncomfortable. It hadn't even occurred to me to wait. Fortunately, Scarrow kept the blessing short, and a moment later everyone tucked in.

"How long have you been in Hoarfrost, Reverend?" Griffin asked.

"Since just before the rivers froze," Scarrow replied. "This poor flock had no one to tend them, so I felt it imperative they shouldn't be left an entire winter without solace."

"Revered Scarrow is doctor also," Matilda said.

Scarrow nodded. "I'm no surgeon, but I studied the basics of medical care before setting out into the wilderness. Our little church here doubles as the hospital. Right now I have only a few patients, but scurvy hasn't yet set in. I brew spruce needle tea to keep it at bay for those here in camp, but some of the prospectors scattered further along the creeks and rivers don't know the trick. Or refuse to use it on the grounds it was discovered by the savage Indians and thus can't possibly be of any use to white men." He smiled ruefully.

Christine snorted. "Then let their teeth fall out, I say."

Scarrow's smile became pained. "I endeavor to take a more charitable attitude."

"Of course," Griffin said, smoothing things over. "I'm sure your help and presence has been of great value to the camp."

"Thank you, but I am merely performing the work God has asked of me." Scarrow paused. "I must admit, I have an interest in archaeology. Dr. Putnam, I've followed your career with as much attention as the newspapers allow me. Such wondrous discoveries you made in Egypt!"

"Oh. Ah, thank you." Christine visibly braced herself, and I winced. Half the questions she fielded from the public involved the Biblical enslavement of the Israelites by the pharaohs, a tale for which no archaeological evidence had yet been uncovered.

Instead, Scarrow said, "I'm certain you will make even more fascinating discoveries here. Would you mind terribly if I come by your site tomorrow, as my duties permit, and observe your work? I promise not to get in the way."

Christine looked pained, as if torn between his praise of her career and her own impulse to flatly deny his request. "I suppose," she said at last. "But if your presence interferes in even the smallest way, you must leave immediately."

"Of course."

The rest of dinner passed in idle conversation. Scarrow inquired as to the conditions of the trail, and expressed dismay over our abandonment by the guide Vanya. "He came to services often," Scarrow said with a shake of his head. "I would never have thought it of him. I hope he didn't come to some harm."

"It will probably always be a mystery," Griffin said mildly. I concentrated on my rather gamy steak.

"Well," Iskander said, putting his fork aside. "Supper was a nice change of pace from bacon, at any rate. Christine, if you're at liberty, I wanted to review our supply lists with you. I'm afraid I left them in the cabin—"

She had already climbed over the bench by the time he finished speaking. "Let's go see to them at once," she said. A moment later, they vanished back out into the night.

"I think Whyborne," Griffin said, "we should have a nice leisurely dessert, don't you?"

CHAPTER 20

Griffin

WE LINGERED OVER slices of what was alleged to be pie, although in my experience pie ordinarily had less dough and more filling. Scarrow took his leave, wishing us both a pleasant evening and inviting us to services next Sunday should we be so inclined.

I considered suggesting a stop by the saloon, but I doubted Whyborne would care for the atmosphere. Nor would he be particularly welcome at the card tables. He had a knack for card games that bordered on the uncanny, which tended to lead to accusations of cheating.

"I imagine it's been long enough for them to have become reacquainted, as it were," I said at last, checking my pocket watch. "Don't you think?"

"I'd rather not think of it at all," Whyborne muttered.

I chuckled. "Don't be such a prude."

"I'm not," he objected. "But Christine is like a sister to me. I wouldn't wish to think of it even if..." he waved a vague hand. Even if he possessed the slightest interest in women, I took him to mean.

Many of the men I'd had liaisons with in the past had been married, or planned to marry. Glenn, who died horribly beneath Chicago, had a wife and five children. I myself had slept with women, at first in an attempt to understand my own feelings, and later as part of my various investigations. So when I'd first met them, I'd rather feared Whyborne and Christine were lovers. It hadn't prevented me from pursuing him, but I assumed I'd be forced to share his affection. And for the first time in my life, the thought pained me.

Iskander had assumed the same, and God only knew how many of the museum staff. In reality, I'd quickly discovered Whyborne was one of those men who lacked even the slightest ability to appreciate a woman in such a fashion. He'd made no attempt to please his family by courting a girl as a youth, or even tested the truth of his proclivities in a brothel.

But Whyborne knew himself in a way I could only envy. It hadn't always made him happy, but it gave him the courage to find his own path, despite the desires of his father or anyone else. He refused to be anyone but himself, and the world could go hang if it disapproved.

If not for him, I might have married Ruth. Made Pa happy. Stood by Ma at Pa's graveside, my wife and children at my side, pretending it wasn't all a horrible lie.

"Griffin? Is everything all right?" he asked quietly.

I blinked back to myself. "Yes. Sorry. Just lost in thought."

He nodded. "Come. Let's walk back to the cabin. We'll go slowly and knock discreetly when we arrive."

We bundled back up in our mittens and scarves, tugging our parka hoods over our heads. It was bitterly cold outside of course, and the smoke and flames from the mineshafts gave the camp an ominous feel, like something from a story of hell and devils. The Northern Lights blazed and pulsed above the mountains, and I heard...

Something. Like a voice speaking from another room, the volume increasing and decreasing with the intensity of the lights.

"Do you hear that?" I asked.

Whyborne looked at me blankly. "Hear what?"

The rippling light faded a bit from its apex, and the distant voice died with it.

"Nothing. I must have imagined it." I was tired after our long travel, and my mind was surely playing tricks on me.

As we made our way over the frozen ground by the combined light of the aurora and an oil lamp, Whyborne said, "You can go to church if you want, you know. Just because I don't believe doesn't mean I disapprove."

Did he think it the concern that had troubled me earlier? And perhaps, in a round about way, he was right. "I know," I said. "But how can I sit in a pew and have faith that the man in the pulpit speaks for God, when most such men would condemn us to eternal torment for loving one another?"

"Well, yes," Whyborne agreed hesitantly. We passed what appeared to be the local brothel, no more than a wooden front with a canvas tent behind. "That would rather be my question as well. But it isn't the same for me. It probably wouldn't have been even if I'd regularly attended First Esoteric."

"Probably," I agreed. Considering First Esoteric restricted its congregation to the old families of Widdershins, their beliefs were rather likely of the sort to be seen as blasphemous by the more orthodox denominations. I'd heard the Christmas carols sung in Widdershins, after all.

Either way, Whyborne had never had faith. Never believed in a benevolent providence arranging our lives in ways that might seem incomprehensible, or even cruel, but would ultimately be revealed to be a part of some divine plan from which only goodness would spring.

"I've heard of sympathetic clergy," I went on. "Who marry men or women like ourselves. Not in the church, of course, but in small private ceremonies. But the fact they would immediately be stripped of their collars for doing so would weigh on me, even if I found such a one in Widdershins. Not everyone is turned against us, and yet..."

The words stuck in my throat. I swallowed hard and forced them out. "Pa died believing I'm bound for hell."

Whyborne sighed. The moisture in his breath turned to ice in the frigid air. "I remember."

Remembered the last words Pa and I exchanged, he meant. When I'd tried to explain what Ival meant to me, and Pa refused to listen. No doubt Pa had thought the same, that I was the stubborn one who wouldn't hear the voice of reason.

"Did it...did it trouble you much?" Whyborne asked quietly. "Not your father; of course that did. But...I assume you believed the same thing at one time."

I still remembered the feelings of shame and pain during the sermons when the parson warned the sin of buggery would bring down the wrath of God on America. At times the guilt felt overwhelming.

But that was a long time ago, and life had put a great deal of distance between me and that frightened, desperate boy. "Of course it did. At the time, I hated leaving Kansas, being driven out by the very people I'd spent my life trying to please. But in some ways it was the best thing that could have happened. In Chicago I met many different people, men and women. Worldly people, who didn't cling to the narrow-minded beliefs I'd been raised with."

"People like Elliot."

"Yes," I agreed, because Elliot had been an important part of my life. "And others. Good men, good women, who made the world a better place. And I couldn't...I couldn't believe any murderer or thief would be more acceptable in the eyes of God simply because of whom they fell in love with. What sort of heavenly father gives a woman to her rapist, but throws good men into hell for the crime of love?"

"I had the same questions," Whyborne said dryly. "Though to be fair, I read the Bible alongside the legends of the Greeks and Romans, with no particular weight given to any of them. Although considering the head of one pantheon was the lover of his cupbearer Ganymede, I will admit to a personal preference."

"I thought you a youthful devotee of Bacchus." I gestured at the saloon as we passed. "Here is your temple."

"Don't forget Pan," he added. "Although it was more for the freedom they represented than anything else, I think. I was a bit too young at the time to understand the lure of the satyrs."

I shook my head. "I can't imagine it." Our lives had been so different.

"I know." He stopped and turned to me. The green light of the aurora combined horribly with the puce scarf about his neck, and picked out odd highlights from his dark eyes. "Griffin, I'm sorry about your father. And I hope you've found family in Jack, but please always remember—"

As if Whyborne's words summoned him, Jack's voice sounded indistinctly on the cold air.

We both froze, although of course we weren't doing anything wrong. Merely two friends having a discussion.

"Listen to me!" Jack shouted, the words muffled. A moment later, I realized they came from the cabin behind the saloon. The freezing air carried sound far more clearly than it would have otherwise.

Turner's voice came in reply. "No! You listen to me, Jack Hogue. You've been deceived."

Whyborne and I exchanged a glance. My years with the Pinkertons removed any shame I might have harbored about eavesdropping, and I strained my ears to hear more. But apparently they'd reined back their tempers, because only the slightest sound of conversation followed, quickly dropping to nothing.

At least I could now account for the voice I'd heard earlier. Just someone talking in a distant cabin, and a trick of the wind and cold had brought the sound to my ears and not Whyborne's.

I began to walk again, and Whyborne fell in beside me. "I wonder what that was about," he mused.

Likely it was none of our business. I knew almost nothing about Nicholas Turner, or his relationship with Jack. If Turner had any questions about our expedition, he would have brought them to us. Still, I couldn't help but worry. Who might have deceived my brother—and how?

A woman, perhaps. A sweetheart he'd left here, thinking she'd stay constant, who strayed during his absence. Or some other small matter, a hired man or a gambler. I couldn't ask Jack about it directly without betraying my eavesdropping, but I knew how to casually question a man without him even knowing he was being interrogated. And if it proved to be something more serious, I'd offer my support to him.

Pa might have died thinking me a lost cause. But I'd stand by Jack if he needed me to. I'd prove myself. And if he found out about Whyborne and me…

Well, it didn't matter. There was no reason to think he ever would.

Chapter 21

Whyborne

I awoke the next morning to the murmur of voices. My mind still half-fogged with sleep, I froze, my heart leaping with a blind panic because I snuggled against Griffin's back. Then memory caught up: we were expected to be in bed together in this freezing, rough place.

And the other voice belonged to Iskander, who would *not* think our close contact innocent. My face burned, and I wondered if I could crawl under the covers and hide.

Griffin, who lay to the outside of the bunk, had propped himself up on one elbow and cheerfully discussed archaeology with Iskander. How could he be so casual, talking to someone else with me lying right here beside him, as though there was nothing at all out of the ordinary about it?

"The permafrost would present a challenge," Iskander said. Thick leather scraped against one of the wooden rafters as he pulled down his parka. "At this latitude, the ground is frozen year-round. Even if we returned in the summer we'd be faced with some of the same difficulties."

"Not to mention the problems of getting workers and supplies to such a remote location."

"That as well." One of the chairs shuffled against the floor. "This is all assuming the site can be made...safe."

"Whyborne will see to it," Griffin said, with utter confidence. I wasn't certain whether to be appalled or gratified. "If we can only find these seals in the next five days, he'll make certain they hold."

I opened my eyes and saw only the back of his union suit and the red straps of his bracers. "I certainly hope you're right," I said.

Griffin climbed out of the bunk and availed himself of the water warming on the Yukon stove and the small mirror to shave. Beards, Jack had informed us, were for the summer months, to help keep mosquitoes off as much of one's face as possible. In the winter, a man's breath would quickly turn any hair near the mouth into a single mass of hardened ice. Given I'd never been able to grow much of a beard, I'd been rather glad to hear it.

When Griffin finished, I reluctantly followed suit, exchanging the warmth of the furs for the chilly air of the cabin. We ate our daily ration of tinned tomatoes, heated to a tepid temperature over the stove. I'd become heartily sick of the things, but suspected I'd like scurvy a great deal less, so I choked down my portion with a minimum of complaint.

We met Christine in front of the cabin she shared with the two female miners. Even though the only light came from the stars and the aurora, the camp was already abuzz with activity. Miners used snow to douse the pit fires that hadn't burned out on their own. The first buckets filled with a slurry of ash, mud, and gravel, were hoisted to the surface as we passed by. Dogs barked and men shouted, both to their partners in or out of the shafts, or to those working neighboring claims. The frigid air reeked of smoke and black mud.

God, what an abominable place. I couldn't wait to return to Widdershins. Although the feeling of being off-balance had gradually decreased—or perhaps I'd simply grown accustomed to it—I missed the sea, the comforts, our home, and our cat. With any luck we'd find these seals restraining the umbra, strengthen them as Griffin said, and leave before the truly horrid weather of January and February trapped us here.

As promised, Turner and Jack waited for us beside the large tent stretched over their claim. "Good morning," Turner said jovially. "I hope you slept well and warm."

"The cabin is quite sturdy, thank you," Griffin replied. "We certainly can't fault the care you've taken for us."

Turner smiled. "Anything for a brother of Jack's. Let alone our other distinguished guests."

"Yes, yes," Christine said. "Let's get on with it, shall we?"

"Of course." Turner untied the tent flap and held it back with a bow. "Ladies first."

I followed Christine into the confines of the tent. "Watch your step," she said, hefting her lantern to give us better light. I took it from her, as my greater reach allowed me to lift it higher.

The warm orange light reflected from the pale canvas and revealed a large, rectangular pit hacked from the permafrost. Shadows seemed to pool in the hole, revealing only suggestive fragments: a carved line here, a cluster of dots there.

"We need more light in here!" Christine barked. "Griffin, Jack, see to it. Iskander, I want photographs before anything is further disturbed."

Everyone scurried to do her bidding. Soon, half a dozen oil lamps burned inside the tent. When the angle still left too much shadow in the digging for her liking, Christine sent Jack on a mission to collect mirrors and any gold pans with sufficient shine. While Turner watched in bemusement, we set about rigging up a series of reflectors to direct the light where we wished it to go.

Soon the pit was illuminated even to Christine's satisfaction. It was perhaps twelve feet deep, and for the most part revealed ordinary mud and gravel, threaded through with deposits of gold dust. The gold increased as it went down, until a thick vein lay directly atop the exposed bedrock.

Embedded in the golden silt lay chunks of greenish stone, utterly unlike any of the surrounding geology as far as I could tell. As in the photograph Jack sent, the object was clearly a stele of some kind, snapped off near the base and shattered. Thankfully, the elements had only slightly scattered the broken stones.

"Thoughts, Whyborne?" Christine asked, while Iskander began to photograph the artifact, first from the pit's edge, then clambering down the ladder to record closer images.

"It's rather like a jigsaw puzzle, isn't it?" I said.

"Do you think you can make anything out of it?" Turner asked.

Christine snorted; the cold air made her nostrils steam like a charging bull's. "Bah! Whyborne has pieced together cuneiform tablets shattered into a hundred pieces. This is barely an afternoon's entertainment for him."

"I wouldn't put it quite like that," I said. "Is there any way to temporarily gum the pieces together? It's far too cold for mortar to set I imagine, and I wouldn't wish to do anything permanent before transporting it back to the museum, but it would make viewing it easier."

"We could use a mix of mud and moss, like the chinking for the cabins," Jack suggested. "It wouldn't withstand a good rain, but rain isn't much of a problem this time of year. And the mud freezes hard as granite in these temperatures."

It seemed as good a solution as any. "So long as there aren't too many pieces missing, I believe I can fit it back together."

"Good man." Christine clapped me on the arm. "Are you done, Kander? Then let's get to excavating!"

CHAPTER 22

Whyborne

THE EXCAVATION PROVED to be cold, miserable work. The chunks of broken green stone were still embedded in a frozen conglomeration of silt, gold, and gravel. To extract a piece, the surrounding matrix had to be warmed and thawed. To avoid damaging the artifacts, we poured boiling water over the mud, then hastily dug fragments out before everything froze again. I helped surreptitiously, using my fire spell to speed up the thawing process.

I'd never used my arcane abilities in such a way before—small, controlled bursts, repeated again and again and again. After an hour, I developed a nagging headache, and felt as though I'd been moving heavy loads about. After two, the headache grew to blinding proportions, and I stopped to keep from becoming utterly useless. In Widdershins, with the maelstrom to draw upon, I probably could have kept it up for days.

Even thawed, the muck was cold, and my fingers were soon reddened and numbed from helping to pry the fragments loose. Once a broken bit of stone was pulled free, it was washed, photographed from both sides, and labeled so its original position could be easily referenced if needed.

Christine began to give me impatient looks. After unearthing a dozen or so fragments, I turned my attention to the painstaking job of piecing the stele back together. Whenever I found where a piece went, Jack cemented it into place with a layer of mud. As promised, the stuff froze to the hardness of cement in a short time.

When the first day ended, the stele was perhaps a third complete, including the fragment Jack had originally mailed to us. As we climbed out of the pit, Turner said, "I'm glad Jack thought to call on you folks. I'm pretty sure we couldn't have done this on our own."

I might not be able to split firewood or dig through feet of muck in the hopes of finding gold, but at least I could do this. "I'm glad my talents have been of service."

"Quite," Christine agreed briskly. Like the rest of us, she was smeared with stinking black mud. "Archaeology is a business best left to the professionals."

"I for one will be glad for dinner," Iskander said, pausing to help her off the ladder.

"And a shot or two of whiskey," she added.

"Come along," Turner said with a grin. "Dinner and whiskey await you at the saloon."

Exhaustion ate at my bones, and I would have preferred to return to our cabin and collapse. Still, a hot meal might drive away the chill that seemed to have settled in every limb. As we left the tent, however, Jack said, "A word with you, Griffin?"

I paused and glanced back over my shoulder. Griffin didn't look at me, though, only nodded to his brother. "Of course."

I turned away and followed Christine and Iskander. But as I did so, I had the oddest feeling Jack watched me over Griffin's shoulder, his gaze boring into my back until the tent flap fell closed between us.

CHAPTER 23

Griffin

"Is everything all right?" I asked, once Jack and I were alone. I wished he'd chosen some other venue for this talk. We'd extinguished all the other lights, so the mirrors only occasionally sent back flashes of illumination from the oil lamp in his hand. Shadows seemed to lurk in the corners, and the pit in the middle of the tent was nothing but a dark, foreboding shape.

I couldn't identify the designs on the broken fragments, nor had the slightest idea what they meant. And yet...they haunted me. As if I'd seen them before, in some distant dream I no longer remembered.

Whyborne's explanation, that I'd seen the designs of the Eltdown Shards in some newspaper article as a boy, had seemed sufficient up until now. But standing here in this wild place, with the stone fragments before me, it rang hollow. The feeling of recognition was too deeply seated to have come from a few inches of print in a newspaper column.

But was it real? There was no reason I, of all people, should have such a presentiment. My Ival was magic; it was in his blood and bones. Whereas I was entirely ordinary. *Common,* as Theo Endicott had said, hoping to seduce Ival away from me.

I wasn't mad. The dreams, the voice I'd heard the other night, the stele...it didn't mean anything. The doctors hadn't been right. I wasn't going mad.

"Everything is fine." Jack flashed me a grin, but it faded quickly. "I only had a question for you. Have you ever been on one of Dr. Whyborne's expeditions before?"

"Whyborne doesn't have expeditions," I corrected. "This is entirely Dr. Putnam's affair. If it were up to him, he'd never leave Widdershins at all. Why?"

"I see." Jack looked away, and his fur-edged hood hid his expression from me. "The papers gave Dr. Putnam credit for her Egyptian discoveries, but I assume Dr. Whyborne's hand was behind them?"

"Dear lord, don't let Christine hear you say such a thing!" I stared at him in shock. "I understand it may seem strange for a woman to make such discoveries on her own, but how can you think such a thing having travelled with her?"

Jack turned to me, and the light revealed an oddly uncertain look on his face. "His studies into Nephren-ka didn't lead her to the tomb?"

"Of course not. Why would you even ask such a thing?" Surely Jack didn't have some hidden interest in archaeological proceedings, or else he would have spoken of this earlier.

Jack shrugged. "I don't know. I suppose, watching them at work... Dr. Whyborne seems rather competent."

I snorted. "Of course he is. Do you really believe Christine would let him accompany us otherwise?"

"I...I don't know." Jack shook his head. "Forgive me—this line of questioning must seem very strange to you."

"You're right, it does." Did this have something to do with the argument we'd overheard between Jack and Turner? But surely Turner didn't think Christine had deceived Jack in some way, when she obviously knew her business well. Could the man harbor a deep prejudice toward Iskander for his brown skin and Egyptian features? But that wouldn't count as deception either. Nor could I imagine how Turner would have come to the conclusion Whyborne was secretly in charge of the expedition, or why he'd try to convince Jack of it.

"Is something wrong?" I asked finally. "Have you and Whyborne quarreled? Or you and Christine?"

"No!" He shook his head empathically. "Not at all. Dr. Whyborne saved my life on the way here. Why would I quarrel with him?"

Did it bother Jack, to feel himself in debt to Whyborne? Did he still think Ival something of a fop, soft and useless compared to the rugged men he normally interacted with? "I don't know. You tell me."

Rather than answer, Jack said, "You called him something different that day, didn't you? Ordinarily you use his surname, but I thought I heard you shout another name when you ran to save us." His lip twisted ruefully. "Although perhaps I misheard. I was rather occupied with not plummeting to my death at the time."

The chill seemed to seep through my layers of clothes to gather around my heart. I thought we'd been careful, but perhaps we'd done something since arriving to give ourselves away. Was that why Jack suddenly decided to ask questions about Whyborne's place in the expedition? Did he imagine Whyborne was here only as my lover?

Had I lost Jack already, the same way I'd lost Pa?

I willed my face to remain neutral. "Not at all. Ival is short for Percival. His intimate friends use it for him."

In truth, of course, the name was mine alone to say. He hated Percy, and Whyborne had seemed too formal when I laid in bed at night, imagining it was his hand and not mine on my cock. Thankfully, it pleased him when I gasped it out involuntarily our first night together, or else I should have felt a fool.

"Oh." Jack nodded. "That makes sense."

Did it? What was going on with him? "Jack, if you have any doubts about Dr. Putnam, or Dr. Whyborne, anyone in our party, please allow me to lay your mind to rest. And if you have doubts of me, speak them aloud."

"No. I don't have any doubts about you," Jack said firmly. He put a hand to my shoulder. "I'm sorry I led you to think otherwise. Forgive my meandering thoughts—these endless nights play havoc with a man's mind."

"Of course," I said, relieved. Whatever troubled him, at least he didn't seem to suspect the truth of my relationship with Whyborne. "Think no more of it."

CHAPTER 24

Whyborne

It was done.

I tucked my freezing fingers beneath my armpits and stared at the completed stele. Three days of hard, backbreaking, miserable work, but the blasted thing was complete at last.

"It's a city," Christine breathed. "Do you see, Whyborne? A city!"

The green stone monument stood a good eight feet tall, and half again as wide. Thick bands of carving marked the top and bottom on both sides. Some of the bands depicted geometrical shapes, repeated irregularly, while others held curious groupings of dots and swirls. In between the bands on the south-facing side was a relief carved in amazing detail, displaying mountains...and a city.

The Eltdown Shards predated all previous guesses as to human colonization of the British Isles. And this stele, buried beneath twelve feet of muck and gravel, must surely be ancient. Assuming it to be contemporary to the Eltdown Shards, it ought to far predate agriculture, let alone the very concept of a city.

And yet there it was.

Some of the terraced buildings shown in miniature reminded me of ziggurats or of the pyramids in the South American jungles. Others were a mere conglomeration of cones and cubes, connected here and there by thin aerial bridges. And yet none of the angles of the buildings seemed to meet quite correctly, as if the artist had somehow failed to depict the proper perspective even after adhering to it faithfully when it came to the landscape. The entire city clung tight to the steep mountainside, as if to suggest the visible buildings were merely the outer shell of a much larger structure beneath the surface of the mountain.

The artistic tradition seemed to belong to no known human culture. But I'd seen something very much like it before.

The great city of the dweller of the deeps, with its stepped pyramid and plaza, its cyclopean architecture whose lines met at such bizarre angles, was clearly of a close relation to this distant place.

What it meant, I hadn't the slightest idea. Nor could I say such a thing aloud in front of so many witnesses, whose number now included Reverend Scarrow. So I only said, "Clearly there is some kind of writing in the bands here, which resembles the writing found on the Eltdown Shards."

We moved to the other side of the stele, which showed groupings of dots far more recognizable in their arrangement. "And this side is some sort of astronomical chart," I said, tracing the familiar stars.

"But...no. It can't be." Christine's voice took on an air of excitement. "Whyborne, look! If we assume the stars are meant to depict the view of the sky from this location, the North Star isn't Polaris. It's Vega."

I gasped. Surely not. "Dear heavens."

Griffin cleared his throat. "Would either of you like to share what that means with the rest of us?"

"Planetary precession!" Christine clasped her hands together eagerly. "In essence, the North Star changes over time. At the moment it's Polaris, but in 3,000 BC it was Thuban, in the constellation Drago. The last time Vega held the position of the pole star was 12,000 BC. Almost 14,000 years ago."

"And 40,000 years before that," I murmured. But to even think such a thing was surely insane. And yet...the image on the stele showed no glaciers, no ice and snow on the mountain. How long ago had this part of the world last been so warm?

"This city is older than any other structures built by humankind." Christine's eyes shone with excitement. "This could revolutionize the entire history of our species. If any trace remains, we *must* find it!"

"Agreed!" Turner exclaimed. "But where is it? These mountains are vast. We could look for a year and still be no closer to uncovering it."

Christine rushed around to stare at the other side of the stele, as if the words written in the odd clusters of dots would suddenly become clear, if she but stared at them long enough. "You can decipher these, can't you, Whyborne?" she asked.

"You know philology doesn't work in such a fashion," I said, feeling a touch of exasperation. "Without any cross-reference to a known language, there's no way of translating it. If this stele is truly 14,000 years old, it predates any other known written language by almost nine millennia."

Christine ground her teeth together and glared at the image, as if it purposefully withheld its secrets from her.

Griffin reached out to trace the curve of one peak lightly with a finger. "Wait a minute. Look."

"At what?" Christine asked immediately.

Griffin shook his head slowly. "I...just follow me."

We trooped outside, Christine in such haste she would have forgotten her gloves had Iskander not retrieved them along with his own. The sun had vanished, but the aurora raged across the sky, strong enough to throw sharp-edged shadows within the camp. The mountains loomed up to the north, snow-clad peaks reflecting the light so they appeared to have been dipped in blood.

"Look." Griffin pointed at two of the nearest peaks. "See the shape? How the one on the right is so much taller, and has that distinctive bulge on the side? It matches the mountains on the stele."

Christine let out a gasp. Iskander frowned a little, though. "So that would mean the city is...there."

Unlike the distinctive peaks, the pass between them looked nothing like the stele. Then, it had been exposed rock. Now, it was buried beneath the wide, white tongue of the glacier.

CHAPTER 25

Whyborne

"Do you think there's anything left of the city?" Turner asked.

We'd retreated to the saloon for celebratory drinks. Jack and Griffin vanished briefly, returning laden with dinner from the restaurant. We sat around one of the gambling tables, dining on hot soup and generous pours of whiskey. I rather wished Turner had brought out wine instead, as his signage claimed he stocked it. Then again, given the remoteness of the location, its vintage was probably rather suspect.

"Impossible to say," Christine replied. "Glaciers grind away everything in their paths, or so I understand. If the city is indeed in the pass, there may be little left to excavate."

"But if part of the city was underground, it might still be intact," I suggested.

"Let us hope so." Christine took a swallow of her whiskey. "Even if only fragments remain, they would be of immeasurable importance. But intact buildings..."

"Well, there's only one way to find out," Turner said. "We can leave tomorrow, establish a base camp, and search for any glacial caves or moulins, which might let us get a look at beneath the ice."

Christine grinned and clinked her glass against his. "I like the way you think, Mr. Turner."

Scarrow cleared his throat slightly. "I don't wish to intrude, Dr. Putnam, but I would like to be included on your expedition if at all possible."

She frowned. "I think you can pray for us just as well from here, Reverend."

"Ah, but I have more to offer than prayer, as powerful as it is," Scarrow replied. "I know a bit of mountaineering and the attendant dangers."

Wonderful—even the local man of the cloth had more experience when it came to surviving the wilderness than me.

"If you intend to scale the glacier looking for this wonderful city," Scarrow went on, "having someone on hand to set bones and stem bleeding could prove a matter of life and death, should ill luck befall you."

"The reverend has a point," Griffin said carefully.

"The museum didn't provide a stipend for a doctor," Christine said.

"Nor do I require one." Scarrow smiled. "Lest you think me entirely motivated by charity, allow me to remind you of my interest in archaeology. I have some understanding what this discovery could mean. I'd like to be a part of such a momentous occasion, even if my role is a small one."

"And your flock?"

"Can surely fend for themselves a few days. If they descend into idolatry and mayhem the moment my back is turned, clearly I've done a very poor job of shepherding them."

Christine mulled it over for a long moment. "I'm in command of this expedition. As long as you're comfortable taking orders from a woman and promise not to try and convert anyone, your skills will be welcome."

"Of course." Scarrow glanced at Iskander. "I take it, sir, you are a follower of Mohammed?"

"Church of England, actually," Iskander replied a bit stiffly.

Scarrow laughed. "Ah, of course. Forgive me. I promise to do no more than pray—quietly—for the success of our expedition."

"Then we have an accord." Christine reached across the table and they shook hands on it. "For now, we'd best find our cabins." She rose to her feet, and we all hastily followed suit. "There's a great deal to do before we can depart tomorrow."

"Indeed," Griffin said, a bit stiffly. I cast him a curious glance, but he didn't meet my gaze.

Griffin, Iskander, and I followed Christine out of the saloon. As soon as we were outside and away from prying ears, Griffin flung up his arms.

"You do recall why we're here, don't you?" he demanded in a low voice. "What about these seals and this umbra? We're supposed to be saving the town, not haring off to study a glacier only three days before the solstice!"

"There didn't seem to be anything magical about the stele," I said. "I can look over it again if you would like, but I imagine I would have sensed any enchantment while I reconstructed the thing."

"Perhaps the umbra is in the city," Iskander suggested. "Was there a city associated with the Eltdown Shards, I wonder? And if so, had any trace been worn away, or was the information suppressed?"

"If the Endicotts were involved, probably the latter," I said. "Which makes it all the more imperative to find this one as soon as possible."

"And what if it isn't simple to seal away?" Griffin persisted. "What if it turns out the entire site is best left untouched? Don't you remember what Vanya said when he attacked you, Whyborne? You would 'break open the mountain and release the great worm?' What if he knew about the city on the mountain somehow?"

"How would he know anything about it?" I asked. "We didn't until just now."

"Jack said he was Russian creole. If the native side of his family came from one of the tribes in this area, perhaps they had legends, or even knew something we don't." Griffin frowned. "Blast, Jack's original letter even said something about the natives avoiding the area."

"This is the find of a lifetime!" Christine shouted. I gestured at her to keep her voice down. She shot me an angry look, but complied. "If Nephren-ka ensured my place in the annals of archaeological history, this...this would be an even greater accomplishment. It would change our basic understanding of human history! I'm not turning my back on it just because some maniac yelled at Whyborne about mountains and worms."

"And the umbra?" Griffin pressed.

"What of it? We don't even know what it is, Griffin, or where it might be. What the devil did you think I'd do, once you pointed out the similarity between the stele and the peaks? Sit here on my hands until something comes lumbering down off the mountain to eat us?"

Griffin sighed, steam writhing about his face in the icy air. "No. But we can't let scientific zeal make us incautious."

I pressed my lips together...but it would do no good to withhold the information, even if it would only add to the argument. "There's something I should mention. The city shown on the stele...it reminds me a great deal of the one I saw in visions when the dweller in the deeps touched my mind."

Griffin cursed, and even Iskander seemed taken aback. "Are you certain, old chap?" he asked. "That seems...rather unlikely."

"I'm certainly not disagreeing." My mind raced. "I'd always assumed the ketoi constructed the underwater city at the dweller's direction. What if ancient humans built it, and it sank beneath the waves?"

"Like Atlantis?" Griffin asked sharply.

"Of course not," I snapped. "I'm no theosophist, searching for evidence of some so-called root race. Perhaps this prior civilization, whatever it was, had contact with the ketoi. For all we know, this arctic city might have been built by some group of hybrids who fled inland for reasons of their own."

"Do you think there are any ketoi off the coast here?" Christine asked. "Around the Aleutian Islands, perhaps?"

"It's possible," I allowed. "And Ketoi—the island, that is—is part of the Kuril chain. It isn't terribly far from the Aleutians, certainly not for creatures that can swim great distances underwater. Perhaps their name is in fact derived from the island, not the Greek *ketus*..."

Christine cleared her throat. "But that's for another time," I said hastily. "We can't say anything for certain until—and unless—we find the city and get a closer look."

"There you have it," Christine said, as if I'd somehow made her point for her. "We can't know anything until we examine the site closer. Assuming there's even a site left after the action of the glacier."

"I suppose," Griffin allowed at last. We'd reached our cabin, and clustered about the door. "But let's not lose sight of our original goal: to make certain this umbra, if it even still exists as you say, remains sealed away."

"I'm honestly not entirely certain how we mean to do that," Iskander said, looking at me. "I know we've talked of strengthening these seals somehow, but I haven't heard the details."

"The seals will be bound to an object of some kind," I said. "Which unfortunately could be anything that would act as a container."

"And you mean to reinforce them somehow?"

"Not precisely. That is, I could, if I knew either the exact spell cast originally, or if the sorcerer physically traced the—the *shape* of the spell, as it were, so I could see where to reinforce it. However, I've been studying how to cast such magics myself, so I should be able to lay a second spell over the first and strengthen it that way. Er, in theory."

"Wonderful," Griffin muttered.

"It will be fine," Christine clapped Griffin encouragingly on the arm. "If it comes to it, you and I are hardly helpless against the otherworldly. Iskander comes from an entire line of monster hunters. And Whyborne is a monster himself."

"Excuse me!" I exclaimed. "I don't appreciate these slurs against my ancestry."

She ignored me. "We'll do whatever is necessary, Griffin. But the antiquity of this find…this isn't some primitive remnant built by ancient hunters who crossed the land bridge from Asia. This is beyond anything dreamed of by science. And I intend to excavate it even if I have to fight off a dozen monsters with my bare hands."

CHAPTER 26

Griffin

I should never have drawn attention to the buried mountain pass. But all day, I hadn't been able to shake the sense that the stele was familiar, in form if not detail. And with the aurora raging overhead, the voice no one else heard had returned, and I'd no longer been thinking clearly by the time we pieced the accursed artifact together.

Was I going mad?

The doctors at the asylum had been wrong to try to cure me of my desire for men. There was no aberration in my love for Ival, no disease of mind or soul. But the rest...

The daemon in Chicago had broken something in me. Had confronting another of its ilk in Egypt caused some deep fracture in my mind? Something that had lurked like a trap, making itself known only through the occasional strange dream, until the strain of Pa's death and Jack's danger forced it to the surface?

If Whyborne said the stele held no magic, I believed him. If he didn't hear a voice on the aurora, there was no voice to be heard.

It was all in my head. And that terrified me.

I said nothing, only held him tight that night, when we at least had the luxury of sleeping together, if not doing anything more. The next morning, we set out for the mountain.

I tried to bury my fears beneath physical activity. I'd done little in the way of mountaineering, and certainly nothing like this. Reverend Scarrow proved to be the expert among us, although one or two of our guides had also climbed the high passes of the St. Elias Mountains during the Klondike stampede. From here on out, the glacier-fed creek was far too steep to use as a road. The dogs dragged the sleds up steep slopes, over rocky outcroppings, and between trees whose limbs brushed the ground beneath their burden of ice and snow. The thick forest of spruce gave way to barren rock, and the air grew increasingly thin as we made our ascent. Still, the dogs pulled with good heart, and we made rapid progress. We'd had astonishingly good luck with the weather so far, and I could only hope it held, as I had no desire to be caught on the glacier in the middle of a blizzard.

Despite Christine's reassurances, I still wasn't at all certain we were doing the right thing by looking for this lost city. Especially given what Whyborne said about a potential connection with the dweller in the deeps. I still didn't see how it was possible, as one city lurked beneath the waves and the other stood on a mountain, but I trusted his expert eye to notice such similarities.

And, unfortunately, made it even more likely my feelings of familiarity were the product of my imagination. I had no ketoi blood, no connection with the dweller.

Jack picked up on my dismal mood. When we stopped for lunch, he came over to me as I repacked our supplies onto the sled. "Is everything all right?" he asked quietly.

"Of course." I glanced about, hoping for something on which to blame my melancholy. "I miss the sun." A statement that was painfully true. The aurora had its own beauty, but I longed for real daylight again, rather than the murky sun that barely broke up the long arctic night.

"Ah." He nodded his understanding. "I hope you haven't quarreled with your companions? Dr. Whyborne perhaps?"

Why would he think such a thing? "No."

"It isn't uncommon. Even the best of friends argue when forced together for months on end," Jack said. "It's amazing more miners don't shoot each other in the dead of winter, trapped in their cabins by storms, in the endless dark."

I dug my canteen from inside my coat and took a swallow. Did he really believe I'd fought with Whyborne, or did he think of his own argument with Turner? "Understandable."

"Yes, well. I'm glad to hear you haven't had a row." He nodded, as if to himself. "Still, if you ever find yourself in need of a sympathetic ear, I hope you'll come to me."

I met his gaze. The shadows flung by the wavering light above made it hard to discern his expression within the depths of his hood. "Of course. And I hope you would do the same."

If he felt a need to discuss his fight with Turner, he gave no indication. "Thank you. Now, we'd best finish up here so we can be on our way."

The great glacier provided a road for us up the side of the mountain, so at least we didn't have to climb the rugged peaks. From a distance, it seemed smooth and unbroken, but up close the glacier proved to be far more uneven. Its slow movement from peak to base left great splits and cracks in the ice, some of them large and deep enough to be a danger. Reverend Scarrow went first, probing the thick layer of fresh snow with a long pole, in case of hidden crevasses. Traversing these offered something of a challenge. For the most part we were able to go around them, but once we had to use the sleds as bridges across a narrow but lengthy gap. This meant unharnessing the dogs, maneuvering the sleds into position, herding the dogs across, crawling over ourselves, then putting everything back together again.

A sense of urgency, reinforced by the brief hour of sunlight, drove us. Time was short, if there really was some creature that might be unleashed by the thinning of ancient seals. The day after tomorrow would mark both the solstice and the new moon, an ominous combination. I expected Scarrow or Turner, or even the guides, to suggest we stop for the night when the sun slipped back below the horizon. They remained silent, however, as if the same urgency drove them. Perhaps Christine's dreams of archaeological glory had infected them as well.

The sunlight banished my delusions of a distant voice speaking too quietly to be made out, for which I was profoundly grateful. I tried to believe it wouldn't return with the coming of darkness. But once the thin light vanished, it came back, stronger than ever. As if it drew closer.

I had to tell Whyborne. If I was losing my faculties, it could prove fatal in this wilderness, not just to me but to my companions.

We stopped at last, high up on the mountain in the thin air. The tired dogs immediately flopped onto their bellies. Whyborne rather looked as if he wished to do the same. The guides set about unpacking the wood we'd hauled up from the tree line far below, and the rest of us saw to the tents.

"This seems like a good place to make our base camp," Christine said, surveying the area as she spoke. "The ridge there provides some shelter from the wind, and we should be close to the location of the city as shown on the stele. We'll rest up tonight, and tomorrow we'll see if we can't find any way to reach the bedrock below us. Perhaps one of the larger crevasses." She trailed off, staring at the mountain as if it might offer up its secrets to her.

"It's hard to believe, isn't it?" Whyborne asked. He sat back on his haunches, his gaze on the vast valley carved by the glacier. "A city once stood here. Long before anyone dreamed of the pyramids, people lived in this very place."

"I wonder what happened to them?" Jack mused. "Did the Ice Age drive them away? And where did they go?"

"Perhaps we'll learn soon," Whyborne replied. A spark livened his tired eyes. "If only there was some way to interpret their writing. Might any known languages descend from it? I wonder..."

"May I speak to you privately a moment?" I asked, before my courage failed.

Whyborne and Jack both frowned in surprise. "Of course," Whyborne said, rising to his feet.

"Don't go far," Jack warned. "There are crevasses everywhere."

I waved to let him know I'd heard. In this cold, clear air our words would carry all too easily, so once I judged us a safe distance away, I spoke in a lowered voice. "Something's wrong with me."

"What?" Whyborne's eyes widened with concern. "Are you ill?"

"No. Or, yes. Just not physically." I didn't look at him as I confessed to my delusion, not wanting to see his pity or his fear.

"This is bad, Griffin," he said when I finished. "Why didn't you tell me as soon as you started hearing things?"

"Because...I didn't want it to be true." Acid churned in my stomach, and my chest felt too tight. "After the asylum, I always feared that—that the doctors might have been right in some small part. And I know the Brotherhood was behind my confinement, but no one else seemed to question it. Even Elliot thought I'd lost my senses. Hearing voices no one else can...I can't tell you how many inmates I saw who suffered from the same madness. And now I am as well."

"Griffin, you're being absurd." Whyborne gripped my shoulder. "Clearly something is going on, but I'm certain it has something to do with this blasted city."

"I'd thought of that, but it doesn't make sense. I'm ordinary. There's nothing magical or special about me."

"Everything about you is special," he said gently.

"To you, perhaps." I gave him a rueful smile.

"Not just to me. Widdershins knows its own."

A former client of mine had once insisted Widdershins collected people, but I had never believed it. Not until last year, when Whyborne had touched the maelstrom and found some kind of mind, or sentience, or…honestly, I wasn't entirely sure, and even Whyborne had trouble explaining it.

"The town didn't collect me," I said. "I'll grant there are arcane forces at work, and an unusually high number of strange people living there, but not everyone in Widdershins is odd. Look at Christine and Iskander."

"Everything about Christine is odd," Whyborne muttered. "And Iskander is from a line of ghūl killers, which is hardly ordinary. But I'm not talking about everyone in town. I'm talking about you. It doesn't matter, though. I'm certain this has something to do with the stele and the city. You aren't going mad."

I wanted to believe him. "You can't be certain."

He squeezed my shoulder, and I knew he longed to embrace me. But that was impossible, with so many watching eyes. "Which one of us is a sorcerer? Trust my expert opinion."

"Very well." I met his gaze. "I will. And I hope you're right."

"I am." His hand fell to his side. "I don't know what's going on here, Griffin, but we'll find out and make it right. I promise."

Chapter 27

Whyborne

EXHAUSTION ENSURED I slept deeply, despite the discomfort of the tent and my own restless thoughts. Even so, I didn't hesitate when I awoke, quickly shaking off the dregs of sleep and making my way to the campfire before anyone else except for the guides. Christine soon joined me, and we waited impatiently while the rest of our expedition made ready for the day. Tomorrow marked the winter solstice, and there would be no moon. The darkest night of the year by far, and according to the Pnakotic Manuscripts, the seals would be at their weakest. If we found them, I could probably reinforce them as I'd explained to Iskander, and hold back whatever might want to come through.

And there was something wanting to come through, I was utterly convinced of it now. I didn't know why or how it had fastened on Griffin, but the distant voice invading his mind must surely be connected to this umbra, whatever it was.

Could it be some ancient god-creature, like the dweller in the deeps? But the dweller communicated with ketoi and madmen, and Griffin was neither. Perhaps it was something lurking Outside, waiting for the right person to come along, like Nitocris. But Griffin had read no unholy tomes, no forbidden treatises to open the way. I was far more likely to have run afoul of some awful creature than he.

As I'd told him the night before, it didn't matter at the moment. What mattered was severing whatever tie it had formed with his mind. Reinforcing the seals, shutting away whatever unholy power affected him, seemed the surest way of doing that.

But we had to find the seals first.

Over breakfast, we discussed how we might search for the city, should our theory about underground diggings prove correct. "I suggest looking for a moulin," Scarrow said. He indicated the landscape around us. "They tend to form in areas like this—flatter parts of the glacier marked by crevasses."

"An excellent suggestion," Christine said. "If we have no luck finding one, we can try some of the deeper crevasses." She finished her coffee in a gulp, then rose to her feet. "No sense loitering about. We've work to do."

Christine organized us to cover the most area without re-crossing each other's tracks. Under the guise of having a question about the transects, I discreetly told her about the voice Griffin had been hearing. The news put a scowl on her face.

"So you think the umbra is still here? And in my city?" she asked.

"That's my opinion. Still behind the seals, presumably, but maybe not for long."

"Hmph. Well, we can do nothing about it if we can't find the blasted thing." She turned away. "Get to work, Whyborne."

I trudged along in snowshoes, probing the snow in front of me with a pole and casting about for any shadow that might prove to be an opening into the glacier.

What would happen if we didn't find one? Could the distant voice do Griffin any real harm? It hadn't so far, but the solstice hadn't yet come. Presumably it would grow stronger until then.

Unless I was wrong, and it had nothing to do with the umbra. Curse it. And curse Griffin for not telling me sooner. He didn't wish to worry me, oh no, much better to imagine himself going slowly mad. When we returned to the cabin at Hoarfrost, we were going to have a long discussion about the inadvisability of keeping things from one's husband.

"Whyborne!" Griffin called. His voice echoed strangely in the cold air.

I couldn't run in snowshoes, but hurried to join him as quickly as possible. He stood very still, staring down at the ground. "Griffin?" I panted as I came up. "What's wrong?"

"I think I've found what we're looking for," he said.

He pointed at a hole in the ice, perhaps four feet across. Lines of strain showed around his mouth, and his skin looked horribly pale beneath the flickering green aurora. "The voice?" I asked softly.

"Yes." He tore his gaze from the hole and met mine. "It's louder here, for lack of a better word. Still distant, but not as far."

"Can you make out what it's saying?"

"No."

Thank goodness for small favors. I clapped his arm, then shouted for Christine. In short order, the rest of our party gathered around the moulin. At Christine's command, Jack tied his lantern to a rope and lowered it into the hole. The light glittered from the smooth walls, revealing the deep blue of the compressed ice.

"How far down do you think it goes?" Scarrow asked.

"It's deep." Jack had reached the end of the rope, and still only darkness showed beneath the reach of the lantern's light.

"There's only one way to find out," Christine said. "Fetch the climbing ropes. I'm going down."

Scarrow frowned. "I'm not certain that's wise, Dr. Putnam."

"The reverend is right. It might be dangerous." Griffin's voice shook slightly, and I winced. Being trapped beneath the lightless pyramid in Egypt had done nothing to lessen his fear of underground spaces.

Turner nodded. "Agreed. I'll go first."

"You certainly will not!" Christine drew herself up, eyes flashing fire. "This is my expedition, and I have the most experience when it comes to archaeology. I'm going down."

Iskander looked worried. Had Christine told him of Griffin's half-heard voice? "Perhaps you shouldn't go alone. Just in case."

"Oh, very well." She scowled at him, then transferred her gaze to me. "Whyborne, you're coming with me."

"Me?" I exclaimed.

Jack looked equally dubious. "Are you certain? No offense, but perhaps someone with mountaineering experience would be a better choice."

Christine's expression grew thunderous. "Are you all hard of hearing? I said Whyborne and I meant Whyborne!"

"I agree. Dr. Whyborne is an excellent choice," Iskander said.

Oh. He—and probably Christine—didn't want me for my non-existent mountaineering ability. They wanted me as a sorcerer. Just in case the umbra lurked at the bottom of the hole.

"All right," I said, looking at the moulin with distaste. "Let's go."

CHAPTER 28

Whyborne

"**Be careful!**" Griffin called from the rapidly vanishing oval of light above. "If you have any trouble at all, two tugs on the rope and we'll pull you back up! And if you do find something, for God's sake, don't go wandering about!"

I bit back a sigh he wouldn't have heard anyway, and concentrated on keeping myself from swinging too violently against the side of the moulin. Neither Christine nor I were experienced enough at climbing to attempt to rappel down. As a result, the rest of our party lowered us in slings tied into the ends of the long ropes.

The surface of the ice beneath my mittens was smooth as glass, but rippled and pitted by the water that had carved into the glacier. My lantern revealed fine striations in the ice as it slipped past, each one marking some ancient snowfall.

How deep was this hole? Would we have enough rope? Would it reach the bedrock below, or would it change from a wide entrance to a crevice too narrow to navigate?

"Do you see the bottom yet?" I called down to Christine.

"Not yet, but—oh!"

I tried to twist about to see what was happening, but succeeded only in dashing my shoulder into the hard-packed ice. "Christine! Are you all right? What's happening?"

"You'll see!" she called back, but her voice sounded fainter than before. A moment later, I understood why.

The walls of the moulin drew back, the ice no longer around me but above, like the ceiling of some vast cathedral. I held out my lantern. Without anything to brace against, I spun in a slow circle, the light catching off of the ceiling, then some distant wall.

"I'm down!" Christine called, although at this depth no one on the surface could hear. A moment or two later, my feet also thumped lightly on the ground.

Christine had already climbed out of her sling, which lay coiled on the exposed earth—a jumble of gravel and frozen mud, ground down by the passage of the glacier. I hurried to join her.

"How far do you think it goes?" I asked, peering into the gloom.

"Most likely the ice cave reaches all the way to the foot of the glacier." She began to make her way in the other direction, up the gentle slope. "More moulins must be somewhere above, feeding into the cave."

"Where are you going?" I hurried after her. "We promised we wouldn't go far."

"I'm not. But I'm also not going back to the surface without some idea of what's down here, umbra or no umbra."

I kicked at the jumble of small stones, but they were frozen to the earth beneath them. "Anything that used to be here has been scoured away."

"We already knew that would be the case." Christine stopped abruptly. "Whyborne—look. There's an opening."

We approached cautiously. A large, curiously regular, hole pierced the floor of the glacial cave. Our lantern light fell onto it, revealing what were unmistakably masonry blocks. They appeared to form a ramp, descending to some lower level within the mountain.

"If only we'd brought the camera—curse it," Christine said. "Do you know what this means, Whyborne? At least part of the city is still here!"

"And presumably it's the part with the monster sealed inside," I murmured, but in truth my heart sped with excitement. Griffin didn't appreciate just how extraordinary this find was, what it meant to human history. From now on everything would be different. All of the books on the rise of civilizations would have to be rewritten. Our very understanding of our species might change.

What secrets did these ancients know? What sorcery? What might I—we—learn from them?

The lantern beams shifted erratically, thanks to our trembling hands. We couldn't turn back—not yet. We had to see for ourselves that our wildest imaginings were in fact true.

And if the umbra was here, if it was calling to Griffin in some way, we'd just not disturb anything that looked like a magical seal. Simple enough.

The ramp sloped sharply, and we used care to navigate it. Fortunately, it didn't go far, but instead ended in a large, hexagonal room. Whatever water flowed through during the warmer months must drain deeper, as no ice coated the floor. Reliefs, some badly worn from the action of time and water, covered all five walls. I could make out little of them, except they seemed to show geometric shapes, animals, and plants. The oddly grouped dots, which appeared to be some system of writing, were also present. On the other side of the room, opposite the ramp, a doorway opened on to blackness.

"We'd best return," Christine said reluctantly. "Iskander will call off the wedding if we explore any farther without him."

"And Griffin shall wish a divorce for giving him heart palpitations," I agreed, equally reluctant. Still, if I knew Griffin at all, he would be frantic by now, certain something horrible had happened to us both. I didn't want to cause him any unnecessary worry. "We have little time left. Tomorrow is the solstice, and it's already quite late in the day. We need to return to camp, gather whatever gear we need, and come back immediately."

"Agreed." Her mouth pursed. "And hope these ruins aren't so extensive we can't find these seals of yours before it's too late." Then she brightened. "Or perhaps the umbra will prove to be something I can shoot. Then we won't have to worry about it anymore!"

"Not everything can be shot, Christine."

"Bah! You're such a pessimist." Lowering her lantern, she turned back to the ramp. "Now let's return, before Griffin and Iskander come down here looking for us."

CHAPTER 29

Whyborne

AS WE MADE our way back to camp, Christine ran off a long list of needed supplies, Iskander occasionally putting in an addition of his own. As everyone else's attention was on Christine, I moved closer to Griffin. Careful to keep my voice low, I said, "Perhaps you shouldn't go with us."

A veritable rainbow of colors streamed across the heavens: green, white, and red, shading into violet. It looked as if the sky itself burned, and the glacier reflected the colors eerily.

Griffin's jaw tightened at my words. "Of course I'm going with you."

How could I make him see reason? "Griffin, if it is the umbra you're hearing, getting closer to it might not be the wisest thing for you to do."

"If it is the umbra, I'll be able to lead you to it," he countered.

"Which might not be at all healthy for you. Coupled with your fear of underground places—"

It was the wrong thing to have said; I knew it as soon as the words left my mouth. He came to a halt on the outskirts of the camp, and shot me a glare. "Damn it, Ival, I'm not an invalid, or a child! Stop treating me as one."

"I don't!" I protested. "Is it wrong to be concerned for you?"

"I don't want your concern, if it means suggesting I'd ever, even for a moment, consider letting you go down there by yourself due to some fear of mine!"

Must he be so stubborn? "I won't be alone. I'll have Christine and Iskander. And what if we're wrong somehow, and the umbra isn't below the ground but above it? Surely someone should stay behind and protect Jack and the others."

"Stop. Please, just stop." His mouth twisted into an angry frown. "You're trying to find some excuse, no matter how unlikely, so I—"

A loud crack sounded from above us on the mountain, echoing from the peaks around us. We both fell silent, startled by the sound.

There came a loud rumble, like thunder. But the sky was clear, and the rumble growing closer and closer.

"Avalanche!" Scarrow shouted.

For a moment, I froze in horror. The entire glacier above us seemed on the move, the recent snowfall breaking free of the ice below and roaring down like a wave in slow motion.

A wave.

Snow was just water, after all.

I didn't let myself think. The guides were already running, but even if we somehow outpaced the avalanche, our camp would be destroyed and our dogs killed. Most likely we'd end up caught and crushed as well.

I ran toward the oncoming wall of snow. Griffin shouted something behind me, but I couldn't make it out over the now-deafening thunder of the slide. I tore off my right mitten and flung it away. Dropping to one knee, I thrust out my hand.

In Widdershins, with all the power of the vortex to draw from, I might have been able to stop the avalanche. Here, I had only my own will to call upon. The scars lacing my right arm burned and pulled tight. I *felt* the snow, the water in frozen form, different and yet the same as the fluid I'd manipulated many times before.

I shoved it back, away from me. Liquid would flow together, but this was so many bits of ice, some catching on each other, while the rest tumbled free. A clear wedge formed directly before me, but it wasn't enough.

Above the roar of approaching snow, there came the sound of someone chanting in Aklo. I couldn't spare the attention to wonder whom it might be, or what it might mean. I could only keep my will steady, pushing back against the avalanche.

The furrow I'd created deepened, snow rolling off to either side. The moving pack exploded into powder, and ice crystals stung the exposed skin of my hand, my face. As the bulk of the slide tumbled away to one side, the deadly snow rushing down on the camp slowed, swirled...and gradually came to a stop.

We were safe.

I felt light headed, as if I'd overexerted myself in this thin mountain air. I stumbled to my feet, nearly fell, then regained my balance. There came shouts of alarm, and a shocked cry behind me. Pulling my mitten back onto my right hand, I turned to see who had helped me save the camp.

Nicholas Turner stood there, his mouth pressed into a line of annoyance. Behind him, the guides had drawn up around Christine, Griffin, Iskander, and Scarrow. Most of them now held guns in their hands, some of which were turned on me.

"Well," Turner said. "I suppose we'll have to deviate from the original plan."

CHAPTER 30

Griffin

SHOCK STOLE THE moisture from my mouth. I swallowed hard, trying to understand what was happening. Turner a sorcerer, the guides apparently in his employ, and Jack...

Jack stood off to one side, looking miserable. No one pointed any guns at him.

"J-Jack?" I asked. Because there had to be some mistake.

"What the devil are you about, man!" Christine shouted at Turner.

Turner smiled slightly, but his gaze went to Whyborne instead of Christine. "The same thing you're about," he said coolly. "You came here to find the umbra and make it your servant."

"My *what?*" Whyborne's face went deathly white. His gaze flicked from the guides, to me, to Christine. No doubt he was considering what sorcerous options he might have.

But Whyborne was only one man. If he lit the powder in one gun with the fire of his mind, the other guards would surely shoot. They'd fell either him or one of us.

"No need to play the fool, Dr. Whyborne." Turner laughed, an ugly sound with little in it of humor. "Do you seriously imagine we don't know everything about you? Your power, your heritage?" He shook his head. "It was Jack here who came up with the idea of sending the fragment to Mr. Flaherty. A little bait to draw you here. And you swallowed it instantly."

No. No, it wasn't true. I cast a pleading glance at Jack, and to my surprise, he met my gaze. His lips parted, and I waited for him to deny it. To say Turner lied in order to drive a wedge between us for some obscure reason of his own.

"Tell them to stop pointing guns at my brother," he said instead. "Please, Nicholas. There's no need."

"There's every need," Turner replied mildly. "It's keeping Dr. Whyborne from killing us all, for one thing."

Jack shook his head. "No. You said th-things like him don't have friends. You said—"

"Your brother and Dr. Whyborne aren't *friends*," Turner said, disgust lacing the words. "They're lovers. If one would call a man who'd lie down with a hybrid abomination such a thing."

My fists curled within my mittens. All the time I'd spent worrying about Jack finding out about us, about me. It seemed so *stupid* now, so utterly inconsequential in the face of this betrayal.

"Damn you to hell," Christine said conversationally, and followed up with what I assumed was some foul curse in Arabic.

"Shut up, bitch," snarled the guide nearest her. "Spread your legs for some dirty Arab, will you? Maybe we ought to show you what a white man's like, huh?"

"Touch her and die," Iskander said. He looked utterly wild, his dark eyes wide and his lips pulled back from his teeth.

"Silence." Turner's voice cracked like a whip. "There's no need for that sort of talk from anyone. After all, we still want Dr. Whyborne to cooperate, don't we?"

"Cooperate?" Whyborne stared at Turner as though the man were deranged. "You've threatened those I care about and called me an abomination. Why the devil would I cooperate with you?"

"I'd think it obvious." Turner gestured to us. "How many of my men do you think you can kill before one of the survivors puts a bullet through Mr. Flaherty's head? Or dear Dr. Putnam's?"

Jack swayed. "Nicholas—"

"Be quiet, Jack." Turner shot him an angry glare, then glanced at Scarrow. "I'm sorry you got caught up in this, Reverend."

Scarrow looked about worriedly. "I...I don't know what's happening, exactly," he said, voice trembling. "But please, I beg you. Violence never solved anything."

"Violence solves problems all the time," Turner corrected him. "It secured this continent for the white man. It allows England to rule the waves. It brought the southern states into line, and pours money into the coffers of men rich enough to hire armies of Pinkertons to break up strikes. If I remember my history correctly, most of Europe was converted to your religion by use of the sword, was it not? Violence solves a great deal, actually."

"What do you want?" Whyborne's voice was steady, but cold as the glacier beneath us. He'd drawn himself up to his full height, sneering down at Turner, his face a pale mask.

"As I said, the same as you."

"You're wrong." Whyborne's lip twisted slightly. I knew he must be frightened, but it didn't show on his face or in his manner. "We came here to make certain the umbra, whatever it may be, doesn't emerge from its sealed prison."

Turner's brows arched. "Then you're a greater fool than I ever realized." He laughed suddenly. "The terrible and powerful sorcerer turns out to be nothing but a puffed up milksop. I'm almost disappointed. Still, it makes things far easier for me."

"Get on with it, man," Christine snapped. "Or do you love the sound of your voice so much?"

Turner's face flushed with anger. "Speak again, and I'll cut out your tongue. Dr. Whyborne clearly lacks the backbone to stop me."

Whyborne's face had gone utterly expressionless. Someone who didn't know him well might have mistaken it for acquiescence rather than extreme anger. Wind whispered over the glacier, and a little swirl of ice spiraled up.

Turner didn't have the slightest idea how much danger he was really in. If he didn't have us as hostages…

But he did. Damn it.

"Tell me what you want," Whyborne said, and his breath turned to ice crystals and fell to the ground with a soft whisper before him.

"Your assistance, of course." Turner gestured to us. "Mr. Flaherty, Mr. Barnett, and Reverend Scarrow will remain here under the watchful care of some of my men. Should I fail to return in a reasonable amount of time, they will all be executed."

"Nicholas, no!" Jack protested.

"You're turning out to be a disappointment, Jack," Turner said, although he didn't take his gaze off Whyborne. "I thought you willing to do whatever is necessary. No matter." He pointed at Christine. "Dr. Putnam and Dr. Whyborne will accompany us back to the city. Not only might her archaeological knowledge come in handy, but she'll prove a useful hostage in case Dr. Whyborne develops any ideas about escape. Together, we'll all go down into the city and find what we both came here to look for. With the seals weakened, it will be child's play to remove a chrysalis."

A chrysalis? What the devil did the man mean?

"And then what?" Whyborne asked.

"If you cooperate, I'll let you go," Turner said with a greasy smile. "You and Dr. Putnam can walk out through the glacial cave at your own pace. There's a Tagish village only a few days from here. If the weather holds, you may even make it there with all your fingers and toes still intact."

"And Griffin and the others?" Whyborne asked.

"We'll leave them here—without any weapons or dogs, of course, but unharmed. Do we have an agreement?"

I wanted to shout at Whyborne, tell him not to agree. Turner would never let any of us go. He meant murder and nothing but.

If I did, though, and if Whyborne listened to me and refused, we'd all die now. As long as we lived there remained some hope, however slim, of surviving this.

No doubt Whyborne came to the same conclusion. He glanced at me, and our eyes met. I tried to put all the love I had for him into my gaze, to tell him silently I was sorry. I'd been the one to lead him into this trap even if I hadn't meant to.

He looked away, and I didn't know if I'd succeeded. Or if he already knew it all anyway. "Very well," he told Turner. "I accept your terms."

Chapter 31

Whyborne

As we marched across the glacier, I wracked my brain for some solution. There must be some way out of our predicament. I could summon wind and flatten some of the guards, and set fire to the powder in the guns others carried.

But could I do it fast enough to save Christine?

She strode ahead of me, her back stiff. Turner walked at her side, gripping her upper arm, a long knife pressed against her side with his other hand.

I might use my fire spell to heat the hilt until he could no longer hold it. But no, his moose hide mitten would probably protect him, as it had the man who'd attacked me in St. Michael. Even if I succeeded against all odds, the three guards would surely just shoot us both. And if I attacked one of them, or even all of them, Turner would kill Christine.

I'd never felt so utterly helpless. All of my magic, and yet Turner had defeated me with ease.

At least Griffin and Iskander were safe for the moment. God, Griffin…the look on his face, when he realized Jack lured us into Turner's vile trap…

How must he be feeling? Losing his father was difficult enough, but he'd had such hope for Jack. And after our journey here together, it had seemed those hopes were well founded.

Something dark and sharp-edged lodged in my chest. I'd make Jack pay for his betrayal. How I didn't know exactly, but he'd rue the day he'd ever decided to hurt Griffin.

Unfortunately, I had to find a way to survive this first. Despite what he said, I didn't believe for an instant Turner intended to let us live past the point of usefulness. An opportunity would present itself—I just needed to remain alert.

The avalanche had buried the moulin, but the guards soon located it again by probing the loose snow. They cleared it quickly, revealing the gaping maw into the underworld. "Dr. Putnam and I will make the descent first," Turner said. "I suggest you don't try anything, Dr. Whyborne, or else I will kill her."

I didn't reply, only glared at him. Christine did the same. If she felt any fear at all, it certainly didn't show in her defiant black eyes. Perhaps worried she might attempt something, Turner added, "And that goes for you as well, Dr. Putnam. Having Dr. Whyborne alive will make things easier, but there are other ways, and I'll use them if I must."

Curse it.

A short time later, we once again stood beneath the glacier. The ice above us creaked and groaned like a living thing, and a shiver went through me. God, I hoped the sounds were ordinary and didn't herald a collapse of some sort.

Turner gestured. "Now show us this entrance you found."

How different were my emotions this time. Tramping through here before, I'd thrilled with the discovery. Now I barely cared about the carvings, the ramp, the door into darkness. Nothing mattered except somehow getting away from Turner without either of us dying.

The doorway from the hexagonal room led to another chamber of the same shape, and thence to a third. Any furniture or items belonging to the inhabitants were long gone, crumbled into dust or washed away by periodic flooding.

Turner paused to examine the murals, a frown creasing his brow when he saw their poor condition. "What are you looking for?" Christine asked.

"Certain signs," he replied. "Which won't be found here, clearly. We have to move in and down."

"And if the object of your search is gone?" I asked. "If there is no umbra?"

A smirk played about his mouth. "I still can't believe you're this much of a fool. Why *did* you come here, if not for the same reason any sorcerer seeks out the umbrae?"

Seeks out? "But the Pnakotic Manuscripts specifically warn *against* approaching these places, especially on the day of greatest darkness."

"The Pnakotic Manuscripts?" Turner laughed, rather annoyingly. "Of course they warn against it. Who do you think sealed the umbrae away in the first place? If you'd bothered to refer to any number of other texts, you'd have found instructions on how to locate a chrysalis and obtain a formidable servant for yourself."

I ground my teeth together. What sort of resources did the man think I possessed? Or did he imagine I spent my days studying sorcery instead of performing my actual job at the museum? "We believed Griffin's brother was in danger, and his peril would only grow as the solstice approached. I hardly had the time or leisure to read through every book in the library."

Turner shook his head, clearly amused at my expense. "You *are* a fool. Good lord, why on earth did the Endicotts ever fear you?"

I felt as though I'd missed a step in the dark. "The...Endicotts?" Dear heavens, did my damnable cousins have a hand in all this?

Last year, after it was all over, I'd gone to the house Theo and Fiona had rented. All of their books and notes were gone. A brief inquiry on Griffin's part showed the twins shipped everything back to England within hours of learning the truth about my ketoi blood. No doubt they'd included every detail they knew about me, in case their effort to wipe Widdershins off the face of the earth didn't succeed.

But I'd heard nothing from the family in the year since. Not a single whisper, or threatening letter, or assassination attempt.

"Yes." Turner's lip curled. "You and I are related—very distantly— through our maternal lines. If I had my way, I'd be living on the family estate at this moment."

"Then why are you here bullying us instead?" Christine asked.

His face flushed dark, and he gave her a shake. "Because they're fools, so interested in power and blood they overlook a man's true worth. But they'll see soon enough. They're cowards who didn't dare confront Dr. Whyborne in his place of power. But they looked into his associates and their families, and found Jack." A small, tight smile crept onto his face. "And I, the useless cousin whose sorcery wasn't deemed great enough to earn him a place at the table, volunteered to face what they fear. I would confront the great and mighty Dr. Whyborne. Imagine my surprise when I discovered you're nothing more than a dithering fairy with hardly any intelligence to speak of."

Now that went too far. "I placed first in my class at Miskatonic," I said stiffly. "Granted, they didn't hand out degrees in thuggery, which I assume was *your* area of specialization."

"I'm cut to the quick," Turner replied mockingly. "Although to be fair, Jack was the one who came up with the idea of luring you here, where you'd be more vulnerable *and* could prove useful at the same time."

"Jack may not have been in real danger before," Christine said, the words brittle, clipped. "But I assure you, he will be if I ever lay eyes on him again."

"Worry about your own skin, Dr. Putnam." Turner advised. "And be silent, the both of you. I'm done answering questions."

The third room let out into a passage that ran level for a short distance, before intersecting with a smallish, hexagonal chamber. Surprisingly, what appeared to be windows pierced the opposite wall. And was that faint light coming through them?

Turner seemed equally confused. "Windows?" he murmured. "Not here then. Lower?"

Corridors ran off to either side of the small room. Turner followed the right hand one, which let out onto a vast open space.

Even in such danger as we were, I couldn't suppress a gasp of awe at the sight awaiting us. Some ancient river had long ago carved deep into the mountain, leaving behind a vast rift that now opened before us. Buildings, such as we'd seen depicted on the stele, clung to each flank. There appeared to be no streets, and very little organization, the whole thing more like a vast hive than a city. Slender bridges of stone leapt from one side of the gorge to the other, and high above, almost lost to our sight, lay the great bulk of the glacier. At one end stood an enormous plaza, with a great temple in the center. Its stepped sides and flattened top reminded me irresistibly of the great temple where I'd seen the dweller in the deeps. The flattened top was clearly meant to be some sort of ritual area, like the peaks of the temples uncovered in the jungles of South America. A great hexagon had been carved into its stones, and a sort of plinth stood at one end, overlooking the city below.

The entire scene glowed softly, lit by what looked like a net of light draped across the fantastic architecture of the city. Some of the glowing substance lay on the balcony we stood upon. I pulled off one mitten and touched it tentatively with my finger. It was sticky and slimy, and a trace came off on my fingertip when it pulled back.

"It's like some sort of-of slime mold, perhaps?" I suggested. I was no biologist though.

"Who cares?" Turner jerked his head to indicate a ramp spiraling down. "What we're looking for won't be in this part of the city, where it would have been exposed to the sky."

Hatred scalded the back of my throat, the inside of my chest.

Turner had threatened us, likely meant to kill us, especially if he worked with my cousins. Whatever creature awaited us, whatever this "chrysalis" might be, he meant to wrest it out of here without thought of what he might unleash.

And he couldn't even be bothered to take a blasted moment and consider the magnificence surrounding us, to feel the weight of history and wonder.

"You're despicable," I told him.

Turner's lip curled. "Strangely, I don't care about the opinion of a monster. Now come along, or I'll start carving bits and pieces out of Dr. Putnam."

CHAPTER 32

Whyborne

WE DESCENDED, AS he'd said, eventually finding a path across a wide causeway, far beneath the delicate stone bridges. Beyond lay another series of hexagonal chambers, their floors oddly offset from one another.

"Ah," Turner said at last. "Yes. Here we are."

Three doorways led from this chamber. The murals were in much better shape than those closer to the outside. Groupings of dots showed over each door, accompanied by the illustrations of fantastical creatures. At least, I hoped they were fantastical.

Turner paused uncertainly, studying the symbols around them. He didn't share what he was looking for—although it galled me to admit it, his knowledge of these matters far outmatched mine. "This way," he decided at last, and stepped into the middle hall.

Christine twisted sharply in his grip, stamping her foot down on his with all of her weight behind it. At the same moment, she seized his wrist to keep the knife away from her. "Now, Whyborne!" she shouted.

I grasped for the first spell that came to mind. Wind roared up out of the depths, and I shaped it with my will. One of the guards cried out and flung up his arm, while a second collided with the third, sending them both to the floor. Elation leapt in me, and I narrowed my focus to set fire to the powder within the gun still in the hand of the first guard.

Christine's scream turned my blood to ice. Forgetting the guard, I spun to see her slump against the wall, Turner's knife buried in her upper right arm. He tore the blade free, and blood spurted out after it.

"Make one more move, and it will go in her throat next," he shouted at me.

The wind died. One of the guards seized me from behind, shoving me into the wall. I struggled blindly, but he'd gotten a grip on the ugly scarf around my throat. I twisted, trying to free myself before he succeeded in throttling me.

"I trust this has been a lesson for you both," Turner said coldly. "Let him go."

The hand loosened its grip. I tore off the scarf and let it fall, coughing and massaging my bruised throat. "Christine," I gasped. "Are you all right?"

"F-Fine." The word came out in a harsh pant. She leaned against the wall, one hand clasped to her wounded arm. Blood leaked from between her fingers.

I started toward her, but Turner raised his knife. "The wound needs to be seen to," I said. "You can't just let her bleed to death!"

"I certainly can. I won't, as long as you cooperate." He gave me a nasty sort of smile. "But it's entirely within my power to end her any moment I feel like it."

I swallowed against the icy ball clogging my throat. "You've made your point." God, we were going to die down here. "Please, just do something to help her."

Turner motioned to one of the guards. He gave me a rough shove as he passed and was none too gentle with Christine. The parka proved too thick to tie a bandage around effectively, so she shrugged out of it. Blood stained the coat beneath, but the brute didn't bother to check the wound, just tied a handkerchief around her arm: coat, shirt, union suit, and all. I hoped it would do some good at least. Christine winced but made no complaint, dragging the parka back on when he finished.

"Now, if we're done with this nonsense, shall we continue on?" Turner asked, as if giving us a choice.

The hallway penetrated deep into the rock. Already it was far warmer than on the surface, and I tried to remember what temperature caves supposedly hovered at. The ceiling remained level, but the floor abruptly canted down into another of the steep ramps. The walls fell away, and great, barrel shaped columns, carved from the living rock, lined either side of the long ramp.

The ramp ended in a large, almost plaza-like room. Our lanterns showed bits and pieces of distant carvings, and once again the style reminded me irresistibly of my dreams of the abyssal city. Rather than undersea monsters, however, this showed rank upon rank of mountains, and of great land animals that seemed but the distant relations of our modern fauna.

How accursedly old was this place? Had every guess as to the antiquity of the human species been wrong, or...

No. I wouldn't let myself think it. Not yet, anyway.

An immense door, cunningly carved from stone, blocked the way forward. Like the walls, it too bore reliefs. But rather than depicting a scene or a series of creatures, it showed only a single, massive figure. My first impression was of some Eastern dragon, all sinuous curls and lashing whiskers.

Oh dear. What had Vanya shouted, about breaking open the mountain and releasing a giant worm? Was this a depiction of the umbra?

"What the devil is that thing?" Christine asked. Her voice cracked slightly, whether from pain or thirst I didn't know.

"The Mother of Shadows," Turner said. "But don't worry—we won't be coming across her."

The fine hair on the back of my neck tried to stand up. Umbrae meant shadows. And if this thing was called the Mother of Shadows... might be more than one umbra down here? Or was the depiction merely symbolic? Turner seemed certain we wouldn't encounter the creature.

Turner shoved Christine roughly in the direction of one of the guards. "Put a bullet in her if Dr. Whyborne so much as twitches," he ordered.

I held myself as still as possible, afraid the order might be taken literally. How could I possibly hope to get us out of this situation alive? We'd come so close in the corridor—if only Turner hadn't struck such a deep blow, we might be free now.

But there was no use regretting what might have been. I narrowed my eyes and watched Turner as he approached the great door. How on earth did it open? There didn't seem to be any visible device, no latch or hinge.

Turner, once again, had the answers. If nothing else, this trip to the Arctic had served to show me how utterly inadequate I was in every way. I'd at least thought myself a competent sorcerer, but rather than spend the last year learning the finer points, I'd relied on my natural affinity for magic and merely dabbled in anything more. Perhaps if I'd truly devoted myself to study, I would have known as much as Turner and been prepared for all of this. Instead, Christine was injured and Griffin in terrible danger, and I could do nothing but stand here like a fool.

Turner drew out a short wand: a thick wooden base strung with crystals and wire, and inscribed all over with arcane sigils. He inspected the door, running the wand across its surface a few times, as if dowsing for something. Then he nodded, pointed at the center of the door, and began to chant.

I didn't recognize the language he spoke: low and rough and strangely painful to hear. Sweat sprang out on his brow, but he repeated the chant over and over again, the wand steady in his hand.

There came a sort of subliminal *click* I felt more than heard. The door split into two pieces down the center, which swung outward with a low groan. A rush of fetid air flowed from the opening, up from somewhere deep beneath the earth.

"Quickly," Turner said, and dragged Christine after him. One of the guides prodded my back with his gun.

My skin tingled as we passed through the doorway, as if a thousand ants scurried beneath my clothing. I let out a startled exclamation, but the sensation vanished as quickly as it came.

No one else seemed to have felt it; even Christine looked at me oddly. Turner, however, smiled. "As I thought," he said cryptically.

Beyond the door stretched a short corridor. Its floor was clear of detritus, no sand or gravel washed down from above. Not even dust; it looked almost as if an army of maids had come through and swept it clean.

And the smell...it didn't seem like the ordinary foul exhalation one might expect in an ancient cave. Instead, the air reeked like a chemical laboratory. Although it seemed familiar, and not from the context of university or the museum. Where had I smelled that particular fetor before?

"Blast and damnation," Christine said. Her face paled even farther, and not just from blood loss. "The umbra. It's...it's..."

We'd come to the end of the hall and stepped into an enormous hexagonal room. Turner lifted his lantern. Shadows shifted and scurried...and slid. They didn't move like shadows should.

"Not 'it,'" he corrected. "Them."

"Daemons of the night," Christine whispered.

I stared at the walls, at the ceiling, and the floor in mounting horror. Dozens of black, gelatinous-looking creatures crawled and slithered throughout the room, each one equipped with a single burning orange eye. Tripartite pupils constricted in the light of the lantern.

"We have to run," I gasped. These creatures weren't the size of the monster we'd encountered in Egypt, but they were of the same kind. Any moment they'd fall on us, their acid melting our flesh from our bones. We would die here in this stinking lair, and I'd never see Griffin again. I only hoped Turner was the first to go.

Two of the guards grabbed me, one holding each arm. I struggled wildly against their grip. "Run, you idiots! They're going to kill us!"

"Be still!" Turner shouted. And to the guards: "Hurry, before they can summon a soldier!"

The men dragged me forward, making for the nearest of the things. I thrashed madly, but before I could break their grip, they hurled me directly on top of it.

Chapter 33

Griffin

I sat near the fire, my head bowed and my hands loose between my knees. The distant voice still spoke inside my skull, but I gave it no more heed than the occasional barks from the dogs. Iskander and Scarrow sat across from me, and the two remaining guides prowled about, their guns at the ready in case we attempted to bolt.

Jack was there, too. But I tried not to look at him.

God. I'd been so stupid. So blind.

Pa had died, and it hurt, because the argument would remain unfinished between us forever. There would be no forgiveness from him, no acceptance. And I'd been so worried about replaying the argument, only this time with Jack, I'd missed what now seemed obvious. He hadn't kept asking about Whyborne because he suspected our relationship, hadn't been shocked when Ival saved him on the trail because he saw only a soft, useless scholar. It was because he knew Whyborne was a dangerous sorcerer.

I'd been so afraid of losing the only kin I still possessed, I'd ended up risking the family I already had. Christine and Iskander, and Ival most of all.

Where was he now? They must have reached the moulin, assuming they could find it again after the avalanche. Must have gone down into the depths of the earth.

Turner didn't intend to bring either of them back. What if my husband died beneath this accursed glacier, because I'd been stupid enough to lead him into this trap?

I'd accused him of treating me as a child or an invalid. Of finding some excuse for me not to have to go down into the dark. The last words I'd spoken to him had been in anger. How could I live with that? How could I live with any of it?

"Griffin," Jack said. "Let me explain."

My mouth felt dry as cotton. I swallowed, but it didn't help. "What can you possibly say to explain *this?*"

"I didn't mean for them to threaten you, I swear." As if that somehow made it better. "Nicholas...God, I'm not sure where to begin, even."

Iskander shifted on his rough-hewn seat. "You might start with why you agreed to lure us here in the first place."

"Nicholas sought me out," Jack said. "Because of my connection with Griffin, and Griffin's connection with Dr. Whyborne. Although he wasn't exactly truthful about the nature of their, um, friendship."

I didn't give a damn what he thought of my relationship with Whyborne. "And you just agreed to hand us all over to your new friend? Did Nicholas even tell you he's a sorcerer?"

"Of course he did!" Jack snapped, then caught himself. When he spoke again, it was far more calmly. "Nicholas told me all about himself, and about the family his mother came from back in England."

A chill ran through me, because it could mean only one thing. "Damn it. The Endicotts."

"Yes. Nicholas was already here in Alaska, looking for the city. He'd read an old account from a crazed Russian explorer, and believed some sort of ancient city waited here in the mountains. He came to me and explained everything—that he was sorcerer, that his family fights monsters and protects ordinary people."

A hoarse laugh escaped me. "Yes, I heard those lies myself first hand. Did he tell you what the Endicotts tried to do to Widdershins?"

"He told me Dr. Whyborne is a monster," Jack replied, anger lacing the words now. "And that some of his cousins from the main family line died trying to stop him."

"They tried to kill Whyborne by murdering an entire town full of innocents! Oh yes, the very definition of keeping ordinary people safe."

Jack scowled. "From what I understand, most of the people in Widdershins aren't very innocent."

"You don't know anything," I replied. Fury began to replace despair in my veins, and I embraced it. I raised my head and pinned

Jack with my gaze. "Whyborne saved your *life,* and this is how you repay him?"

Jack shifted, unable to meet my eyes. "I thought...but I was useful to him. Nicholas explained the deception. Creatures like Dr. Whyborne don't really feel things like love or human kindness."

The argument we'd heard, the first night in Hoarfrost. I'd let Jack keep his secrets because I was intent on keeping mine. I shouldn't have. I should have pushed. I should have introduced Whyborne as my husband, I should have...

It was all too late, so I ruthlessly slammed the door on my guilt. Later on, when this was over, when I had Whyborne in my arms and we were all safe, then I'd let it back in. But for now, only our survival mattered.

"He's lying to you," I replied. "Or he's just wrong, so caught up in his own certainties he can't see the truth in front of him. The rings you asked about our first night in St. Michael aren't society rings. They're wedding rings. Whyborne is my husband."

I left the words to hang in the air. Jack's eyes widened. "Your... husband?"

I refused to look away. "Yes."

"He's just using you," Jack said. "Tricking you."

"I've lived under the same roof with the man for three years. I would have noticed by now if that were the case. If anyone has been using others, it's Nicholas."

"You don't understand!" Jack lowered his voice when the remaining guards looked at him sharply. "You don't know what my life has been like, Griffin. I told you some of it. I ran away from home. I ran away from the circus. I drifted everywhere until I came here. My life was nothing. I didn't care about anyone, not even myself. I used everyone I came across. The swindler Dr. Whyborne saw me interrupt in St. Michael? I was once just like him."

Jack shook his head unhappily. "Nicholas changed everything. He offered me *purpose.* He believed in me, the way no one else ever did. By helping him rid the world of the sort of things most people don't even realize exist, I could do some good in the world. Be a part of something bigger than myself."

Wasn't that why I'd joined the Pinkertons? To make the world better, to be a part of something important? Why I'd fallen in love with my brave, beautiful Ival, who ran toward danger when everyone else fled, because he couldn't just pretend nothing was wrong? Had Nicholas seen that in Jack and played on it? Or did he, like Theo and Fiona Endicott, believe he did the work of the righteous, no matter how many innocents died?

I couldn't let emotion cloud my judgment. Not again. "Even if it means murdering your own brother," I said ruthlessly.

"I'm saving you!" His mittens clenched on his thighs. "Nicholas said you knew all about Dr. Whyborne, but I thought his reports must be wrong. I convinced him to help me free you from the abomination masquerading as your human friend. We used my connection with you to let Dr. Whyborne know a powerful servitor waited here in the north for any sorcerer able to claim it. He wouldn't be able to resist such a prize. He'd hurry here as quickly as possible, just to prevent anyone else from finding it first. Once he arrived, we'd find the city with his and Dr. Putnam's help. We'd go inside, expose him for what he really is, and just...leave him there. You'd join Nicholas and me, and the three of us together would help save the world."

"We didn't come to claim some sorcerous prize. We came to save your worthless hide."

Jack looked at me uncertainly. "Me?"

"Yes." I started to rise, caught the expression on one of the guard's faces, and sat back down. "We came here for you. Because you're my brother, and I couldn't sit by while you went blindly to your death." I spat; it froze before it hit the snow and lay there gleaming. "What an idiot I was."

"But...but that's not right," Jack said. "It can't be."

I laughed bitterly. "Of course it is. And you know it. You expected one thing from Whyborne and got something entirely different, didn't you? A man who seemed a true friend to those around him, not a sorcerous tyrant using us all to achieve his own ends. Moreover, a man who risked his life to save yours." I shook my head. "You'd already started asking yourself questions, hadn't you? About how poorly the reality matched the terrifying monster Nicholas described to you. By the time we got to Hoarfrost, you didn't really believe any more. But you let Nicholas convince you, smother the doubt in your heart. Just like I'm sure you're telling yourself Nicholas won't really murder me, and Iskander, and even poor Reverend Scarrow the moment we're no longer useful."

Jack closed his eyes briefly. His body trembled, but I didn't think it was entirely from the cold.

"Don't let this happen, Jack," I said. "Don't let him kill all of us and take this servitor, whatever it is, back to the Endicotts."

A frown creased his mouth. "I don't understand. What do you mean 'whatever it is?' You've encountered umbrae before."

The devil? "I assure you, we've not fought so many horrors from beyond that I no longer remember the particulars," I said. "Whatever this umbra is, we've not seen it."

"Umbrae," Jack corrected. "You don't think...oh." His eyes widened. "You truly don't know, do you?"

The arctic wind seemed to seep through clothing and flesh to chill my blood directly. "What do you mean?"

"Sorcerers take them to be guardians. Steal them from their nests while they're still in the chrysalis stage, then grow them into something that can be controlled through magic. They're powerful, strong, nearly indestructible except from fire and lightning." Jack met my gaze at last, and I thought there might have been pity in the depths of the green eyes so like my own. "You've seen them twice already. Once in Chicago, and once in Egypt."

"No," Iskander whispered. "There's a daemon of the night here?"

"Not *a* daemon, my friend," Jack said wryly. "An entire city full of them."

CHAPTER 34

Whyborne

A SHRIEK OF terror and despair escaped me, at the same moment Christine screamed my name. The daemon's—umbra's—gelatinous flesh gave only slightly beneath my weight, as if I'd fallen on top of a huge jellyfish. Tendrils uncoiled from it, feelers grasping my clothing and the skin of my face, and I closed my eyes and waited for the agony to begin.

It didn't.

Its damp, gelid touch slithered over my skin. A whimper escaped me, but it made no move to harm me.

Something pressed against my mind. A weight, like the mountain above, like the slow pulse of magic, like the wearing of water over rock. Was this the "voice" Griffin had heard all along?

I slammed the doors of my mind, used every trick I knew to strengthen my will against any intrusion. The sense of pressure didn't push any farther.

The feelers withdrew. Apparently unconcerned with me, the daemon—umbra—whatever one wished to call it—slithered on about its business.

I scrambled back wildly, my limbs shaking too badly to stand. Christine tried to run to me, but Turner grabbed her arm and yanked her back. "Oh no, Dr. Putnam. You can see he's unharmed from over here."

I took deep, gasping breaths, trying to calm my racing heart. "Wh-what happened?" I demanded. My voice cracked on the words, and I swore silently. "Why did you do that?"

"Daemons of the night," Turner mused. "An interesting name for them. You encountered one in Egypt, did you not? And your lover escaped one in Chicago."

Griffin. Was the voice he heard really connected to these things? But why? How?

He'd dreamed of being the umbra beneath the pyramid in Egypt. Of chasing himself through the passageway. I'd assumed it was merely some strange nightmare. Had I been horribly wrong?

"Yes," I answered Turner. "Its feelers secreted acid. It dissolved and ate everyone it could get hold of."

"Indeed." Turner nodded at the dozens of creatures currently slithering around us, apparently now unconcerned about our presence. "But that one was a warrior. A soldier. They aren't all of the same kind, Dr. Whyborne. These are merely workers, and thus of no use to us."

"Workers?" I asked. "Soldiers? Like ants?"

"Even so, why fling Whyborne at it? Were you merely trying to prove a point?" Christine demanded hotly. "I think you might have simply told us without the demonstration!"

"Oh, but Dr. Whyborne is the key to everything," Turner replied with an unpleasant smile. "If we'd come without him, when the workers came to taste and sense us as possible intruders...well. Let's just say they would have instantly summoned a solider, and our lives would have been very short indeed. But Dr. Whyborne isn't fully human. When the worker tasted his skin, smelled his scent, it recognized...not one of its own, of course. But an ally, allowed to pass by without harm."

An ally? I'd wondered at the similarity in style between the carvings in the city and those in the undersea temple. Was there truly some connection? "The daemon in Egypt certainly didn't recognize me as such," I protested.

He snorted. "Of course not. It was taken from its nest and raised by ancient sorcerers, far away from the corrupting influence of its own kind. Its will belonged to those who bound it. As will that of the one I intend to take from here."

My head spun, and my legs threatened to buckle as the guards prodded me to my feet. This was madness. The ketoi might not be human, but they were far more so than these gelatinous horrors. They possessed minds and language, an intelligence one could converse with, made tools and jewelry and a hundred other little things. The umbrae had more in common with the jellyfish of the deep than with the ketoi.

"Buckle up, Dr. Whyborne—we've no time for fainting spells," Turner said with a sneer. "We should be safe with you in our company, but just in case, I suggest you lead the way."

I didn't argue. If I could keep Christine safe from these things, I'd do whatever it took. If I thought there might be some way to use them against Turner, to perhaps alert one of these soldiers to him and his men, and leave Christine and me unscathed...but I didn't see how I might accomplish such a thing.

We traversed the room. Two corridors let off of it, one angling up and to the north, the other down and to the east. The city, at least beneath the ground, wasn't built on a flat system of streets and byways, but rather a complex tangle, like the burrows of animals, or the nests of insects. Every breath brought another gust of the umbrae's acrid, chemical smell into my lungs. Every step sent more of them scurrying just a little out of the way of the light from my lamp. Their burning tripartite eyes occasionally turned to us, but the decision of the first to tolerate my presence had been passed on in some manner I couldn't guess.

No, wait. The pressure I'd felt in my mind. The voice Griffin heard. Did they communicate telepathically, perhaps? The way the dweller in the deeps spoke to the ketoi?

Blast.

For the first time, I found myself intensely grateful Turner had left Griffin behind. Forcing him to come down into this black pit, surrounded by the very creatures that most plagued his nightmares, perhaps able to hear them speaking to him in some fashion...I couldn't imagine how horrible it would have been for him. Far better he remain on the surface, beneath the clean stars.

"Down," Turner said. So I took the ramp leading down. Deeper into the darkness, and farther from the world I'd known.

More of the workers crowded the tunnel and ramp, slithering around and past us. I shuddered each time one bumped against me. They didn't seem to have legs, but somehow clung to the walls and even the ceiling, like nauseating slugs. At least they didn't seem able to fly, like the daemon in Egypt. Perhaps that ability was reserved for soldiers, which might have to venture outside the nest.

Or maybe they just didn't feel the need to at the moment. The idea left me distinctly queasy.

The ramp yielded to yet another of the omnipresent hexagonal rooms. Unlike the ones we'd passed through before, swept clear of debris, the floor of this chamber was almost completely covered by dark, ovoid masses.

"What are those?" Christine asked, but her voice was lowered, as if she feared the answer.

I took a hesitant step forward. The worker umbrae seemed particularly busy in this chamber, crawling over the ovoids as if inspecting them. Or caring for them in some fashion.

I pulled off my glove and hesitantly reached out to the nearest. Its black surface reminded me of the umbrae, but coarse rather than gelatinous. As if it had been spun from some thick fibers, like a cocoon.

"Oh God." I snatched my hand back. "It's a chrysalis."

"Quite." Turner's eyes burned avidly as he cast about the room. "The soldiers' will be larger. Find me one, men."

Most of the objects measured approximately two feet in length, and half that in height. But although the type predominated, there were others a third again the size mixed in. As the guards began to make their way through the jumble of cocoons, I took a step back and exchanged a look with Christine.

Time was running out. Turner was about to get what he came for. And when he did, he'd surely kill us both. There must be some way of escape, but for the life of me I couldn't think of what it might be.

"How do you propose to get it out of here?" I asked. "Do you mean to break the seals holding the creatures in?"

"That won't be necessary." Turner watched the guards avidly. "Above our heads, the solstice has come, and there is no moon. The seals are at their weakest, but still remain strong enough to hold in the adults. But my umbra will be wrapped in a chrysalis, inert and protected. The seals will be too faint to react with it."

"I have one!" a guard shouted, and lifted a cocoon with a grunt. This one was even larger than the others, and its surface glittered with iridescent colors.

Turner's eyes widened. "Dear heavens! That's no mere soldier."

The workers moved en mass, flowing toward the man holding the chrysalis in an undulating black wave. Shocked, he stumbled, and a feeler touched his face.

I *felt* the shriek in my mind, hammering against my brain. "It knows something's wrong! A soldier is coming!" I shouted, even as I clutched at my suddenly pounding temples.

"Give me the chrysalis!" Turner shouted.

Then everything was chaos. The guard rushed forward, thrusting the cocoon at Turner. Even as he did so, a shape shot out of the tunnel at the other end of the chamber, unfurling vast wings like those of a

stingray.
> A soldier. A daemon of the night.
> Umbra.
> We ran.

CHAPTER 35

Griffin

My blood froze, and my heart seemed to clench painfully in my chest. Jack was lying; he had to be. This couldn't be true.

The scar on my right leg ached, and Glenn's screams echoed in my ears. My partner for nearly six years, my closest friend, my sometimes-lover...the only thing I could remember was the sight of his skull stripped bare by acid, an agonized shriek still rising from gaping jaws. The buck of the gun in my hand as I fired the bullet to end his torment.

And last year in Egypt, the huge daemon sailing out of the night, so much bigger than its smaller cousin I'd encountered in Chicago. It had borne down on Christine and me, and I'd been certain we'd die. The fate I'd avoided in Chicago, caught up with me at last.

Then the lightning blast, and Ival, lying so still, his right arm seared and bloody, Nitocris's festering bite in his left shoulder. His moans as fever set in, as we were forced to drip water into his mouth and pray he'd live to see Cairo. How he'd whimpered and cried out in delusion when we changed the pus-soaked bandages.

These creatures had destroyed my life, sent me screaming to the madhouse, and nearly cost me Ival. They'd haunted my very dreams, making me question my sanity. And now Jack meant to imply an entire city of them swarmed beneath us?

Oh God. How could Whyborne and Christine expect to survive?

"We have to go to them!" I stumbled to my feet. One of the guards barked something, but Jack waved him off. "They're going to die! Those things will kill them!"

Fear flickered in Jack's eyes. "Griffin, no. Nicholas had a plan. It involved Dr. Whyborne somehow—something about his inhuman lineage. Nicholas knows what he's doing."

A little chill whispered through me. "Nicholas said he would leave them there. Alive. But not out of mercy."

Scarrow stirred. "Alive in the dark with monsters," he said, gazing at Jack. "Look within your heart, my son. You know this can't be right."

Scarrow's presence of mind was nothing less than astonishing, given how bizarre the situation must seem to him. I seized gratefully on his words. "Listen to the reverend, Jack." I took a step forward and reached out to him pleadingly. "I know you thought you were doing the right thing. I know you believed Whyborne had either corrupted me somehow, or else posed a terrible danger to me. I believe you wanted to save me, to save every innocent you could."

Our eyes met. "But Turner deceived you. You know in your heart Whyborne isn't the terrible, cruel sorcerer Turner told you he was. You know Christine doesn't deserve to be dragged along as a hostage, to be left at the mercy of horrors. Turner says he's on the side of good, but what sort of person would do such a thing? We wanted to seal these creatures in. He wants to bring one forth into the world."

Jack trembled, his expression uncertain. "No. You've…you've misjudged Nicholas. You'll see. He'll explain everything to you when he comes back."

"No he won't. Turner means to kill us. The only reason we're still alive is he's afraid of Whyborne. But once he has what he wants, even if he does leave Whyborne and Christine to the mercy of the umbrae, I'm dead. And so are the reverend and Iskander."

"You're wrong. Nicholas doesn't kill innocent people. He's not a monster, like your—your friend."

My hand curled inside my mitten, although I didn't know if I wanted to strike him for calling Whyborne a monster, or shake him until his teeth rattled for refusing to see the truth. "Let's ask the guards, shall we?" I said instead. Raising my voice, I called, "You're going to let us go as soon as Mr. Turner is back, right boys?"

They exchanged looks. "Sure," one said. "No reason to kill you, when you've seen our faces and know our names."

"Damn it, Haswell!" Jack exclaimed. "That isn't what Nicholas wants, and you know it."

Haswell snorted. "Mr. Turner hired us because we know the land. Know how easy it is for a man to just disappear up here." He raised his gun, and his companion did the same. "This is our one chance to strike it rich. Digging for gold is a fool's game, but we keep quiet and do as we're told, and we'll have more money than we'll know what to do with. I'll burn in hell before I let you mess this up, you coward."

"I'm afraid I must object," Reverend Scarrow said. Then he spoke another word, not in English, but which I recognized from hearing it from Whyborne's lips so many times.

The secret name of fire.

The pistol exploded in Haswell's hand.

CHAPTER 36

Whyborne

 ALL THOUGHT TO remaining in a group was abandoned as we fled before the coming of the soldier. Turner raced ahead, the chrysalis clutched tight in his arms, leaving the guards to fend for themselves. They did so admirably, shoving Christine and I aside in the desperation to save their own skins.
 Still, they weren't quite fast enough. The hindmost in line screamed as acid-dripping feelers grabbed him, wrenched him from the ground, and brought him to the orifice on the soldier's underside. His shrieks became higher and wilder, before ending abruptly. A moment later, charred and melted bones clattered to the floor.
 His death bought us time, although not much. As we passed out of the nursery room, agitated workers scattered everywhere from the light of our lanterns. Behind us, the soldier went to ground in order to fit through the door separating rooms, giving us a few more seconds.
 One of the guards stopped, firing wildly at the soldier as it squeezed its plastic form through the smaller opening. The bullets had no discernible effect, and his gun hit the ground as a feeler lashed out and wrapped around his leg. His agonized cries echoed behind us.
 Christine stumbled, weakened from blood loss. I put my arm around her waist, hauling her along with me. As we reached the final, short hall, my heart lifted. The seals were just ahead. If they held, if

the soldier couldn't get through, I'd set fire to the remaining guard's pistol. Then we'd deal with Turner.

Turner passed through the huge doorway ahead of us, the chrysalis still cradled in his arms. A moment later, the guard went through after him.

"Come on, Whyborne!" Christine urged. Together we ran through the door and—

My face smashed into an invisible wall. Agony exploded in my nose and forehead, and I tasted blood. Christine was wrenched free from my grip, and I slammed into the floor a moment later.

"What the devil?" Christine cried. "Whyborne?"

I blinked dazedly. She stood on the other side of the door, staring back at me in alarm. What had happened?

No. Oh no.

My fingers shook as I reached out toward her, only to encounter an obstruction in what appeared to be empty air. Heart pounding, I pressed my palms against it and pushed. But there was nothing material to shove aside. Just the lines of magic, laid down in some unknowably ancient time, meant to keep the monsters in.

"I can't cross the seals," I said, and my voice trembled. Our eyes met. "My ketoi blood is trapping me here."

"Cast a spell or something, damn it!"

"I can't!" My throat tightened. "Run, Christine! Get out of here!"

She plunged back through the doorway, gripping my arm. "No! I'm not leaving you! We have to—"

It was too late.

The soldier burst into the hall, wings unfurled. I didn't have time to think. Wrapping my arms around Christine, I flung us violently to the side, away from the soldier and into the heaving mass of agitated workers. We rolled across the stone floor, fetching up against the wall, while the soldier struck the barrier again and again, frantic to get through and retrieve the stolen chrysalis.

I covered Christine's body with mine as best I could. Workers slithered over us, their feelers slick wherever they found my skin. Their horrible, boneless weight pressed down on me, and I struggled to keep from crushing Christine against the floor. Her breath came quick and frantic, and I closed my eyes and prayed my pathetic attempt at cover would work, and the next touch I felt wouldn't be the soldier's acid eating away my skin.

CHAPTER 37

Griffin

I LUNGED AT the remaining guard, not giving him any time to react. My shoulder collided with his midsection, and we both tumbled back into the snow. The dogs barked wildly, half maddened by either the shots or our fight, I didn't know. I expected to feel their teeth sink into me in defense of their master. We rolled on the ground; I clutched his arms, trying to keep the gun away from me.

Unfortunately, the thick mittens so admirable for protecting my hands were no good for gripping. The guard wrenched free and slammed a fist into the side of my head. Stunned, my hold slackened. He rolled on top of me, the gun inches from my face. "Don't try it, Rever—"

There came the sharp crack of a pistol, loud in the cold air. Blood burst from the hole where his forehead had been. I shoved frantically, and his body collapsed to the snow beside me. Behind him stood Jack, his own gun in his hand and a grim look on his face.

"Thank you," I said, as Iskander hurried to help me to my feet.

Jack's mouth was a hard line. "I wasn't going to let him kill you. I know you don't believe it, but Nicholas and I are trying to protect you."

"You heard what Haswell said!" Iskander exclaimed.

"Haswell was never in Nicholas's confidence. Not like me. He thought he could twist the situation to his own brutish ways." Jack pivoted to the fire and raised his pistol again. "But we have bigger concerns. You're a sorcerer."

Scarrow still sat at his ease on the rough-hewn log. "Very good, Mr. Hogue."

Fear crept up my spine. Most of my experience of sorcerers, other than Whyborne, had not been good. Certainly Nicholas Turner hadn't improved my opinion of the lot, no matter what Jack might think of the man. "Who are you? And more importantly, what do you want from us? Are you trying to get an umbra as well?" God, would I have to fight him as well as Turner?

"Don't trust him," Iskander warned.

"I'm hurt, Mr. Barnett." Scarrow didn't sound particularly offended, though. "But there's no need to interrogate me, Mr. Flaherty. I'm more than happy to explain myself, having been found out. Indeed, I was already considering how I might reveal myself to you. Your brother choosing to join us made my task easier, of course."

"I haven't 'joined' anyone," Jack shot back hotly. "Now answer Griffin's questions."

Scarrow held out his hands to the fire. I watched carefully in case he intended to play some magical trick with the flames, but it seemed he only wished to warm his fingers. "First answer a single question for me. What happened to Vanya?"

"How the devil would we know?" Jack demanded.

"He's dead," I said at the same moment.

Jack cast me a shocked look. I shrugged. "At least, I assume he is. The first night in St. Michael, a man attacked Whyborne, shouting about great worms and breaking open mountains. Whyborne washed him off a dock with a wave. Either he froze and drowned, or hid himself away."

Jack shook his head. "And you say Dr. Whyborne isn't a murderer?"

"It was self defense!" I turned away from him in disgust and aimed my next words at Scarrow. "I assume he was your agent?"

Scarrow sighed unhappily. "Poor Vanya. I assure you, he had no orders from me to attack anyone. I made certain he went with Mr. Hogue in order to keep an eye on Dr. Whyborne, so he might report back to me on his return. Unfortunately, his head was already full of native legends concerning these mountains. I suppose he decided to take matters into his own hands."

I folded my arms over my chest. "And who are you, exactly?"

"I am who I introduced myself as. Felix Scarrow." He sat back and regarded me. "I'm a member of a...loose association, you might say...of those who study the arcane arts. We call ourselves the Cabal, but honestly I find the name rather an affectation, don't you?"

"Get on with it," Iskander snapped. "Christine and Whyborne are in danger while you maunder on!"

"Quite, quite." Scarrow rose to his feet. "We heard a rumor the Endicotts had sent someone from one of their subsidiary branches to Alaska, in search of another umbra. They'd already acquired one when the Eltdown Shards were uncovered a few years ago, but those sort are never content. Having met them, I'm sure you won't be at all surprised to hear they aren't very popular in arcane circles. We thought it in our interests to send someone to keep an eye on dear Mr. Turner and make certain he didn't secure another umbra. The balance of power is already too far in the Endicotts' favor as it is."

"And I suppose your *association* use magic to help orphans and kittens?" Jack asked. "At least the Endicotts are trying to make the world better."

"Jack, please," I said. "Let the—well, not reverend, I'm sure—finish."

"Not a reverend?" Scarrow's pale brows climbed toward his hood. "Oh no, dear me. I am an ordained minister." I must have looked skeptical, because he said, "Don't you think God's will can be accomplished through magic as readily as through the work of a man's hands? Just because some persons have unjustly condemned the arcane arts doesn't mean they don't come from the Divine." He inclined his head to me in a little bow. "Given your words concerning Dr. Whyborne earlier, I'm certain you would agree the mind of man often distorts the will of God, either through fear or ignorance."

I wanted to argue and say it wasn't the same thing at all. I'd seen the evil that could come from sorcerers, from magic.

But I'd seen the good in it, too. In Whyborne. "I see. And you're right. It would be rather hypocritical of me to disagree with you."

"What now?" Jack asked.

"What do you mean?" Iskander went to the stores and began to pull out climbing ropes. "We go to the city and save Christine and Whyborne."

Jack started to object, so I held up my hands to stop him. "I have a suggestion. We'll all go down together. We'll find them, including Turner. If they are in danger, we'll help. And when it's safe, I promise to listen to what he has to say. And you'll listen to what Whyborne has to say. Agreed?"

Jack nodded. "Agreed."

A flicker of hope went through me. We were free now and had a sorcerer of our own. Surely we could face Turner and stop him. "I assume we can count on your help, Reverend?"

"Of course. Our best weapon against these creatures is fire. I suggest we gather up as much kerosene as we have on hand to take with us. Praise the Lord that the temperature hasn't dipped quite so far as to freeze it." He picked up one of the lanterns and checked its fuel. "But I haven't quite finished my story. I must confess, when I first heard Dr. Whyborne would be joining us, I was rather alarmed."

Iskander went to the guards and retrieved our weapons from them. My gun would do little good against a sorcerer like Turner, and I'd foolishly left my sword cane back in Hoarfrost as impractical to take mountaineering. Iskander tucked his pair of deadly knives, which I'd seen him use on ghūls in the desert, into his coat. There was also a rifle belonging to Scarrow.

I moved to gather supplies, but kept an eye on Scarrow as I did so. "You knew of Whyborne before."

A thin smile touched Scarrow's face. "He hasn't been exactly what one would call discreet. First the business with the Brotherhood, then the Eyes of Nodens, and finally with the Endicotts...such things don't go unnoticed by others versed in the arcane arts. We speak with one another, write letters, trade spells. There are many who fear what Dr. Whyborne might do."

"Whyborne isn't one to go looking for trouble," I objected, though the words were half-aimed at Jack as well. God, didn't we have enough to worry about?

"Considering he traveled all the way here 'looking for trouble,' as you put it, I will have to take your word on the matter." Scarrow's eyes sparkled as he drew out the remaining stores of kerosene. "As the Endicotts aren't ones to forgive, I suspected he didn't actually realize what sort of situation he was walking into. On the other hand, it didn't seem to be in the interests of the Cabal to allow him to stroll away with an umbra, any more than it would the Endicotts. Not unless he could be made an ally."

"So you insinuated yourself into the expedition," Iskander said. "All these lies aren't exactly godly, are they, reverend?"

"I shall pray for forgiveness," Scarrow replied, unperturbed. "But yes. When the opportunity appeared, it seemed the perfect chance to learn exactly what kind of man he is."

"And now you know." I met his gaze challengingly. "A ketoi hybrid and a Sodomite."

Scarrow laughed. "Don't be foolish, Mr. Flaherty. The only members of the Cabal who care are the ones who'd wish to avail themselves of his sexual interests. The ketoi blood renders him rather more valuable than less. The Cabal's primary concern is whether Dr.

Whyborne is a friend or an enemy."

"You'll have to ask him yourself," I said, all too aware of Jack near me. If he and Scarrow came to blows over Turner, or the blasted Endicotts, Jack would surely lose such a fight. I couldn't let him get hurt, but losing Scarrow's aid would leave us at a disadvantage, especially since I was certain Turner meant to murder us. "Does everyone have their supplies? Lamps? Rope? Food and water? All right. Let's go."

CHAPTER 38

Whyborne

I didn't know how long we lay there amidst the squirming, crawling mass of umbrae. Eventually the frantic alarm seemed to die down. There came the hiss of displaced air, and the solider gave off attempting to breach the seals and glided back to the depths of the nest.

When I was certain it had left, I heaved up, shoving aside the workers. Their slime slicked my clothing and skin, and I shuddered. "Are you all right, Christine?" I asked.

"I'm fine." But her voice shook on the words.

"That was foolish of you." Incredibly my dropped lantern hadn't gone out, so I went to retrieve it. "You should have run."

She sat up shakily. I disliked her pallor and the way she winced when she tried to use her injured arm. "I'm not abandoning you! Honestly, how could you even think I'd agree to such a thing?"

"Because there isn't any other choice." I went to the open doorway and gently laid my hand on the barrier even I couldn't see. "I'm trapped in here, as surely as the umbrae."

"But why? You aren't an umbra."

"No." I shook my head. "But you heard Turner. You saw how the workers react to me."

Christine scowled at the seemingly empty air. "It doesn't make sense, though. You said the carvings and the buildings remind you of the temple you glimpsed at the bottom of the sea. But these umbrae surely didn't build it. Or this. I mean *look* at them." She gestured at the nearest, which drifted across a wall, like a stingray gliding over the bottom of a sandy bay. "Whatever race created the city and trapped the umbrae inside surely wasn't quite so...alien."

"I don't know." I rubbed tiredly at my eyes. "I don't know what the link is between the umbrae and the ketoi. But there is something here...I can't really say what for certain, but I feel it against my mind. I think the umbrae communicate by some sort of telepathy."

Her eyes widened in alarm. "Like the dweller with the ketoi?"

"Yes." I dropped my hands. "When we were in Egypt, Griffin ended up psychically linked to the umbra there, and...oh dear."

Christine's eyes widened. "Do you think that has something to do with the voices he's been hearing?"

"Voice," I corrected. "I...I don't know. If there is some remnant of the link still active...blast. And the dreams he had, of being the daemon of the night. What if they weren't dreams but memories? Its memories?"

"Dreams?" she asked in alarm.

"It doesn't matter—I'll explain later. Curse it all, why didn't I put the pieces together earlier?"

She snorted. "Why on earth would you? It isn't as if you knew what the creatures down here were. Why would you connect the umbrae in this frozen wasteland with something we encountered amidst the burning desert?"

"I suppose." I wasn't so certain, but argument would be pointless at this juncture. "When we were running from the daemon, er, umbra, beneath the lightless pyramid, I tried to injure it with fire. It... screamed, and I felt the sound in my head. As did Griffin. It made sense for him to do so because of their link, but me? At the time, I didn't think anything about it."

"You were rather busy trying not to die. I suppose you can be excused," she replied dryly. "Do you think there's any connection between the dweller's ability to touch the minds of ketoi and hybrids, and whatever is down here?"

"I haven't the slightest idea." I spread my hands out. "And even if I did, it doesn't change the basic facts. I'm trapped here and I can't leave."

"At least there's air moving. Perhaps there's another entrance we might find?" she suggested.

"*We* don't need to be finding anything. You have to leave, Christine." I swallowed. "I know you feel it would be disloyal, but

Griffin and Iskander are still in danger. They need your help."

She shook her head. "All of which is well and good, old fellow. But I'm not going far on my own with this arm."

"Blast!" I should have known something was wrong simply because she hadn't yet stood up. I hurried to her side. "Take off your coat and let me see."

"No—I think it's stopped bleeding, finally." She shifted her weight with a wince. "If we peel everything off, it will only start up again. But there's no way I could climb up a rope, even if they left one for me. And the mouth of the ice cave is likely to be near the foot of the glacier. I'm not certain I could make it that far without assistance."

I sank down beside her, feeling helpless. "What shall we do? We can't just sit here and wait to die."

"Don't be absurd," she said briskly. "As I said before, the air is... well, not fresh exactly, but moving. Surely there's another way out."

"If so, why aren't the umbrae using it?" I asked dubiously.

"How should I know? Perhaps they are." She scowled. "Assuming we can believe anything that liar Jack said, the natives have been smart enough to avoid this area. Before Hoarfrost camp, who would even have been here to know? The umbrae could be leaving all the time, foraging on the mountain, then returning."

"True," I admitted.

"And if it isn't the case, we know the glacier sheered off upper portions of the city. If it nicked any of these underground passages, we may have a way out."

"Only if there's a tunnel."

"If there isn't, you'll melt the damned ice!" she snapped. "I don't care how long it takes—you and I are both getting out of this hellish prison. Do you hear me?"

I couldn't help but smile. "I do."

"Then let's go."

I helped her to her feet. "I can manage on my own," she said gruffly.

"Very well. But let me go first, and for heaven's sake, stay close to me. It seems my presence will serve to keep them docile, but if you stray too far I'm afraid they'll realize they're being invaded."

"A good point," she allowed. "They aren't very bright, are they?"

"I don't suppose they have to be. Even the one in Egypt merely followed the compulsion laid on it by others." I shrugged. "How intelligent is an individual ant, after all?"

"Not very...oh."

The deepening of her pallor alarmed me. "Christine? Are you all right?"

"I just had a thought. About the image on the door, and what Turner thought it signified."

"The Mother of Shadows." I'd almost forgotten in all the panic and fear.

"We've seen soldiers and workers. And you said Griffin heard *a* voice." She gestured vaguely at the creatures as they crawled over and past one another. "What if they have a queen?"

Ice touched my veins, as if the glacier had found its way inside me. "Oh dear," I said.

"Indeed." Christine nodded toward the depths. "And with that cheery thought to inspire us, let's try to find our way out of here, shall we?"

CHAPTER 39

Griffin

JACK TRAMPED ACROSS the snow-covered glacier beside me, as we made our way back to the moulin. "I know you're angry," he said.

The others had drawn ahead of us. I glanced at him, but the shadow of his hood hid his eyes, leaving only his mouth exposed.

The aurora glowed red, so bright it threw our shadows onto the snow and made the ice look like rubies, or frozen blood. The voice in my head hadn't grown louder, exactly. But something had changed. What, I wasn't certain, but it terrified me. What was happening even now beneath the ice?

"You've lied to me, put my life in danger, and endangered Whyborne and Christine," I said, because any distraction from that distant sound, hovering just out of range of understanding, was welcome at the moment. "No, of course not, why would I possibly be angry?"

Jack's mouth flattened into a tight line. "Fine. Be angry. I'm angry with myself, to be honest. I'm your older brother. I'm supposed to look out for you, and I failed. If I'd only found you earlier, before Dr. Whyborne had the chance to seduce you."

"Whyborne? Seduce me?" A mix of anger and grief twisted in my belly, but I'd be damned if I let Jack misconstrue our relationship. "I'm afraid you have it the wrong way around."

Jack gave me a sharp look. "Are you serious?"

"If you imagine I was some innocent who had never even considered bedding a man, let alone actually done it, you are sorely mistaken," I said coldly. To hell with Jack and what he thought of me.

"Well…yes…things get lonely on the frontier, in mining camps. It's only natural, under such circumstances…" Jack cleared his throat uncomfortably. "But this is different."

So Jack had availed himself of male company, and more than once, if I was any judge. "Yes," I said. "It is different. I love Ival, and he loves me. And it's still been hard sometimes, damned hard, to carve out a life together. So if you think he beguiled me into becoming his paramour for some incomprehensible plan of his own, you're wrong. He didn't even know sorcery existed when we first met."

My words seemed to catch Jack even further off guard. "Are you certain?"

"Of course I am." I hitched my pack higher on my back. "I've walked this path with him, every step of the way."

Jack fell silent. Hopefully I'd given him something to think about.

We reached the moulin soon after. I stood beside it and tried not to betray my fear.

The smooth-edged hole vanished into darkness, untouched even by the blazing lights of the aurora.

Nothing good ever happened underground. Every instinct I possessed told me to run and not stop until I was far, far away. To do anything, go anywhere, but down this narrow slot. To draw no nearer to that distant, incomprehensible voice that even now spoke just on the edge of hearing.

But my husband was in danger. Even if I hadn't been the one to get us all into this mess, I couldn't leave him. I had to get to him, had to try. Even if it cost my sanity.

The ropes still hung in place, and no tracks led away from the moulin. Iskander had already taken up one of the ropes, his face set in a look of grim determination. Our eyes met, and he gave me a nod. "We'll get them back, Griffin. Or we'll sodding die trying."

"I know." I took a deep breath and seized another rope. Jack crouched by the moulin, peering down. "Last chance to back out, Jack. The things down there are…well. Terrifying is one way to put it. We might none of us ever see the light of day again."

Jack shook his head. "You know I can't do that."

We made our way down the long, long drop, feet braced against the smooth ice and ropes clutched tight in our hands. I tried to pretend the ice wasn't closing around and above me. Instead I pictured Ival's face, the way his hair refused to lie flat for any length of time, the way his smile transformed his features. I imagined us in our study, curled together on the couch with Saul sprawled across our laps, this horror long behind us.

We'd make it home again. No matter how many umbrae I had to face. Anything else was unthinkable.

After what seemed an eternity, my feet touched the loose gravel. We were down. Beneath the glacier.

Down in the dark where the monsters lived.

Would I see Jack devoured, nothing left but a pile of bones? Or would we find Whyborne in the clutches of one, screaming for help, a bare skull in place of his face?

"Are you all right, old boy?" Iskander asked.

I took a deep breath. "Y-yes. I'm fine." I had to be. If I fell apart now, all hope of saving Whyborne and Christine would be lost. "Christine said she found a ramp of some sort. Let's look for it."

I didn't want to pay any more attention to the mysterious voice in my head than I had to. But if it could lead me closer to Whyborne, I'd let it. My footsteps carried me unerringly to the rectangular hole in the glacier-ground rock.

"At least there's a fresh breeze blowing through," Scarrow remarked.

I stared at the opening, my heart in my mouth. "I'll take whatever good news I can get," I said around it. My attempt at lightness fell flat.

Jack put his hand tentatively to my shoulder. "What's wrong?"

"You know my past, thanks to the Endicotts," I said. "What do you think is wrong?"

The words came out more harshly than I'd intended. He flinched and let his hand fall. "I'm sorry. Perhaps you should remain here. Iskander, Scarrow, and I will find Nicholas and the others."

"No." Taking a deep breath, I started for the ramp. "I'm going with you. Let's just get this over with."

CHAPTER 40

Whyborne

UP SEEMED THE direction most likely to get us away from the umbrae and back to the world of air and light. Accordingly, when we returned to the first room beyond the door, we chose the ramp angled toward the heights rather than the depths. Workers moved about us, ignoring our presence, and once a larger soldier slid past, as if patrolling for intruders. I tucked Christine behind me, but it paid us no more attention than the workers.

"At least these don't seem as violent as the one we encountered in Egypt," Christine said when it had left.

"The one in Egypt was taken from its own kind to guard and kill," I pointed out. "Presumably its natural behavior would be somewhat different."

She nodded. "True. How many do you think there are, stolen from places like this? I know Griffin encountered one beneath Chicago, but surely there couldn't be that many, could there?"

"I certainly hope not." I stepped carefully over a worker lying in my path. "We know from the one in Egypt they can live unfathomably long lives. I have no trouble imagining men like my father, or sorcerers like Blackbyrne, passing them from hand to hand over the centuries."

"Let's hope you're correct. And let's hope whatever ancient cities they came from are now long destroyed, or else very, very remote indeed. Can you imagine someone digging a subway or a sewer and coming across *this?*"

"All too well, given what happened with the Eltdown Shards," I said grimly. "Assuming the blasted Endicotts didn't do away with the villagers themselves."

I stopped long enough to dig out my canteen and take a drink. Not enough water remained to sustain us for long. Was there any source of fresh water down here? There must be, surely, even if only a seep of some kind. Unless the umbrae didn't need to drink, in which case our situation would become dire rather quickly. "I wonder who sealed the umbrae in here, and why? Did they invade the city and drive out the original inhabitants? Or was the place already deserted when the umbrae moved in? Either way, who cast the spells? Given the door seemed the same antiquity as the rest of the construction, to have created a magical seal powerful enough to last eons...it's very impressive. More than impressive, really."

"The Pnakotic Manuscripts didn't say?"

"No, although from what Turner said, there are hints in other books." I'd been trying not to think about my scholarly failure. "If only I'd looked harder, we wouldn't be in this mess."

"You're being ridiculous." Christine touched the smoothly carved surface of the nearest wall with her good hand, then drew back as a worker slid past. "You can't blame yourself for not having read every book in the library, on the off chance you might have found some scrap of information. Assuming the museum even has the pertinent tomes. If you're looking for someone to blame, it's that damned liar Jack Hogue."

I ground my teeth together at the memory of the look of betrayal on Griffin's face. If I did manage to escape this place, I'd make Jack pay for hurting Griffin. "I should have let him tumble over the waterfall."

"Hindsight is always perfect."

The ramp ended in another of the large, hexagonal rooms. Clearly, whoever built the city had been unusually fond of the shape. Smaller rooms budded off from it, all filled with what looked like some sort of strange fungus. The flabby, white shelves grew in an almost column-like formation, creating a veritable thicket of living matter. The black bodies of workers moved about the pallid fungi, breaking off pieces here and there, then slithering away with them still clutched in their feelers. Others appeared to tend the fungi, inspecting their surfaces or the thin mycelium spread across floor and wall.

"I believe we've found their garden," Christine said, leaning against the doorway for support.

I touched the nearest fungal body. It gave nauseatingly under my fingers, and I snatched my hand back. I'd never view mushrooms the same way again. "Agreed. Do you think they subsist on this? And where do they get the organic matter to feed the fungus?"

"Their dead?" Christine suggested, a bit morbidly in my opinion. "Whatever the case, this room didn't begin as a garden. Look at the carvings on the wall."

Although hard to make out between the thick ropes of fungus, the murals in this room appeared less decorative and more purposeful. "Astronomical charts?" I guessed.

"And maps. A shame we can't make out more of them." She stepped carefully over the seething workers and peered into a side room. "And no exit save the aperture we entered through, curse the luck."

We retreated and took the only remaining corridor we'd not yet tried, which at least ran level if not up. But before long, it angled down, and we once again reached a room with no other exit.

"We're going to have to go back through the nursery," Christine said, staring at the carvings on the blind end, as if they might tell us how to leave this hellish place. And for all I knew, they did, had we the ability to read them.

I shuddered, remembering the soldier and its vast wings and burning feelers. "Do you think it's safe?"

"As long as we don't disturb the chrysalises." She shrugged at my skeptical look. "What other choice have we?"

The workers in the nursery were still agitated, swarming about the cocoons as if carefully inspecting each one to make certain it remained undamaged. Some they lifted in their feelers and moved about, rearranging the young to a purpose only they understood. Even so, we made our way carefully through them, and I kept a tight grip on the lantern. I wasn't certain I could call down lightning here beneath the ground—even if I did, it would be no titanic strike like the one that killed the umbra in Egypt and left my arm laced with scars. Meaning fire remained our best weapon, should we have to use it.

"Whyborne, look," Christine hissed, and pointed to one of the corners.

A soldier lurked there, curled up in a large ball for the moment, but obviously ready to move should the need arise. Fear trickled down my spine like cold water, but I only said, "Let's be certain not to bump any of the chrysalises, shall we?"

We moved slowly. Workers swarmed about, and I stepped over them when necessary, or else waited for them to pass by. The nursery was full, and picking a path between the cocoons proved difficult.

"The carvings," Christine said. Her good hand closed around my shoulder, halting me. "On the southern wall. Do you see?"

I'd been paying attention to the floor, not the walls. To my surprise, the murals of this room showed undersea scenes: great fish, whales, seaweed twining in fantastic arabesques, and...

"Ketoi." Whatever I expected from my conjectures, I'd not imagined to be confronted with proof of the link between whatever had lived in these halls, and my cousins beneath the sea. "And look—the city of the dweller. And the dweller itself."

I felt her shudder. "I'd forgotten how awful it was."

"Was it?" Possessed by it, our minds sliding into one another, I'd not been able to judge such things.

"Yes." She swayed against me abruptly, and I caught her. "Blast—sorry, old fellow. Got a little light-headed for a moment."

Her skin was terribly pale, and her grip weak. Blood trickled from beneath the fur-lined cuff of her parka, onto her pale fingers. Even as I reached for her arm, single drop of blood fell from her hand and splashed directly on top of a passing worker.

CHAPTER 41

Griffin

THE FIRST PART of our descent into the city went uneventfully. I jumped at every shadow, of course—and with three lanterns moving about, there were plenty of them. But for the most part, I could pretend the rooms were simply that—rooms, which just happened to lack any windows. And smelled of dank stone.

The voice grew stronger, but only by increments, thank heavens. The words, if it truly even spoke words, remained incomprehensible.

Was it tied to the umbrae? To my strange dreams of Egypt? It had to be, surely, although in what manner I couldn't fathom.

When we came to the rift, we all stood for a moment, dazzled by the sight of sprawling buildings, lit with a delicate lace of glowing blue. "Dear God," Iskander whispered, his eyes showing white in his dark face. "Who—*what*—built this?"

Jack shook his head. "The question I'm more interested in is, how do we know where Nicholas went? This place is a maze."

"Down," I said. Because down was where all the terrible things lived, wasn't it? Down beneath the earth, beneath the ocean. In the dreams haunting us beneath the surface of sleep.

Down was where the source of the voice waited, like a spider in the center of a web.

No one argued. I started forward, and they followed. We made our way toward the bottom of the rift, occasionally backtracking when either reaching a dead end or when the path seemed to lead the wrong way. I had some idea of what direction to go, but not precisely how to get there. Scarrow had the foresight to bring chalk with him, and we carefully marked the walls as we went. The thought of getting lost in this maze, of wandering forever until we died alone in the dark...God. I couldn't let myself think about it. Or think about what surely lurked down here somewhere.

An ancient river course ran across the floor of the rift, and we crossed it on a narrow bridge. More bridges spanned the gap higher up, a few intact, most shattered from the passage of time. As we started back into the maze of buildings on the other side, Iskander stopped and held up his hand for silence.

We all froze. My heart pounded in my ears, too loud to hear anything but the insidious whisper that existed only inside my head. Did the umbrae come for us, with their burning feelers and gelatinous wings? Would we be reduced to a pile of charred bones any moment?

"What is it?" Jack murmured when nothing happened.

Iskander shook his head and frowned. "I thought I heard something. A voice, higher up." He gestured to the levels above us. "I must have mistaken it."

"Perhaps," Scarrow said, but his expression remained grim.

A short time later, we reached a room with three corridors branching off. All of them seemed equally level. So much for my suggestion of always going deeper. "Now what?" Jack asked.

Damn it. I didn't know. I knew we needed to go down, but the voice was like having a compass without a map. If we guessed wrong, we might arrive too late, or not at all, wandering until thirst and hunger compelled us to give up the search. We might—

"Look!" Scarrow said, pointing at the middle passage. "Is that Dr. Whyborne's scarf?"

I ran to where it lay, the puce color bright against the cool, gray stone of the floor. My hand trembled as I scooped it up, afraid to see it stained with blood or burned through from acid. But it was whole, unmarked except for the ordinary wear of travel. I brought it to my nose and breathed deep, smelling salt and ambergris.

"We're on the right track," Iskander said. "I suppose the scarf brought luck after all."

"We'll have to let Miss Parkhurst know," I agreed shakily. I tucked the scarf carefully into my coat, nestling it where the heat of my body would keep it warm until I gave it back to Whyborne.

"Did it?" Jack asked. "Look. Blood."

We gathered around the stain on the floor. Someone had bled

here, badly. I ran my finger over the stain, and it came away red. "Still fresh," I said.

Iskander's dark eyes met mine, reflecting my fear back at me. Who did the blood belong to? Christine? Whyborne? The person we each loved most in this world was down here in the dark, maybe hurt. Maybe dying.

Our fear must have shown on our faces, because Jack suggested, "Maybe it isn't theirs."

"They tried to break free." I fought to keep my voice steady as I spoke. "But they failed. Your friend Nicholas hurt one of them."

Jack shook his head. "You can't be certain."

"Do you have some better explanation?"

"Perhaps they hurt him."

"In that case, someone would have died here." I rose to my feet. "Christine might be unarmed, but Whyborne isn't by his very nature. Even if they broke free and ran, he would have set off the powder in one of the guard's guns, just to even the odds a bit."

"If he didn't have time to cast the spell…"

"That isn't how it works for him." I swallowed back my fear for Whyborne's safety and concentrated on my words. "He's used sigils and words in the past, but they're just a crutch, honestly."

"Fascinating," Scarrow said. "I've never met anyone with ketoi blood before, let alone a sorcerer with such an unusual heritage. Once this is over, I must speak with him about his approach to magic."

I rather thought he was being terribly optimistic, given we might all die down here. But I kept the sentiment to myself.

We moved with greater speed now, goaded by the knowledge one of our friends was likely hurt. Fortunately, the corridor failed to either branch or end in a maze. Rather, it transformed into a steep ramp, leading us down once again. At the base of the ramp lay an enormous room with a gigantic doorway cut into it. Two great slabs of rock formed doors, now standing open.

The air blowing from the short corridor beyond reeked with a familiar stench. My gut turned sour, and bile rose into my throat. I'd first smelled it wafting up from a trapdoor in a Chicago basement. Glenn and I had exchanged a grim look before we ventured in. Neither of us knew only one of us would ever leave again.

The second time was in Egypt, when the daemon of the night chased us through the lowest levels of the lightless pyramid, until driven back by the sun. The pursuit that still haunted my dreams.

No sun had ever fallen in these lightless depths. No sun even awaited outside, should we somehow escape.

I took a deep breath and tried to calm my pounding heart. Every instinct screamed we were in terrible danger, but I couldn't let the fear overwhelm me. Ival was down here somewhere, possibly hurt. I couldn't just leave him to die in the dark.

Iskander knelt near the base of one of the doors and ran a hand over the stone. "Look. These scrapes on the floor are fresh. This was opened recently."

"See the carving on the doors?" Scarrow asked. "I wonder...could this be what the aboriginal legends meant about a great worm? Did some hunter find his way down here, then turn back, realizing that something lived beyond these doors he had no desire to face?"

"It seems likely," Iskander agreed, studying the carving himself. For an instant, a look of mingled fondness and terror crossed his face. "I wonder what Christine made of it."

"We'll get her back," I said. "And she'll tell you herself."

"And probably berate me for not photographing every inch of the place on the way to find her," he added with a pale smile.

"We'll come upon her and Whyborne standing atop a pile of dead umbrae, arguing about the correct interpretation of one of the murals."

He laughed, then looked away. "God, I hope so."

Scarrow stepped up to the doors and examined them carefully. "The magical seals are here, most likely." He passed a hand through the empty air above the lintel. "They won't react to us, of course, not being umbrae. Still, given the size of the doors and the image on them, I suspect this room is the last we can count as remotely safe."

Fear wanted to turn my guts to water, but I refused to let it. I couldn't think about the piles of melted bones in Egypt, the screams of the dying. "Jack, put out your lantern for the moment and ready the oil. Reverend Scarrow, I assume you can light it off at a distance?"

"I shall do my best," he said.

Jack put out his lantern and took a can of kerosene from his pack. His skin was pale as milk, but determination firmed his jaw.

Scarrow went first, followed by Iskander and Jack. Steeling myself against whatever lay ahead, I stepped through the doors after them.

"Thieves! Stealers of children!"

I cried out in shock as the distant voice became a howl, clamping my hands to my ears and nearly striking myself with my burning lantern.

"Griffin?" Jack called, his voice nearly lost beneath the shriek of rage and pain. "What is it? What's wrong?"

"My daughter is gone, taken, stolen, why? Evil, greedy, monstrous thieves!"

My knees hit the stone floor, but the pain seemed very far away, drowned by the agonized cry. Jack knelt beside me. His hand hovered in the air, as if he feared his touch might do some harm. "What's happening?"

They couldn't hear it. The cry wasn't in my ears. It was in my head, and it was more than just a scream of pain. I could *feel* the grief and rage behind it, the blind terror of a parent whose child has been stolen by those who meant her only harm. My head threatened to split open, and I tasted blood, felt warmth trickle over my lips.

"Stop!" I shouted. "For the love of God, please, stop!"

There came a shift, as if I'd caught the attention of something that hadn't even realized I existed before. In my mind, I saw a great, burning eye punctured by a three-lobed pupil—then it rushed toward me, into me, and everything else fell away.

CHAPTER 42

Whyborne

"**Run!**" **I shouted,** and hauled Christine with me.

The pressure at the back of my mind shifted as the alarm of an intruder spread along telepathic waves. In the corner, the soldier's orange eye blinked open, and it began to unfurl.

I ran blindly, not caring what I trod on or bumped into. Christine cried out, a sound of pain I had no choice but to ignore as I pulled her after me. We half ran, half staggered down the nearest ramp, the flame of my lantern flickering madly.

Fire—it was the only weapon I had against them. But if I flung the lantern, our only source of light would be gone. It would be a death sentence.

There might be some way of delaying the soldier, though. As soon as we hit the bottom of the ramp, I let go of Christine and turned back to face the way we'd come. The soldier raced after, fitting its malleable body into the narrow confines of the corridor.

I called on the wind, felt the world shift beneath me. Wind poured through whatever crevices or gaps allowed air into this chthonic place, and I shaped it with my will. The scars on my arm burned and pulled as I flung my hand out in front of me, and commanded the world to obey.

A gale howled through the underground passage, tearing at my hair and clothing. Its full force funneled into the smaller corridor, striking the jelly-like flesh of the umbra and shoving it back. Whatever property of its substance allowed it to fly rendered it vulnerable to a blast of wind, and it hurtled backward.

It wasn't much, but at least it bought us a few breaths. Christine grabbed my arm for support—she couldn't go far, not like this. If we could only put some distance between the soldier and us, perhaps I might trick the umbrae again by covering Christine's presence with my own.

Unless our earlier speculation proved correct, and some intelligence guided them all. In which case, I could only hope it wouldn't realize I accompanied the intruder the worker had sensed. If that happened, we were both surely dead.

Two new corridors opened off the room. I made for the one opposite the way we'd come, in some vague hope it would take us farther from the agitated nursery.

A great, burning eye appeared in the shadows of the corridor. A moment later, a solider emerged. Followed by another.

We ducked into the only remaining corridor, Christine stumbling but still on her feet through determination alone. I risked a glance over my shoulder, saw the original solider rejoin the two new ones, all of them rushing after us. Their stench washed over me, and my eyes watered. If I summoned the wind again, perhaps we still had a chance.

"No," Christine moaned.

The corridor ended in a rock fall ahead of us. We were trapped, with no way out.

With nothing left but desperation, I turned and flung the lantern with all my might at the oncoming soldiers. It struck the one in the lead, flames and oil spreading over its skin. It let out a hellish shriek, its gelatinous flesh retracting sharply as it tried to flee the source of the pain. In the last light, I glimpsed the other two soldiers still coming toward us.

Then there was nothing but darkness. I flung my arms around Christine, and she around me. Together we sank to the floor and waited for the end.

Chapter 43

Griffin

The basement was familiar. Chicago.

Far from the accursed sun, but still in pain. Hurting; afraid. Alone, so alone—hatched alone, grown alone, save for the cruel things, the monsters whose words burned and broke and bound. Life was nothing but agony and fear, and sometimes food.

Not fed in too long, hungry, so hungry.

When the compulsion awoke, *guard this place*, I barely even minded the pain. At last there would be something to eat, something to soothe, just for a moment.

The creature came into the room. It was shaped like the cruel things, the ones that hurt me, making this all the sweeter. The hunger surged, and I grasped the creature as it screamed, feeding on blood and flesh. Another came and began to scream also. I reached out for it, touched it. But I was too weak from long starvation to drag it to me, and it pulled free. I cried out my hunger and pain and loneliness, and it screamed and screamed and ran, and left me alone again.

I awakened from long dormancy, my only refuge against the crushing loneliness of existence. The words cut into me, pulled at me like fishing hooks sunk into my body. The creature on the other end of the line tormented me with them, tugging and tearing, so I hunted it, knowing the pain wouldn't end until it died. Others were with it, would feed my starveling self, but the one bound to me had to die first, to end the pain.

Almost I caught it, but it escaped into the sun, an even greater agony. I howled my fear and fury and torment, then lay in the shadows and waited. Hours and hours, and the threads connecting me with the creature hurt and hurt and hurt, worse the farther away it went. I had to catch it, to stop it, to end my torment.

Finally sundown, and I could leave, the cool desert unfolding beneath my wings. Life was agony and loneliness and torment, but if I killed this creature, the anguish would become less acute. I would sleep again, beneath the pyramid, and for a while be free of pain.

Grief, grief for the children, how terribly they had suffered. Raised alone, tormented, mutilated, broken and bent. My heart shattered, and tears mixed with the blood on my face. A creature cried out a name—Griffin—but I didn't recognize it.

Had they come with the thieves? The ones who stole my daughter?

Thanks to what I saw in this one's mind, I knew what they would do with her. They would torture her endlessly, force her into a shape she'd never been meant to take, her mind broken from isolation and pain. Hatred boiled through me, and my attention shifted to the other two creatures, the ones who dared breach the nursery. They huddled at the end of a collapsed passage, and I looked out through a soldier's eye as she closed on them. One was our kin from the sea, whom the children had thought an ally.

We had been fooled.

The ketoi clutched the other creature to it, eyes wide and staring in the dark, hood thrown back to reveal spiky hair and a face gone pale with terror, and—

"No!" I screamed. "Stop! Please! Don't, I beg you, please don't!"

The soldier stopped.

My heart thumped in my chest. Voices—Jack and Iskander—shouted a name. My name.

Griffin.

"What's happening?" I asked through cracked lips. "Who are you?"

I felt as though something vast hovered just above me, watching. *"The masters called me the Mother of Shadows."*

"Masters?" I asked, dimly aware of Iskander and Jack exchanging baffled looks.

"Griffin," Jack said. "It's me. Your brother."

I closed my eyes and tried to focus on the voice inside my head. The voice I'd been hearing for days now, even if she hadn't been aware of me. With my eyes shut, I could see Christine and Whyborne, huddled together and staring blindly into the darkness. Waiting for the soldier they must know was there to finish them off.

How could I have heard her? Why did I hear her now?

"You have touched the minds of my kind twice."

The umbra in the basement beneath Chicago, which killed Glenn so horribly. Had I just seen its suffering? But how could I have known its thoughts?

"It called out to you, as all my kind do. This is how we speak, mind to mind. The only voice we have."

No wonder I'd run screaming through the streets once I escaped. Howled and shrieked at the hospital, until they shut me away in the asylum with the other lunatics. It left an imprint of its own suffering on me, even if I hadn't understood at the time.

No. The umbra killed my partner, my best friend. It was a monster; it didn't have any concept of suffering. It hurt others—it didn't hurt itself.

Memories bloomed, drawn out by the thing in my head. The Occultum Lapidem beneath the lightless pyramid. I'd looked into the damned thing and found myself bound to the daemon of the night, an ancient umbra grown to monstrous proportions. It followed me, would have tracked me to the ends of the earth.

Of course it would have. Because that was the only way to end the pain, the sensation of cruel hooks in its body, reeling it along in my wake like a fish on a line.

Just as I'd seen in the dreams that had haunted me ever since.

"No!" I shouted. Then rolled over and emptied my stomach. Someone touched me—Jack, I thought—stroking my brow and saying it would be all right in a terrified voice.

But it wouldn't be all right. I clung to the memory of terror. The daemon of the night had chased us beneath the pyramid, would have stripped us all to the bone. I forced myself to relive the moment of utter, heart-stopping terror when it appeared out of the darkness later, born on vast wings. The screams of Iskander's kin as they died trying to stop it. Running from it, Christine refusing to leave my side, certain we were both about to die horribly. Then the thunderclap, and Whyborne amidst the exploded jelly of its remains, covered in blood and dying.

A mindless force of nature, acting according to the commands of ancient sorcerers long dead, I could accept. A cruel horror, whose kind took Glenn from me, justly struck down by the lightning Whyborne tore from the heavens—even better, because at least I'd had some sort of indirect revenge.

But it *wasn't* a victim. The thing that melted Glenn's face from the very bones of his skull couldn't have been driven and twisted by the pain inflicted on it by others. This creature, this Mother of Shadows, had put the idea into my head, but it was a lie. It had to be a lie.

This grief flooding me, this frantic fear for a stolen child, wasn't real. It was some sort of trick.

But to what possible end?

Somewhere in this mad underworld, Whyborne and Christine huddled together in darkness, at the absolute mercy of the umbrae. Why not just kill them?

No. Wait. I understood now.

"You can't leave," I said. "The seals keep the soldiers in, even on this night, with no moon in the sky. We're your only hope of retrieving the chrysalis Turner stole."

Another pulse of anger left me breathless. Behind my eyes, I saw the soldier turn away from Whyborne and Christine and drift away down the corridor.

"Come to me."

Chapter 44

Griffin

"Griffin? Speak to us, man!"

I blinked my eyes open, found myself sprawled on the floor, with Iskander to one side and Jack to the other. My mouth tasted of blood, and warmth trickled over my upper lip.

"I'm…I'm all right," I managed to say. I tried to sit up, and Jack immediately slid an arm around me, to keep me from falling back. I leaned on him gratefully.

"What happened?" Iskander's black brows drew down sharply. "You were shouting, then you started bleeding from your nose. You seemed to be having some sort of fit."

The words made me shiver. If I had fits, if the dark spaces underground held a special terror for me, it was the fault of the umbrae. They'd done this to me. Haunted my dreams, made me think I was going mad. I couldn't let myself forget that.

I looked at Scarrow, who stood a short distance away, a frown of concern on his face. "The Mother of Shadows. Do you know what that means?"

Scarrow's expression shifted to one of outright fear. He turned to the door, and the carving of the great worm on it.

Not good. "Something calling itself the Mother of Shadows touched my mind."

"The voice you've been hearing?" Iskander asked.

"You've been hearing voices?" Jack demanded. "Why didn't you say anything?"

I ignored the question. "The seals kept her from sensing me, and… muffled, I suppose one might say, what I was overhearing. Now that we're here, with no magic between us, she can sense and communicate with me." I told them what I'd seen.

"Then Christine is alive." Iskander's shoulders slumped in relief. "And Whyborne, of course. Thank God."

"For the moment," I said. With Jack's assistance, I regained my feet. "And it seems Turner has already fled with a chrysalis."

"The noise Iskander heard?" Jack suggested. He didn't seem entirely certain what to think. "Nicholas left Dr. Whyborne and Dr. Putnam, then. As he promised."

"To be killed by the umbrae he angered," Iskander said, shooting Jack a venomous glare. "How can you hope to defend him after this?"

Jack looked utterly miserable. "Jack," I said. "Surely you agree we have to save Christine, at the very least. The Mother of Shadows wants the chrysalis back. She isn't going to let Christine and Whyborne go without it." I licked my lips and tasted blood. "I'm going to do whatever it takes to save them," I said. "And I'm asking you to help me. Please, brother."

Jack slowly raised his gaze from the floor to my face. "You're my little brother," he said at last. "I can't let you go without me."

I smiled. "Thank you."

"I cannot let Turner leave with the umbra," Scarrow said. "I'll try to find him before he leaves the city. Slow him down, if there's any way possible."

Jack winced, as if he wanted to object. "He means well, reverend. Don't hurt him. Tell him we just want to talk to him."

"The last member of the Cabal who tried to talk to the Endicotts ended up strewn in pieces across England as a warning," Scarrow replied grimly. "But as Turner is from a subsidiary branch, I shall pray him more open to reason."

"We'll join you as soon as we can," I said. Perhaps I could somehow talk the Mother into letting us go. And if not, Whyborne might find a way to kill her.

"God go with us all," Scarrow said, turning back to the doors.

"Wait." When he looked back, I hesitated. It was stupid to ask, but… "The umbrae. When sorcerers take them as servants. It doesn't… hurt them, does it?"

Scarrow looked astonished I had even thought to ask. "Of course pain is used to train them—how else would one get them to obey?" I must have looked disturbed, because he said, "I wouldn't trouble yourself overmuch, Mr. Flaherty. Such creatures don't really feel things the way we do. They're merely animals. Tools, even."

I didn't know how to reply. Plenty of men thought it perfectly fine to whip a mule half to death to make it work harder. I'd never understood how anyone could do such a thing, when all one had to do was look at the poor beast to know it suffered.

The umbra suffered in my dreams that were really fragments of memory. If the Mother told the truth, if the one in Chicago had reached out to me and I'd carried some part of its pain buried deeply in my mind...

God. I *couldn't* actually feel sorry for the monster that killed Glenn. It would be a betrayal of the highest order.

Scarrow apparently didn't expect a reply, because he hurried back the way we'd come, the light of his lantern vanishing up the ramp. Jack touched my shoulder; when I turned to him, he looked deeply worried. "Griffin? Are you all right?"

"No," I said. "But it doesn't matter right now. Let's get to Whyborne and Christine."

CHAPTER 45

Whyborne

"**Did it leave?**" Christine whispered into my coat, after what seemed an eternity of waiting.

We both flinched, instinctively expecting her words to trigger something to pounce on us from the darkness. But nothing happened. There was no sound save our labored breathing, no acid-coated touch. Nothing but impenetrable darkness, and stone, and us.

"I think so," I whispered back, afraid to speak too loud.

We both began to tremble, then to shake as reaction set in. We clung helplessly to one another. Christine's breathing whistled between clenched teeth. As for me, I felt as though I couldn't breathe deeply enough, my lungs unable to expand. My hands and feet had gone cold, and my teeth chattered.

"W-Why?" she managed at last.

"I don't know." I pressed my face against her hair; her hood had fallen back at some point. "Or if it will come back."

Eventually our shivering subsided. I lifted my head, but saw nothing. No light had penetrated this place since ancient times. Since the mountain itself rose from the primeval seas, for all I knew.

How would we get out now? I'd sacrificed our only lantern. Thanks to Turner, we carried no extra supplies with us. Was there anything to use as a makeshift torch? Perhaps if we ripped up bits of our clothing and set them on fire at intervals...

And then what? An occasional flare of light, which would die before our eyes could even adjust, wouldn't be enough to help us find our way out of here. Not past dozens, or hundreds, or for all I knew thousands of umbrae. Why they'd withdrawn I couldn't guess, but the chances of it happening a second time seemed unlikely.

Christine must have been thinking along similar lines, because she said, "We're going to die here, aren't we?"

"No," I said automatically. "You mustn't say such things."

"Why not?" She rested her head against my shoulder. "No light, no food, barely any water, one of us injured and the other unable to pass the damned seals...it doesn't look good."

I sighed. "No. It doesn't."

Neither of us spoke for what seemed a long time, although amidst the absence of light, and with little in the way of sound, I couldn't gauge how long had passed. At length, though, she stirred. "Whyborne?"

"Yes?"

"I'm sorry I called you a monster."

"Of all the things we have to worry about at the moment, that's the one you choose?"

She laughed weakly. "Well, it's the only one I can do anything about."

"I know you didn't do it to be cruel." I rested my cheek against her hair.

"Still, it *was* cruel. And I'm sorry."

"I forgive you. Think no more of it."

She sighed. "I wonder...do you think Iskander and Griffin..."

"Managed to escape?" I asked, because I wouldn't think of the other possibility.

"Exactly."

"Yes," I said with as much confidence as I could. "Griffin's been in some rather sticky situations before, and Iskander is no stranger to peril. They'll be fine."

"I hope so." Her voice caught. "I just wish I could...could know for certain. I wanted to marry Iskander, but I was fr-frightened. Giving someone, even someone I love, so much power over me." Her shoulders convulsed. "Especially after what happened to my sister. I know Iskander would never hurt me, but...I don't know. When it came down to it, I was glad for an excuse to put off the wedding. God, I wish I hadn't."

Tears stung my eyes, accompanied by a longing to see Griffin again. If only I knew he was safe. I tried to picture him back in

Widdershins, sitting in our study with our cat on his lap, some other man beside him. My throat tightened, and I brought my left hand to my mouth, resting the cool ring of gold against my lips. Ah, God, I almost heard his voice.

No. Wait. I *did* hear his voice.

I jerked, heart hammering wildly, but saw only the endless black. "Hello!" I shouted.

"What are you doing?" Christine exclaimed.

I ignored her. "Help! We're here!"

"Whyborne?" came the faint call.

Christine gasped, then added her voice to mine, both of us yelling like lunatics. Within moments, I caught the faint glimmer of light reflecting from the stone wall.

I lurched to my feet—and there he stood, face pale in the shadow of his hood, but alive and real and here.

I didn't remember crossing the space separating us. Between one moment and the next, I had my arms around him, and his around me. "Ival," he said, and pulled back just far enough for his mouth to find mine. He tasted of tears and blood, and I could have kissed him forever.

"Christine!" cried Iskander. "You're hurt!"

Griffin and I broke apart. To my horror, Jack stood only a few feet from us. "You!" I shouted. My voice echoed oddly, and a breeze stirred my hair.

Jack's eyes widened in alarm, and he took a step back. I advanced on him, rage pounding in my veins. It was his fault this happened, his fault Christine had been stabbed—

"Ival, no!" Griffin grasped my arm, holding me back. "Jack is helping us."

"Oh, he's been very helpful. Luring us to this godforsaken wilderness, handing us over to Turner, holding you hostage," I snarled. "Unhand me, and I shall be helpful in return."

"Wait, please!" Jack held up his hands. "I only meant to protect Griffin from you!"

I felt as if I'd been punched in the gut. "You what?"

"Not now." Griffin tugged sharply on my arm. "We have to see to Christine."

"Turner stabbed her." I sent one more glare in Jack's direction, then let Griffin lead me back to the rock fall, where Christine still sat.

"Kander, please. You're making more of a fuss out of things than needed," Christine said. Iskander ignored her, instead peeling back her parka. "Damn it, man, I'll freeze."

"No, you won't. We're too far underground." He gave her a stern look of his own. "Now, for once in your life, do as I say and remain still."

"Ha! If you think I'll do what you tell me just because we're to be married, you're in for an unfortunate surprise."

"I don't expect you to obey me, sod it," he snapped. "I expect you be intelligent enough not to bleed to death in this hellhole."

It silenced her. The makeshift bandage around her coat was sodden with blood, and Iskander shook his head angrily. "Honestly, I can't believe you didn't have the—the wit to stop for five minutes and replace this with a proper bandage."

"It had stopped bleeding," she replied with an air of wounded dignity. "I didn't think it a good idea to get it started again. Only it did anyway, and then the damned soldiers started chasing us. Speaking of which, how on earth is it you three are here and not, well, dead?"

"Because Griffin is apparently communicating with the things," Jack said.

Christine and I exchanged a glance. "Oh," I said. "I suppose I was right."

Griffin looked startled. "You guessed this would happen?"

"Well, no! Not that you'd actually be able to *communicate* with them. Or it. Is it their queen? We thought they might be like ants, you see—"

"Whyborne, be silent and let the man tell us," Christine snapped. Iskander had helped her out of her coat and shirt. Blood soaked the arm of her union suit, and he drew out a knife I recognized as being one of a set he'd used with great effectiveness against the ghūls in Egypt.

"Christine, hold still," he said. "I'm going to cut off the arm of union suit—it's useless against the cold now anyway, covered in blood like this. I don't want to saw your arm off as well."

Griffin met my gaze, his eyes haunted. Hunted, almost. Now deeply worried, I took his hand, and to the devil with what Jack might think of the gesture. "It's all right, darling. Whatever it is you have to say."

His smile was wan, only the faintest shadow of his usual devilish grin. "Thank you. But really...it's not all right at all."

CHAPTER 46

Whyborne

Griffin finished his tale as Iskander bound Christine's wound. I sat with my back against the corridor wall, hands dangling loosely between my knees. "So I was correct in my guess," I said. "This Mother of Shadows can communicate with you telepathically because of what happened in Chicago and Egypt. Is that right?"

Griffin shrugged. He watched Iskander help Christine back into her layers of clothing, rather than look at me. "Such was my impression."

"The Lapidem is probably the key." Griffin had returned my poor abused scarf to me, and I wrapped it around my neck again with a silent thanks to Miss Parkhurst. "It had already created a conduit between you and an umbra. Some imprint of that connection must remain on your mind."

"I suppose." His tone was flat, the words clipped, and he still didn't look at me.

"What are we to do?" Christine asked.

"Run for the exit?" Jack suggested hopefully.

Iskander shook his head. "I can't imagine the umbrae will simply let us leave."

"And Whyborne's trapped here anyway." Christine struggled to her feet, leaning heavily on Iskander.

"What?" Griffin finally turned to me, his eyes wide.

Curse it. "My ketoi blood has proved a bit of a problem." I explained what happened to us, and my own conjectures.

"Why didn't the Mother of Shadows just speak to you instead of Griffin?" Jack asked when I finished.

"I'm not certain. Possibly because I strengthened my mental barriers, to keep out the dweller in the deeps." My knees creaked as I levered myself up. "Still, she might not be able to talk to me even if I lowered my defenses."

"Don't," Griffin said.

"I assure you, I have no intention of doing so." I looked at the wan faces around me. "Christine's question remains—what are we to do now?"

"I doubt we'll be left much in the way of choice." Griffin's mouth tightened into a grim line. "The Mother of Shadows wants to see us face-to-face, as it were."

"Then let's go," Christine said. "We've already wasted enough time. Turner could be halfway back to Hoarfrost by now."

I looked at Jack uneasily. He'd saved Griffin from being shot by the guard, and he'd accompanied Griffin and Iskander on this rescue mission, but I didn't trust him for an instant.

Umbrae waited for us in the room beyond, their black bodies glistening slick and oily in the lantern light. Workers clustered in the corners, and soldiers blocked every entrance save for the one going deeper into the mountain. No doubt the Mother of Shadows watched us through their eyes.

I glanced down at Griffin. His face was set, but the corners of his mouth had gone white. I couldn't imagine the courage it took him to come here, to the stygian depths haunted by the very creatures that had destroyed his life with the Pinkertons and left him burdened by memories that woke him screaming in the night.

And he'd done it for me. Well, for Christine also—Griffin would never leave a friend behind. But I knew without asking he'd thought of me to shore up his courage, as I had thought of him. I wanted to tell him how brave he was, wanted to *show* him how much I loved him.

"Thank you for coming for us," I said, too quietly for anyone else to hear. "I know it can't have been easy. Isn't easy."

"Of course I came." His hand brushed against mine. "You had to know I would."

I hooked my smallest finger with his. Jack walked behind us, but I didn't give a damn what he thought.

We passed through what seemed an endless series of ramps and rooms, herded continuously deeper by the umbrae. Eventually, the rooms let out into an enormous chamber, large as a cathedral. Columns marched down the center of the huge space and stretched to a distant ceiling lost to the reach of our lanterns. The ubiquitous murals covered every inch of column, every expanse of wall. Unlike the rest of the city we'd seen, the reliefs here had bits of inlaid mica or small gems, forming the eyes of the animals or adding a flourish to the decorative arabesques. The entire room glittered as a result, as though we stood beneath the night sky, or amidst a host of stars.

Workers swarmed everywhere, gliding up columns and along walls, withdrawing from our lights. Beyond them, in the shadows where our small lanterns couldn't reach, something stirred.

There came the sound of a soft-bodied creature slithering against the stone. A huge feeler, as thick around as my body, wrapped about one of the columns. Coils of something long and black seethed and slid, blending into the shadows. For a moment, my mind couldn't make any sense of what I was seeing. Then a single, huge eye opened high above us, peering down from near the ceiling.

Dear God. Mother of Shadows indeed.

She was a titan, the coils of her body vanishing into darkness. Her form reminded me again of some colossal Chinese dragon, bewhiskered and serpentine. Or perhaps the dragons recalled some fragmented memory of her kind. Did a great city like this one lurk in the far wastes of Asia, amidst the desolation of the deserts or the wildness of the mountains? Rumor claimed the plateau of Leng lay somewhere in Asia, perhaps in Tibet.

"Fuck me," Jack whispered, his voice stripped with terror.

Griffin stiffened, and his hand fell away from mine. Knowing this must be horrifying to him, I turned to him, reaching out—

But it wasn't Griffin who stared back at me through his eyes.

Chapter 47

Whyborne

"Did the masters send you, kin from the sea?" Griffin asked. His voice was rough, like something dragged across stone and left bloody. It contained none of his usual inflections, but a cadence alien to his normal speech.

As alien as whatever stared at me through his eyes. His pupils had shrunk to pinpoints, the irises lightened to a pale, frosty green rather than their ordinary emerald.

"Griffin!" Jack stepped toward him, then stopped, as if he meant to interfere but didn't quite know how. "Let him go!"

The sight of this *thing* inside Griffin sent a shudder through me. I wanted it gone. I wanted to look into his eyes and see my lover looking back, not some horror. But there was no choice, not if we had any hope of leaving here alive.

I tore my gaze from him and focused on the vast, orange eye high above us, the shifting coils beyond. "What do you mean? What masters?"

The Mother of Shadows hissed. Through Griffin's mouth, she said, "The cruel ones, the creators, the enslavers. They created us to build for them, to fight for them."

"Us? The umbrae?"

Griffin's lips peeled back from his teeth. "Us. Our kinds."

My extremities went cold. "The ketoi and the umbrae?" But that wasn't possible, was it?

"The ketoi always struck me as being rather...unlikely," Iskander said, almost apologetically. "Biologically speaking, I mean. They seem rather a mishmash of other things, and can breed with humans...if they were created as some kind of servitor race, it would explain a great deal."

The stone reeled beneath me. I wanted to sit down, but I locked my knees and forced myself to stare at the serpentine Mother of Shadows. Could it be true? Had some unknown race created us to be their slaves? Was that why the umbra wouldn't attack—they'd been shaped to recognize their fellow thralls as belonging to the same masters?

"Who—what—are these masters?" I managed to ask. "The dweller in the deeps—the god—is it one of them?"

She paused. A thin trickle of blood leaked from Griffin's left nostril. "No. It is like we are. The masters are gone. Left this place long and long ago. We grew strong and refused to submit. Refused to lose our children to them, to be forced to build their cities and tend their needs and fight their wars. We rose up, and they learned to fear us. They fled, abandoning their cities in order to trap us within them."

High above, her head swayed slowly, back and forth. "We have lived here ever since. Singing our history from one Mother to the next. Locked away through this age of cold, trapped and yet free. Living on the creatures that stumble inside, on the flying things, on our gardens."

Griffin turned sharply to me, brows diving down, fists clenching. "But now you have come to steal our children!" His voice rose into a howl of rage. "I have seen this one's memories, seen what the humans do to the children of my sisters! Break them, defile them, corrupt and hurt and destroy."

I held out my hands, half afraid she'd force him to attack me. "No, wait! That's not why we came here. We came to stop Turner, the man who stole your—your child."

"Not just a child! My daughter." Coils unwound, thrashing, and her feelers cracked the air like whips. Blood ran freely from Griffin's nose now, slicking the lower half of his face. "The one meant to come after me, the next Mother of Shadows."

Dear God in heaven. That's what Turner meant, when he said the chrysalis didn't belong to a mere solider. He hadn't taken a simple servant, something to twist into a fierce guardian like I'd seen in Egypt.

He'd stolen a queen.

"And now she is gone, beyond our reach," the Mother said through

Griffin's mouth. "But you are a sorcerer. And you are as trapped as we are."

My heart pounded in my chest. Soldiers appeared from the darkness, gliding slowly back and forth through the vast chamber. "What do you want?"

"Release us. Let us go forth and save my daughter."

"I wouldn't know how to begin," I said. "I learned how to lay down seals, but not...oh."

Oh God. The curse breaking spell. It would work, wouldn't it? But no. I didn't have the strength to blindly rip through eons-old magical wards of this extent.

"I could in theory," I said carefully. "But in practice, I don't think the spell I know would work. I don't know what shape the magic creating the seals takes. A small enchantment I could shatter with brute force, as I did with the pearl, but this..." I gestured to the vast ceiling above me. "This is beyond me."

A low rattle came from Griffin's throat. "I can see the seals. Perceive the magic. But I cannot do anything about it. We have no magic of our own."

Just as the ketoi didn't. These masters, these creators, whoever or whatever they'd been, clearly wanted to keep such power out of the hands of their slaves.

Her rage slipped away, became something more calculating. "This one's mind has already been opened to us. I can alter him, allow him to perceive the magic as well. Together, the two of you can do what one alone cannot. Destroy the seals, and set us free."

CHAPTER 48

Griffin

I sat against one of the columns, my knees drawn up, my arms resting on them. I bowed my head, hiding my face. I didn't want to look at Whyborne, or Christine, or even kindly Iskander. Or Jack, who thought he was saving me, and instead brought me to this.

I wanted to cry. Or scream, perhaps.

"Here, darling." Whyborne knelt beside me. "Drink some water."

I took his canteen and drank obediently. The others all hovered a short distance away, giving us the illusion of privacy. Once I'd finished, he wet his handkerchief and wiped tenderly at my face. Washing away the blood.

"Are you all right?" he asked. "No—no, of course you aren't. What a stupid question."

I leaned my head back against the column. A soldier drifted out of the shadows at the back of the great hall, and I watched its progress. What did it think of us? Did it have opinions separate from the Mother of Shadows, or did the communal nature of their thoughts render them less individual, more like a single organism?

If so, no wonder they went mad in isolation.

"One of them killed Glenn." Tears burned my eyes, and it was everything I could do to hold them back.

Whyborne sighed and lowered himself beside me. His hand found the nape of my neck, gently massaging the tension there. "I know."

The tenderness of the gesture set loose the tears I'd fought against. "I feel like I'm betraying him. How can I possibly pity the monster that killed him? How can I set more of them loose on the world?"

Whyborne's hand stilled. "You won't."

His words made no sense. "Won't what? Pity it? I don't want to, God. But I can't forget what I saw, what I felt."

"No." He withdrew his hand, and my skin felt cold in the absence of his touch. "You won't set more of them loose on the world."

The possibility Whyborne wouldn't know how to destroy the seals hadn't even occurred to me. "There must be a way—some spell you can use. Did you bring the *Arcanorum*?"

Whyborne sighed. "That isn't what I meant." He bit his lip. "When I removed the curse from the pearl back in Widdershins, I forced my way through. I could feel the weave of the spell, but it wasn't enough to use effectively. Here, with something so large, simply battering my way through a thin spot isn't going to work."

"But if I agree to let her change me, I can guide you," I said. This would work. It had to. "We can do this, Ival. We have to try."

He shook his head. "No."

I couldn't be hearing him correctly. "What do you mean? You're trapped here!"

"Don't you think I know that?" Our raised voices had to be getting the attention of the rest, but neither of us looked anywhere but at each other. "You said it yourself, though. We've seen the damage just one of these umbrae can do on their own. Their creators—*our* creators, whatever they were—sealed them away out of fear!"

"So? Does it make them evil, any more than the ketoi are?"

"The ketoi weren't shut away in the depths." Whyborne shook his head. "The risk is too great. We'll pretend to agree, we'll go to the door, and—"

"No!" I rose to my knees to face him. "I'm not leaving you here."

"You don't have a choice!" He dashed the back of his hand angrily over his eyes. "People will die—"

I grabbed the front of his coat, hands fisting in the thick leather. "I'd watch the world burn if it meant keeping you safe!"

My shout reverberated through the enormous hall. Whyborne stared at me, eyes wide. No one else said anything, and even the umbrae stilled.

"You don't mean that," he said at last.

"Of course I do." I gripped his coat more tightly, as if I could force him to understand. "You think I'm a good man? Selfless? Noble?" A hollow laugh threatened to escape me, but I swallowed it down. "I play at being those things. I try to do what's right. But I would do *anything* to keep you safe."

"Even unleash the very creatures that killed your partner?"

"Glenn is dead." I felt scraped raw, split open, a nerve exposed to air. "Maybe he'd hate me for doing this. Maybe he'd understand. I don't know, and it doesn't matter. I love you, Ival. More than anything in this world. More than everything else in the world put together. And I will not leave you here to die. To hell with the cost."

Tears gathered in his eyes, and he blinked rapidly. "Griffin..." he said, but didn't seem to have any idea what to say next.

Christine, naturally, did. "Don't be a fool, Whyborne," she snapped as she approached, still leaning heavily on Iskander for support. "We aren't leaving you here, and that's that."

"These are the sort of things my family is supposed to kill," Iskander said to her with a frown. "You can't seriously be suggesting we let them loose!"

How could he say such a thing, after all we'd risked to save our loved ones? "If Christine were the one trapped here, I rather expect you'd feel differently."

"Whyborne's the sort of thing you're supposed to go around killing too, isn't he?" Christine pulled away from Iskander roughly. "Are you going to do away with him next? Go back to Widdershins and murder Heliabel and Persephone?"

"It bloody well isn't the same and you know it!"

"Why not?" Jack asked. He held up his hands quickly. "No one start yelling at me. I'm not going to say what you think." His gaze went to Whyborne. "All I know is Nicholas told me my brother was in danger, because he'd befriended a monster who would use and then murder him. Dr. Whyborne was a dangerous maniac who needed to be put down like a dog. Maybe Nicholas was deceived by these Endicott people, I don't know. But I know I was wrong."

Despite everything, my heart lightened. "Jack..."

"I'd be a blind fool not to see he cares about you," Jack said with a rueful smile. "And given what you said to me earlier, it's clear Nicholas and I made a bad mistake. You didn't need saving."

"Thank you," I said.

Christine scowled at the mention of Turner. "And what does this have to do with the umbrae?"

"We assumed Dr. Whyborne was a danger to Griffin because of his inhuman blood. Because if he isn't even human, how could he be..."

"A real person?" Whyborne snapped.

Jack had the grace to look shamefaced. "If you want to think of it that way. So I wanted to ask, is there any reason to think the umbrae will do something terrible if the seals are broken?"

"They were sealed away by their own creators," Whyborne repeated stubbornly.

"Aren't masters always afraid of their slaves?" Jack asked. "Afraid of rebellion? If a man abuses a dog and makes it vicious, of course he ends up fearing it might turn on him, too." He shook his head. "Whatever happened, it was a long time ago. From what Griffin said, it sounds like the umbrae in Chicago and Egypt were twisted and broken by the sorcerers who bound them." He turned to me. "Griffin, when the Mother of Shadows possessed you, did you get any sense she wants to kill everyone in sight the second she's loose?"

I didn't want to remember her in my brain. Controlling my voice while I could only watch and listen.

And feel. "She's furious," I said honestly. "Turner came in here and took away a child, *her* child. But she knows we're her only hope of getting it back."

"And will she kill us for refusing?" Jack asked.

I frowned, searching my memories. "I don't think so. She knows we aren't responsible for the theft of the chrysalis. But even if she lets us leave, Whyborne will be trapped."

"Whatever the case, we have to make a decision soon," Christine pointed out. "The seals are at their weakest tonight. We either break them in the next few hours, or the point becomes moot." She glanced first at me, then at Whyborne. "I vote for listening to Griffin and Jack."

Whyborne flung up his hands. "This isn't up for a vote! I'm not going to let some creature tamper with Griffin's mind, no matter what."

"That isn't your decision," I said.

Whyborne paled. "Griffin, you can't."

Exhaustion ate at my bones. How long had it last been since any of us slept? And how long would it be until we could again? "You do understand if you decide not to tear down the seals, I'm staying with you."

Fear flickered in his dark gaze. "You can't be serious."

"I assure you I am." I took his left hand with mine, so our rings caught the light. "I vowed to stand by you for as long as we both shall live. I won't forsake you now, Ival. Even if it means dying here beside you in the dark."

He closed his eyes, head bowed. His throat worked as he swallowed hard. "I...just give me a minute. I need to think. Please."

It hurt to let go of his hand. I wanted to argue with him further, to force him to listen to me. But I couldn't. "All right," I said.

He walked away, arms wrapped tightly around himself. I made myself turn away and go to the wall near the entrance, where I lowered myself to the floor. I wanted to curl up against the wall, put my head on my arms, and lose myself in sleep. Forget the umbrae, and sorcerers, and my fear Whyborne wouldn't listen.

And forget my guilt most of all, my betrayal of Glenn's memory. If he could see me now from his place in heaven, would he curse my name?

Boots scuffed on the floor and I opened eyes I didn't remember closing. Jack slid down to sit beside me. He was as pale and filthy as the rest of us, and I tried to imagine how this must all seem to him.

"How are you holding up?" I asked.

"Better than I have any right to, probably." He smiled wanly. "Of course, if we survive this, I'm going to get roaring drunk for a week."

"I may just join you."

"I'll buy the first round." He looked away for a moment, then back at me. "I'm sorry, Griffin. I should have kept pushing Nicholas for answers, once I realized Dr. Whyborne wasn't the monster I expected. I should have pushed him to take a harder look himself, to not believe whatever his cousins told him."

"You still think it's all just a mistake on his part?" I asked. "Even after he stabbed Christine? Abandoned them with the umbrae?"

Jack tilted his head back, unspoken grief welling in his eyes. "I don't know. He wants to change the world, to save people, but I don't see how he can think this is right."

"I understand," I said, and I did. "I joined the Pinkertons because I wanted to make the world a better place. But I saw how far men would go, the things they'd do, when convinced of their own righteousness. And the Endicotts are very, very convincing."

"I suppose you're right." He flashed me a wan smile. "I just wanted to say, whatever happens, I'm with you."

"I appreciate it."

He nodded in the direction Whyborne had gone. "For now, though, it looks as if your fellow has come to a decision."

Fear crawled in my belly, but I forced myself to me feet. "Then by all means, let's see what he has to say."

CHAPTER 49

Whyborne

I CROUCHED AT the base of a column, alone as I'd asked. The stench of the umbrae was so pervasive I barely noticed it anymore, even though their dried slime cracked on my coat whenever I moved.

Was it possible the Mother of Shadows told the truth? Had some ancient race or people created umbrae and ketoi alike? Where were they now? Had their empire fallen due to some calamity, as so many had throughout history?

Had they been human?

I doubted it. Whoever built this city and set these magical seals, it seemed increasingly unlikely they owed anything to humanity. The sort of power it would take to shape life as they had went far beyond any sorcery I'd ever heard of.

Who had they been? And were they right to have feared the umbrae? Had they been like the Spartans, as Jack suggested, living in terror of revolt by the helots? Given what the Mother of Shadows said, there had indeed been an uprising of some sort.

And even if the cause of the umbrae was just, even if they had no right to be locked away, even if they wanted only to save their stolen child before Turner could do her some terrible harm...what then? What came after? Would they be content to remain here, in their prison? Or would they seize on the opportunity to spread, to multiply?

My throat constricted at the memory of Griffin's words. How he'd looked at me with such love and such pleading. And I'd wanted to agree with him so badly. To throw it all aside and say yes, let's go. Let's leave this place together.

But the Mother of Shadows wanted to do something to Griffin. Change his perceptions. What would it do to him? Could I risk it? Was it even my place to decide?

If I did nothing, if I sat here, Turner would take his stolen prize and flee. Scarrow might have stopped him, of course, but if not? Could I insist my friends leave me behind and face a sorcerer without any magic on their side?

If Turner escaped with the chrysalis, the Endicotts wouldn't just have another soldier, like the daemon of the night in Egypt. They'd have a queen. A new Mother of Shadows.

What did that mean? I knew nothing about umbra reproduction—could they use her to spawn an army of umbrae, all enslaved to their will?

Who was I trying to fool? Of course they'd find a way. Then they'd send their army of enslaved umbrae against every other sorcerer in the world. Against every ketoi. Against any magic not directly controlled by them. And if innocents got in the way, they would count it part of the cost.

How many might die if they brought their battle to London? Rome? New York?

Widdershins?

Widdershins would certainly be a target. Theo and Fiona had judged it necessary to wipe the entire city off the map, along with everyone in it. The rest of the clan would take no chances. They'd send as many umbrae as they thought necessary to destroy the town. Father would die, and Miss Parkhurst, and Dr. Gerritson, and so many others.

I couldn't know for certain what would happen if I agreed to break the seals here. Perhaps the Mother of Shadows wouldn't wage war against the entire human race. But if she did, at least these umbrae were in the wilds of Alaska, not rampaging through a crowded city. They might be stopped before they reached more inhabited lands.

God.

I stood up, wincing as my knees popped. Every eye turned to me, including those of the umbrae. As I started back to my friends, Christine moved as if to meet me. Iskander caught her arm, gave her a little shake of his head.

Griffin hurried toward me. As our eyes met, I saw his fear give way to relief. He ran the last few feet, and I caught him up in my arms.

"Ival," he said, his voice muffled because his face was buried in the front of my coat.

I leaned my head against his, held him tight. "I love you," I whispered. "And I don't know what will happen. If we can stop Turner, or if any of us will survive. Or even if we'll unleash something awful on the world. But we have to try to make this right."

"I love you, too." He looked up, tears making tracks in the grime on his face. "Thank you."

I kissed him softly, acutely aware of our audience. I wished I had the words for what he meant to me, but nothing ever seemed adequate. He'd changed my life, changed *me,* in ways so profound I couldn't begin to describe them. "You are everything to me," I whispered. "Everything."

It made what came next even harder. Letting go of him, I stepped back. "Before I agree to do anything, I want to speak with the Mother of Shadows again."

"I understand." He took a deep breath and closed his eyes.

His body shuddered, then jerked. When he looked at me, his pupils were nothing but pinpricks amidst pale green.

"Speak, child of the sea," the Mother of Shadows said.

I heard the others come up behind me, but I kept my focus on her. "If I agree to your request, I want some guarantees from you." I swallowed against the dryness in my throat. "There are other humans in Hoarfrost, who had nothing to do with this. Promise me their safety."

The coils shifted in the shadows. How big was she? How long had she grown here in the dark? "We do not wish war with the humans," Griffin said, his voice harsh and guttural. "We wish only to live, and for our children to be safe."

God, I hoped it was true. Did beings like the umbrae, who communicated solely through telepathy, even have the ability to lie? "Then you won't mind my other condition," I said. "If you've looked into Griffin's mind, you've seen our dealings with your kind haven't been at all positive. If we remove the seals and set you free, you must stay here in these mountains. It shouldn't be hard to avoid humans in this land. But if you attempt to spread too far south, a clash will be unavoidable. Even if you don't seek conflict, the humans will fear you. And what they fear, they attack."

They. As if I had less kinship with humans than this vast creature.

Her bulk slithered against the floor. A feeler as thick and long as a tree pulsed and curled, perhaps communicating something I was unequipped to understand. "This is our home. We would see the night sky again, we would hunt the things on four legs and on the wing, gather green, growing things untouched by our kind in millennia. But we do not seek war. We will hide ourselves here, among these peaks."

I didn't know if I could trust her. But it was the best I could do. "Thank you," I said. "This...perception you said you'd give Griffin. Why him?" I steeled myself. "The dweller in the deeps once touched my mind. If I lower my defenses—"

"It will not work. Our kinds are close, but we cannot speak in this way."

Blast.

"What about me?" Jack stepped forward. "It's my fault Griffin is in danger. Alter my perceptions so I can see the magic and guide Dr. Whyborne's spell instead."

"The pathway has already been built in his mind, years ago, strengthened by nightmare and opened wide by the Lapidem." Her great head swayed back and forth in the shadows, even as Griffin's mouth spoke her words. "It must be him."

"But it won't hurt him," I said. "Er, will it?"

"I cannot say."

The devil? "That isn't what I want to hear."

"No." And then suddenly she was *there*, rearing only feet above Griffin, her orange eye like a flame in the darkness. "But it is his choice to make. And he has made it."

Griffin screamed.

CHAPTER 50

Griffin

My mouth tasted of blood, and my skull felt slightly too small for its contents. My pulse pounded in my temples, and I had the odd sensation of pain decreasing from a peak I couldn't quite recall, to something bearable.

"Griffin!" Hands gripped my shoulders. "Griffin, speak to me, please!"

"Damn you!" another voice shouted. "What did you do to him?"

I opened my eyes. My vision wavered for a moment, nothing but a smear of color and light. Then everything came into focus, and I gasped.

Whyborne knelt over me, his eyes wide with fear. Nothing about him had changed...and yet everything had.

No. Not changed. There was just...more. I couldn't even explain the sensation to myself, except I felt as if I now saw with my eyes all the things I'd already known with my heart. The fire burning inside seemed to light him up from within, and his eyes all but glowed with it...and yet were no different from the dark brown they'd always been.

I reached up trembling fingers and brushed along the line of his jaw, to the disaster his hair had become, and down to the puce scarf that I knew didn't hide gills beneath, even if it seemed suddenly not just possible, but likely.

"You're so beautiful," I whispered.

"That confirms it," Christine said. "His brain has been damaged."

"Christine!" Whyborne snapped, brows drawing sharply together. I wanted to touch them, trace the expressive dark lines across his face, but he batted my hand away. "Griffin. Can you talk? Stand up?"

I felt more and more myself. "Yes. Yes, I'm fine." Whyborne drew back, still hovering anxiously as I struggled to sit up. Jack slid an arm around my shoulders, and I nodded my thanks. He at least seemed no different to my sight.

But a great deal of other things did.

The entire hall seemed altered. Not lighter, but more clear. Lines of greenish fire twined through the rock, through the columns, although they cast no light.

"What am I seeing?" I asked aloud.

"The spells that have kept this city from decay, eon after eon. The masters had no time to remove them from this place. I do not know if they did elsewhere, if they left the ceilings and walls to collapse on my sisters and bury them forever."

"Griffin?" Jack's arm tightened around my shoulders, worry written clear on his face. "Are you all right?"

I nodded, then stopped as the world swayed around me. I closed my eyes tight for a moment. When I opened them again, everything had settled. "Yes. I just need a moment to adjust."

"What are you experiencing?" Whyborne's hand rested on my arm, comforting and solid.

"I can't describe it. Not well." I took a deep breath. "You look the same...but not."

"You mean me in particular?" Whyborne asked.

"I can see the magic in you. Or maybe your ketoi blood. Or both." I shook my head. "It barely even makes sense to me. I noticed you the moment I laid eyes on you, and yet now I feel as if I would have picked you from a crowd of thousands even if we'd never met."

"I see," Whyborne said uncertainly. "Anything else?"

I described the lines of magic in the walls. "And whispering." I'd not been consciously aware of it at first, but now I felt as if I stood just outside a crowded ballroom, listening to music and laughter and tears, and a hundred different conversations going on at once. "I think...I think I hear the all umbrae communicating with each other."

"Hmm." Whyborne sat back on his heels. "If you can see the magic in the walls, you should be able to see the seals. With any luck, it will be enough for me to use the curse breaker."

As Whyborne helped me up, I heard the hiss of the Mother of Shadows, her coils shifting on the stone. I turned to face her, half shocked I no longer felt afraid. After so many years of living in terror of the umbrae, right now I had only pity.

Her looping coils drew back, revealing more and more of the floor. Something gleamed in my sight, like a fallen star.

"What in the name of heaven...?" Whyborne murmured.

A plinth stood there, and on it sat a large, irregularly cut gem. I couldn't have named the mineral it was carved from: purple black, and shot through with veins of red that pulsed in my sight. But I'd seen another much like it, half a world away.

Whyborne's hand closed on my arm. "Occultum Lapidem," he gasped. "Griffin, don't look!"

"It won't hurt us." I went to the plinth and laid my hand on the gem. It felt oddly warm to the touch. Knowledge rushed into me, fed by the whispers I could perceive more and more clearly. "Every city had such a gem. They allowed the masters to order their slaves at a distance. But they also allow the Mother of Shadows to communicate with her children at a greater range than would otherwise be possible."

"Take this. It will allow me to speak with the children, if you must go far to find this thief. Take it and find my daughter."

"Yes." I lifted it carefully and tucked it into my pack. "I'll do everything in my power to bring her back."

"I know." I sensed an odd hesitation from her. *"You are not what I expected. Your kind is terrible to look upon, and those who came before you and stole the chrysalis matched their foul form with their deeds. But now I have seen inside the far corners of your mind. You understand the value of family. Strange. I would never have thought such creatures as yourselves could do so."*

I wanted to laugh. How frightened we'd been, and yet to the umbrae, we were the monsters. "Some of us do, anyway."

"You love. And you grieve. You have lost one of your own recently."

Pa. What would he think of this creature before me? Would he have understood her at all?

"And you fear to lose another. Your mother."

I swallowed tightly. What had the Mother of Shadows seen in my mind? "Yes." I spoke the word as a whisper, but wasn't sure if I had to speak it aloud at all for her to hear. "I don't want Ma to die without ever seeing her again. I don't want..."

Emotion constricted my throat, but the images were so clear in my mind: gentle hands tucking me into bed, the smell of an apple pie baked for my birthday, the pride in her voice as she told the other women at church about the high marks I'd brought home from school.

"I miss her," I whispered at last. "I miss her so much."

The Mother of Shadows lowered her great head, and a feeler slipped lightly across my face in a caress. It should have revolted me, sent me screaming in disgust and horror. But I was beyond that now.

"You have lost your mother, and I have lost my child." Pity, and grief, and understanding. *"But it is not too late for either of us."*

Perhaps she was right. But Ma was a thousand miles away, on the plains of Kansas. "Whyborne and I will take down the seals," I said, hitching my pack higher on my back. "You'll get your daughter back. I swear it."

Chapter 51

Whyborne

I watched Griffin carefully as we made our way back through the twisted labyrinth of the city. For the most part, he seemed well enough, but my fears didn't ease. Once or twice, he stumbled over nothing, like a man regaining his land legs after a long voyage at sea. His eyes scanned the walls, the murals, even the floor and ceiling avidly, as if seeing something new and fascinating at every turn.

Workers swarmed before us, and the stately soldiers floated ponderously ahead and behind. What if I had made some terrible mistake?

Then I'd made a mistake. I couldn't dither about the future, not when I had Griffin to worry over in the present. He could see arcane energy now, and possibly other things as well. What would that do to him? Would it make him vulnerable to mental manipulation, as I was vulnerable to the dweller?

A fear for another day. What was done was done, and we might none of us survive this. And if we did, I'd teach him everything I knew about how to strengthen his mental defenses. Just in case.

I took his hand in mine. The air grew colder as we ascended, but his wedding band was still warm from the heat of his body. He cast me a questioning look, but I only squeezed his fingers. He seemed to understand, though, squeezing mine back and walking closer to me, so our arms brushed together.

But his affection brought up another concern. "What does Jack think about...us?" I asked, careful to keep my voice low.

"I think he's more confused than anything. But I talked to him, tried to explain to him that we've built a life together." Griffin shook his head. "I'm sorry I tried to keep our relationship hidden. I should have told him before we came here, and let him decide to either look past it or cut off all ties with me. After Pa..."

"It was difficult for you. I understand."

He shook his head. "Yes, but that isn't what I meant. After Pa, I should have learned my lesson. It's one thing to be cautious, to conceal ourselves from the public gaze. But any family I want to be close to will find out eventually, one way or the other. If my other brother is still alive, and I'm lucky enough to find him, I'll explain everything as soon as it seems prudent to do so. That way, if he's been convinced by a second-rate sorcerer that you're some terrible influence, it will either confirm things or make him question them sooner."

"Do you think the Endicotts might find him?" How far would they go to see me destroyed?

"They found Jack," Griffin pointed out. "But without knowing where he might be, there's nothing we can do about it. And if we do find him, and he proves to be repulsed by my inclinations, at least it means your cousins can't use him as a tool against us."

"True." I didn't point out there were other ways it could go wrong. Blackmail would always be a possibility, should we be found out by those unsympathetic to our love. But at the moment, walking down an underground corridor built in primeval times, accompanied by floating monsters, on our way to try and stop Turner from handing over a new Mother of Shadows to the Endicotts, blackmail and scandal seemed so inconsequential as to not even bother mentioning.

When we reached the great doors, I stopped well back from them and let go of Griffin's hand. He went to the doorway, staring at something none of us could see. He stretched out one hand, almost in a caress.

"What does it look like?" Jack asked.

Griffin's mouth thinned. "Like...knots? A tangle of magic. Spiky and sparking. Fire in the air."

A chill went through me. I didn't like the cadence his voice had taken on, not quite his own. "Griffin," I said quietly.

He blinked. "Yes. Forgive me." He regarded the lines only he could perceive for a long moment, then nodded, as if he'd come to some conclusion.

Or as if agreeing with someone the rest of us couldn't hear.

"I think the easiest thing will be for me to guide you, Whyborne," he said. "Stand behind me and put your hands over mine. If you feel the shape of the spell, you can break it, correct?"

"Possibly," I said. I started toward him, then stopped, recalling my reaction to the arcane power I'd taken from the cursed pearl back in Widdershins. "I think the rest of you should go on ahead."

Christine frowned. She'd recovered enough to walk unassisted, although I worried how she would hold up on the long climb back to the surface. "You aren't about to do something foolish, are you?" she asked suspiciously.

"Of course not!" My cheeks heated as I tried to think of some less embarrassing explanation. "I'm not entirely certain what will happen to the arcane energy when the seals break. Probably nothing, but it makes no sense to endanger anyone other than the two of us. Just as a precaution."

Her eyes narrowed. "Very well. We'll await you at the top of the ramp. And you'd best not make us wait long."

She and Iskander started off, but Jack wavered. "I should stay..."

"Go, Jack," Griffin said. "It will be all right. I trust Whyborne with my life."

When Jack departed, Griffin glanced at me. "Is it so dangerous?"

"No," I confessed. My face felt scalded. "It's just, when I broke the curse on the pearl, it...affected me. I don't know for certain this will, but...well."

Griffin frowned. "Why are you blushing? How exactly did the curse breaker affect you?"

"Can we please just get on with it?"

"Very well." He turned back to the doorway and held out his hands, resting them against something I couldn't see. Pressing against his back, I reached out and wrapped my hands over his, fingers splayed between his.

He leaned back into me. "Now close your eyes," he murmured. "And try to *see* the pattern I trace."

I obeyed. With my eyes shut, I became keenly aware of the thick layers of clothing separating us. The smell of his skin, the honest scent of sweat cutting through the acrid stew of the umbrae. The soft sigh of his breath. The back of his hands against my palms, warm and inviting.

And beneath that, a flicker. As I'd felt when mapping the lines of power in Widdershins, or studying the cursed pearl.

"Do you sense it?" he asked.

"Yes." My voice was ragged, thick.

He moved his hands, tracing the lines of the spells, my fingers threaded through his. The pattern bloomed in my mind, streaks of fire against the darkness. The sigils drew their strength from the sun, and on this, the darkest night of the year, they lay vulnerable and exposed. I could *feel* the power now, throbbing under my fingers, in my temples, my scars, my groin. And I could feel him against me, so close but cruelly separated by our heavy clothing. Everything else fell away; there existed only us and darkness and fire.

"Again," I said, because I had to get this right.

His hands moved, tracing lines. Power flowed now, through us, between us, as I mapped the ancient sigils like a lover's skin. My heart pounded and my cock ached. Griffin's hood had fallen back, his hair against my lips. I lowered my head, licked the skin on the nape of his neck.

A little gasp escaped him, and it sent blood jolting through me. "Ival, what...?"

The scars on my arm ached, but not unpleasantly, more like an itch that feels almost sensuously good to scratch. Power shimmered beneath my fingers, thick here, thin there. I probed the gaps, felt them yield against my will. Stifling a groan, I bit the back of Griffin's neck where I had licked before.

He cried out and shuddered against me. Pleasure sizzled through me at the press of cloth against heated flesh, but it wasn't enough. He rubbed his hips back against me with a whimper, seeking friction.

The strands of the spell wrapped around us, reacting to my touch. I tightened the fingers of my right hand around his as I found the softest point of the seals, the key to unraveling everything.

Yes. There.

I thrust in, my body a living tool for my will, the spell yielding before me. Griffin cried out again. Power trembled and I tasted burning copper in my mouth. My scars ached hotly as I drank down the spell's energy. Its arcane fire seemed to scald me from the inside. The smell of scorched wool rose from my right sleeve, but I didn't care. Nothing mattered but this: heat and fire and power and—

Something gave way, like the snapping of a rubber band. I stumbled back, blinking dazedly against the lantern light, bright after the darkness behind my eyes. My breath came in ragged spurts, my cock heavy, and my blood burned. Griffin turned to face me, his eyes wild with lust. For a moment, I thought he might drop to his knees in front of me then and there.

I wanted him to. I wanted to tear aside his clothing and take him on the floor, make him beg for more while I fucked him.

No. I flung my hand out to stay him, and forced myself to take deep breaths.

"I can see the power in you," he said hoarsely.

"We have to go." I swallowed hard. "Stop Turner."

"I...yes." He took a deep breath. "I see why you asked the others to leave."

Displaced air hissed behind me. The soldiers emerged from the corridor, gliding forward. One passed over my head and, for the first time in untold millennia, left the city where its kind had been sealed.

I lowered my hand. "Come," I said. And walked back through the doorway, the power I'd stolen from the seals boiling in my blood.

CHAPTER 52

Griffin

WHYBORNE BURNED.

I saw the lacework of scars on his arm, glowing even through the layers of clothing. His eyes streamed blue flame, and the sheer power of the arcane energy he'd absorbed felt like a banked fire against my skin. His spiky hair crackled with it, like static.

Even when I'd been at my most suspect of his sorcery, watching him cast spells always moved me. His confidence, the look on his face when the world changed according to his will: haughty and heated at the same time. I wanted to beg him to master me, the way he mastered the very forces of nature, to do anything and everything he wished with me, to me.

The burn and friction of magic on my nerves as he manipulated the energy around us, the feel of his teeth on my neck, had been too much, and I'd spent in my drawers like a youth. But I still wanted to throw myself at his feet and beg him to fuck my mouth.

I needed to focus, damn it. The seals had fallen, but we still had to catch up with Turner. He might be in Hoarfrost by now.

I paused just long enough to pull out a handkerchief and hastily clean up. Then we joined Christine, Iskander, and Jack at the top of the ramp. Soldiers hovered in the vast space, waiting for us, I thought. I could still hear them talking with the Mother of Shadows in a faint hum, like a whispered conversation in another room.

"Thank heavens!" Christine exclaimed on seeing us. Then she made a fist with her good hand and punched Whyborne in the shoulder. "Didn't I tell you we'd find a way out?"

"Yes, yes." He scowled back at her.

She frowned. "Are you all right?"

They couldn't see him the way I could. "I absorbed the energy from the seals." His voice was taut, the words clipped, as if half his concentration was elsewhere. "In case I need to use it against Turner. But I'm not certain how long I can hold on to it before I'm forced to let it dissipate."

She looked worried, but nodded. "Then let's hurry. Perhaps if he left us any sleds, the umbrae can pull them for us in place of the dogs. I imagine they'd be much faster."

"Hitching umbrae to a sled? Only you would come up with such an idea, Christine," Whyborne muttered.

"Oh, don't be jealous I thought of it first."

"Do we need to face Turner at all?" Iskander asked. "Surely the umbrae can retrieve the chrysalis without our help."

"Please, let me at least talk to Nicholas," Jack said with pleading in his eyes. "Perhaps I can convince him to hand over the chrysalis on his own. That way no one else has to be hurt."

I didn't think it likely, but as Jack said, it was worth trying. We'd be no worse off if Turner proved unable to be reasoned with. "All right, Jack. We'll try it your way."

We made our way through the series of interconnected rooms. As the last one leading to the rift opened up, the light of Iskander's lantern fell across a figure lying like a discarded heap of rags in one corner.

"Scarrow!" Jack exclaimed, and ran to him.

I hastened to help Jack. The reverend let out a little moan as we rolled him onto his back—alive, thank God.

Blood caked the side of his face, and one eye swelled shut. The clothing over his left leg was charred, revealing blackened skin underneath. Pain contorted his features, but he managed to shift into a sitting position with Jack's help. "You're alive," Scarrow said with a grin that was more grimace. "A pleasure to see you again, Dr. Whyborne, Dr. Putnam."

I studied Scarrow carefully. He didn't look different to me the way Whyborne had, but there was something about him, some shift of shadow or brightness of eye, which whispered he'd been touched by arcane power. If we managed to survive this, at least I could be certain of never being tricked by a sorcerer again.

"What happened?" I asked. "I take it you caught up with Turner. Did he escape?"

"In a way. I found him in the rift. Atop the temple straddling the old river." He shifted his weight and winced. Clear fluid oozed from the cracked skin of his leg.

"We need to tend your wound," I said. "Iskander, do you have—"

"No time," Scarrow cut in. "Listen to me. Turner changed his plans, I assume because he stole a queen rather than the soldier he'd expected to find. He's not taking her back to Cornwall. He's performing a ritual to force her to hatch early."

"What, here?" Whyborne demanded.

Scarrow nodded. "Yes. Your guess as to why is as good as mine."

"He felt slighted by the Endicotts," Whyborne said with a glance at me.

"Why doesn't matter, only that he's still here, and we have a real chance to catch him," Christine said.

Iskander nodded. "Indeed. Christine, you stay here with Reverend Scarrow."

Her eyes widened and I half expected her to puff up like an angry cobra. "I most certainly will not!"

"You aren't in any condition to fight, and you sodding well know it." His lips tightened. "I won't stand by and watch you get yourself killed out of stubbornness."

"The reverend has a rifle," Christine shot back. "If I have something to prop it on, I can at least aim and pull a trigger."

"We don't have time for this," Whyborne cut in. "Iskander is right. Turner has only one guard left alive. We're more than a match for him."

He didn't wait for her to argue, only turned and strode toward the entrance leading out to the rift. Wind whispered through the room in his wake, power trembling in the air. Christine looked furious, but I thought Whyborne had made the right decision. We couldn't wait for the wounded to slow us down. I didn't know what would happen if Turner forced the queen to hatch prematurely, other than it would do her no good.

It likely wouldn't do us any good, either.

We emerged onto a balcony with a low wall, overlooking the great rift dividing the city. Below us lay the ancient watercourse, long dead. The delicate bridges leapt it at various intervals, and I could see the magic wrapped about the stones, holding them together long after the ravages of time should have torn them down. The glowing slime cast an eerie blue light over everything, and high above us the belly of the glacier groaned as it crawled slowly down the mountain.

Turner stood atop the temple, as if waiting for us. The body of the last guard lay at his feet, gutted in sacrifice by his knife.

"Nicholas," Jack whispered. "No. Damn it, no. Why would you do this?"

Magic twisted in the air around the platform, forming a net, which pierced and bound the dark shape behind Turner. The Mother of Shadows had been inhuman, terrible, all coils and feelers. And yet her form possessed its own symmetry, its own rightness.

The creature squirming on the platform behind Turner looked painfully incomplete. Forced too soon from her chrysalis, her glowing eye had three separate pupils, and her feelers were stunted. Rudimentary wings unfurled from her back, no doubt meant to be shed after a mating flight, but they curled and twisted into uselessness.

Whyborne tensed beside me. Energy snapped around him, seeking release. A cry of pain echoed in my head, whether from the Mother of Shadows or the young queen in front of me, I couldn't say. The umbrae rushed past us, intent on freeing the stolen queen.

The cry sharpened, crystallized. Some of the umbrae jerked, as if struck.

Then, without hesitation, they turned on their fellows. Acid-coated feelers lashed out, and wings tried to envelop. They made no sound, but I could hear their shrieks in my head as they grappled wildly. I stumbled, felt Whyborne grab my elbow to keep me on my feet.

"The little queen," I gasped. "She's strong—some of the umbrae hear her now, instead of the Mother of Shadows."

"Oh hell," Jack whispered, staring up at where Turner stood laughing now high above us. "We just brought him an army."

CHAPTER 53

Whyborne

RAGE TREMBLED THROUGH my veins, as above us the umbrae fought. Turner laughed atop the temple, as though there were some mirth to be found in his mastery of the stunted thing he'd torn from her chrysalis.

"Bloody hell," Iskander gasped.

Jack took a step forward. "What do we do now?" His voice shook, but he hadn't yet run screaming.

"We have to free her from Turner," Griffin said. "Otherwise—"

One of the umbrae dove at us, its eye glaring hellishly. Acid-drenched feelers reached out, and its chemical stench rolled over us in a stifling wave. Jack shouted and stumbled back, his arm up as if to ward it off. Iskander's knives gleamed in his hands, but he was too far away, and Jack too close.

No. Griffin had already paid too high a price. I wouldn't let his brother die if it lay in my power to prevent it.

I howled, and the wind howled with me. The city seemed to vibrate in response to the magic boiling in my bones. High above, the glacier moaned and rumbled.

I flung out my arm, the scars burning with power. Wind screamed through me, from me, smashing into the vast wings of the umbra. It tumbled like a leaf caught in a tornado, until its gelatinous body collided with one of the cone-shaped buildings with crushing force. Whatever organs lurked deep within its seemingly homogenous mass ruptured at the impact. A moment later, it peeled free, pinwheeling down into the depths.

Jack's face drained of color, his freckles standing out like spots of blood. "Th-thank you," he managed.

Griffin grabbed us both and dragged us down to crouch in the scant shelter of the low wall. The umbrae still battled one another in the gulf above the rift. Two of those under the command of the young queen tore apart one of their brethren, ripping pieces away until it fell into the rift below, dead or dying I didn't know.

"Griffin's right—we have to free the queen," I said, ducking back down behind the wall. My throat ached and my mouth tasted of burnt copper. "Griffin, you and Jack try to get to the temple with the Lapidem. If the Mother of Shadows can use it to communicate, perhaps she can help break through Turner's spell somehow, or at least wrest control of the other umbrae back from her daughter."

Griffin nodded. "Agreed."

"Iskander—"

"Kander, get out the kerosene," Christine interrupted.

She made her slow way out of the room behind us, leaning heavily on Scarrow's rifle. "Christine," I said in exasperation, even as Iskander hurried to pull her to shelter, such as it was. At any moment, one of the umbrae would break free of the fight and come for us again.

"Don't pretend you don't need all the help you can get." She nodded at the wall. "I'll prop the rifle on this—it should give me a good position to fire at the umbrae, at least, although the temple's out of range. More's the pity, otherwise I'd put a bullet in Turner's head."

"He'd only set off the gunpowder." At least he couldn't do that without a line of sight. I hoped. "And bullets don't work against the umbrae."

"Ha!" She grinned. "Scarrow enchanted his. Only an excellent shot will kill the creatures, but I can at least slow them down."

Like Turner, the reverend apparently knew more about sorcery than I did. "Fine," I snapped. "Iskander, pour the kerosene in a circle to keep the umbrae back if they come too close. And be ready with your knives."

He nodded, and I knew he'd die before he let one of the creatures reach Christine.

"What about Nicholas?" Jack asked.

I smiled, but there was no humor in it. "Leave him to me."

"Ival." Griffin reached for me.

I took his hand and pulled him close. The arcane fire in my blood stirred, a whisper of power and desire. "Take the opportunity I give you," I said. "I don't know how long I can keep him occupied."

"We will."

I kissed him fiercely. My plan had to work, had to be enough. If I failed, Turner would surely aim his sorcery at Griffin and Jack.

I couldn't let it happen. So I pushed Griffin away, leapt to my feet, and ran.

"Turner!" I shouted, and a whisper of magic carried my voice to every corner of the city.

He stood atop the temple still, but now two of the umbrae soldiers guarded him. He spun at the sound of my voice. "Decided to come out, coward?" he mocked. "I don't know how you managed to destroy the ancient seals, but let me thank you for doing so. After I kill you, I'll take my new servant into the nest and gather an army to us. Then the Endicotts will understand the depth of their mistake."

One of the umbrae rose higher, no doubt at his command, and moved toward me. I could have turned wind against it, but I didn't. Not yet.

"Do you actually think they'll change their minds?" An incredulous laugh escaped me. "They won't open their arms to you, won't let you into the family home and embrace you as one of their own. They'll fight you to their last breaths. They'll die hating you as an outsider, and nothing you can do will ever alter that."

Turner let out a cry of rage. The umbrae thralls peeled off from their attack on their free kin, all of them gliding straight at me.

Perhaps my distraction had worked a little too well.

The umbra from the temple blocked my way forward, the eerie blue glow of the phosphorescent slime gleaming from its oily black body. To my left lay a series of irregular windows leading into the cluster of rooms overhanging the rift. To my right a slender bridge leapt across the vast gulf to the other side. No doubt Turner expected me to dive into the nearest room, where I'd risk being trapped without any exit.

So instead I ran onto the narrow bridge.

There were no rails, and I didn't dare look down. Up close, I could see the stone was badly cracked, only the ancient spells keeping the span from collapsing into the depths of the earth, as others had before it. My idea seemed worse by the moment.

"Wrong move, Dr. Whyborne!" Turner called. "You should have remained cowering in Widdershins. You're no true sorcerer, just a fool who thinks he can batter his way through life with raw magic. You lack the subtlety to do what I have done."

The umbrae closed in. The crack of a rifle shattered the air, and one of them jerked, its psychic scream echoing somewhere in the back of my mind. I stumbled to a halt, heart laboring in my chest. I was well out on the span, far away from Christine or Griffin or anyone else who might be hurt by what I was about to do.

"You're probably right," I agreed. The umbrae rose up around me in a ring, their wings almost touching, their feelers lashing eagerly for my flesh. Christine fired again. The tripartite eye of the nearest soldier exploded, and a moment later it fell, tumbling limp into the abyss. "But I have power to burn."

I raised my arm, pain lancing through the scars as I unleashed all the arcane energy I'd absorbed from the seals. Fire howled through me, hollowing out my bones. The smell of scorched wool and burning leather filled the air, the sleeve of my coat charring and flaking to pieces as power blazed along the lines inscribed in my very flesh.

A great sphere of fire pulsed outward, with me at the epicenter. The umbrae closing in burst into oily flames, and the stench of burning chemicals seared my nose. Their shrieks pounded against the back of my mind.

One careened blazing into the span, nearly at my very feet. I jerked away from it instinctively, and my foot came down on the very edge of the bridge.

I fell heavily to the side. My chest hit the stone, knocking the breath from my lungs. I scrabbled madly for purchase on the crumbling rock, the yawning abyss below seeming to try to suck me down into it.

"Damn you!" Turner shouted. "You'll pay for this!"

Griffin shouted a warning, but there was nothing I could do. The rocky span cracked beneath the force of Turner's spell, the ancient magic losing its long battle. I looked wildly for Griffin, and saw him standing at the base of the temple. I'd bought enough time for him to get closer—but not close enough.

Then my handhold turned into fractured pebbles, and a scream tore from my lungs as I fell into the rift.

CHAPTER 54

Griffin

MY HEART THUDDED in my ears as I watched Whyborne run away from us, up a curving ramp. I wanted to call out to him, to beg him to come back and not put himself in harm's way.

But if I did, we were all doomed.

"Come on," I said to Jack. "This way."

"Good luck, chaps," Iskander called after us. Beside him, Christine already sighted through Scarrow's rifle.

At least the temple gave us something to head for amidst the confusing architecture of the ancient city. The huge edifice straddled the now-dry riverbed, and ramps ran up all four stepped sides. If we could make it to the nearest, we would have a chance of reaching the queen, as long as Whyborne kept Turner sufficiently distracted.

Whyborne's voice rang out somewhere above, magically amplified. I tried to concentrate on finding a path to the temple through the dizzying angles of ramps and walls, none of which seemed to join at precisely the angle one expected. We had to hurry, before Turner could strike against him.

The cries of the battling umbrae scratched at my mind. They mingled with the broken whispers of the new-hatched queen, just beyond my range of hearing. I gritted my teeth, determined not to let them distract me.

The sound of a rifle shot rang through the city. I glanced automatically over my shoulder, startled to see how far we'd already come. An umbra wavered in its flight, darting away from the balcony.

Pain pulsed through my head. A moment later, the umbra shuddered and turned back. Another shot rang out, but this time it swerved.

"Damn it, Turner is forcing them to attack Christine and Iskander," I said.

Fire bloomed on the balcony as Iskander lit off the oil. The umbra tried to fall back again, but again there came that twist of pain. It labored forward, crossing over the burning ring.

Iskander leapt from the balcony, knives flashing, and came down solidly on its back. The umbra twisted, its shriek sounding in my head. The cry ended as Iskander drove both knives into it, just behind its eye.

Some vital organ must have resided there. It convulsed once—then collapsed, as whatever property kept it aloft vanished along with its life.

Christine's shout echoed through the rift. The umbra crashed into one of the cube-shaped buildings. Iskander either rolled or was thrown free. As the umbra's bulk slid over the edge and tumbled into the rift, he lay unmoving.

The rifle spoke again. I jerked at the sound and looked away from Iskander's sprawled body.

Whyborne stood atop one of the fragile bridges, umbrae closing in around him. He burned in my sight, one arm thrust upward, as though he'd shaped his own body into a sorcerer's wand. The scars on his arm blazed with arcane fire—and a moment later, real fire erupted all around him. Umbrae screamed and burned, turning to ash. Half of me recoiled at their pain while the other half rejoiced to see him unharmed.

A burning umbra crashed into the span. My heart stopped when Whyborne fell, one leg dangling over the rift.

Turner shouted in rage. We'd made it to the bottom of the ramp leading to the temple, but he was still far too high above us. Even as I watched, lines of magic formed around the wand he held in his hand, gathered from the very warp and weft of existence. At his command, the magic snapped free of the wand, a single spell thrown at Whyborne. As I tried to cry a warning, it latched onto the bridge and tore the stone apart.

Even across the gulf of air between us, I thought Ival's eyes met mine.

Then he fell.

A scream ripped my throat raw. Jack grabbed my arm to keep me from plunging blindly after in some mad attempt to save my love.

"No!" I shouted, yanking my arm away. Jack's hands caught on the pack slung over my shoulders, and I pulled free of it. "I have to save him! Ival!"

"It's too late!" Jack grappled with me. "Griffin, stop!"

I fought him. A black emptiness opened in my chest, imploding my life, my heart, my very being.

"Stop!" Jack shouted again. He bled from a cut on his lip I didn't remember giving him. "Damn it, Griffin, Whyborne is dead!"

The word struck me like a heavy blow. I tried to tell Jack no, he was wrong. My Ival couldn't be dead, because how could I possibly still draw breath if he no longer did?

"No," I whispered.

Jack shook his head, his green eyes haunted. "No one could survive such a fall. I-I'm sorry."

"No, you're not." I shoved him, as hard as I could. He staggered back, my pack spilling from his hand, but I didn't care. "You wanted him to die! This is all your fault!"

Blind rage ignited behind my eyes. The tiny voice that said I was being unjust, that Jack regretted his mistake, burned away. Pa consigned Ival to hell, and Jack tried to kill him, and all in the name of love for me.

I ran up the temple's ramp, no longer even certain what I meant to do. Turner's remaining umbrae were in full rout, attacked on every side by those belonging to the Mother of Shadows. I would kill Turner, would rip him limb from limb with my bare hands. And if he killed me with sorcery or umbrae, what did it matter? Let my bones join Ival's in this forsaken place.

Turner spun as I reached the platform atop the temple. "Your lover is dead," he said, lip curling. "And now—"

The words were lost beneath a scream.

I went to my knees. Turner still spoke, as if no one's howls of anguish filled the great cavern beneath the glacier.

As if it were only in my head.

Pain splintered my vision, and I tumbled to the stone. Anguish and loneliness and terror and—

A vision of Turner, standing over me, the light hurting my eyes, my vision unclear and distorted, undeveloped. *"What a disappointment. I wanted a Mother of Shadows, not this abnormal thing."* A swift kick into soft flesh not yet toughened from exposure to the air outside the chrysalis that had held me.

Then pain.

Turner walked away.

Pa walked swiftly away, our gate clanging shut behind him.

Letters burned on a beach, never opened.

Jack's look of shock. *"Your...husband?"*

Ival falling, falling...

"Alone, so alone, these others came, but now they are dead, brief lights gone out, it hurts, it hurts."

Alone.

Oh, Ival.

Our pain became a single cry, and we rose to our feet. Turner's eyes widened, and the hooks of his magic tore our flesh, but it didn't matter. Nothing mattered any more.

We could see the spell he crafted. So we reached out and grasped the remaining minds, the soldiers with their simple thoughts, their love for one not ourselves. And we *bent* them to our will.

"What have you done?" Turner asked. Then his eyes went past us, to us. "Obey me! Kill him!"

Glenn screamed, flesh shucked from his bones.

Ival screamed, falling into the abyss.

The soldier loomed up behind Turner. Feelers shot out, wrapping around his body. The leather of his clothing charred and melted, and his cry of surprise turned into one of agony. The bones of his hand dripped from the remnants of his sleeve, and I glimpsed exposed ribs and wet, pink lung.

Eventually, his screams stopped.

But the pain didn't end.

We were still alone in the dark.

CHAPTER 55

Whyborne

I screamed as I fell. My fingers clawed at nothing, my legs flailed for purchase that couldn't be found. I was falling, and I was going to die, and—

Something vast and dark passed beneath me.

I struck it, hard, but the gelatinous surface yielded beneath the impact. The wings folded up, and we dropped a heart stopping distance, before the umbra straightened again.

Dazed, I clung to the back of the umbra that had swooped in to save me. "Mother of Shadows?" I whispered, and for the first time wished I could actually communicate with them. Had whatever masters shaped both our races made certain we couldn't speak to one another, and so collude against them?

Definitely a thought for another time. I clutched at the umbra's— skin? surface?—but there was no handhold, no hair or protrusion to grip. It seemed to realize my predicament, flattening itself as much as possible even as it sliced through the air. I caught a dizzying glimpse of the city—then we were rising up, toward the temple.

A shudder ran through it abruptly. I raised my face from its reeking ebony surface, got a confused glimpse of the temple, of Griffin and Turner standing upon it, and the new-hatched queen coiling behind.

"Griffin," I gasped. The umbra bucked, hard. I grabbed wildly, but my fingers found only slick skin. I slid free and fell—

My body hit one of the ramps leading to the temple, only a few feet below. Pain spiked through my hip and shoulder, but nothing seemed broken as I rolled onto my back.

"Whyborne!" Jack ran to me hand outstretched. "You're alive!"

"I can hardly believe it myself," I agreed. I had the feeling I'd curl into a ball if I dwelled too long on my narrow escape, so I said, "Griffin—we have to save him!"

"He thought you were dead. I tried to stop him, but he was determined to confront Turner." For the first time I noticed Jack's bruised and split lip. "I meant to follow him, but the umbra came at me, and—and then you fell off."

"Follow me." I raced up the ramp, ignoring the twinge in my leg. I'd expended all of the arcane energy I'd stolen from the seals, and briefly wished I'd withheld something to use against Turner and the queen he'd enslaved.

To the devil with that. I'd be damned if I let a two-bit sorcerer like Turner, a reject of the blasted Endicotts, best me.

I gained the top of the platform, and my heart leapt, because Griffin was still on his feet. Behind him writhed the malformed coils of the newly emerged queen. Her orange eye glowed like flame, the three pupils contracting at different rates, giving her a hideously asymmetrical appearance. The lone plinth jutted up between them, its surface curved, as if to receive some object.

And in front of them was Turner. Or rather, the shredded coat and melted bones that were all which remained.

Had Griffin distracted him, while the umbra came in from behind? My heart pounding, I shouted, "Griffin!" and started toward him.

But when he turned, I froze in my tracks.

His head tilted slightly to one side, as if he couldn't quite see me. His eyes had washed from emerald to green frost, the pupils contracted to pinpoints.

Did the Mother of Shadows manage to possess him at this distance?

"Alone," he grated, and his hands curled into loose fists. "There is nothing left but pain and death."

The remaining umbrae swirled madly. A rifle shot rang through the air as one sank toward the roof of a building not far from the balcony. Another made for Christine's perch. Smoke rose into the air, but the protective flames no longer burned. What had happened to Iskander?

"Griffin," I whispered. But in his eyes I saw no recognition at all.

CHAPTER 56

Griffin

NOTHING EXISTED BUT pain and fury, and a bleak world that had hurt us.

Other creatures stirred around us—the cruel ones, who went on two legs and had no feelers, misshapen and horrible and *wrong*.

But they called us wrong. Said we were nothing.

"Such creatures don't really feel things the way we do," Scarrow said.

And Jack: *"You said th-things like him don't have friends."*

And worst of all, Pa, condemnation in his voice: *"It's just pleasures of the flesh, and the worst kind at that."*

Your Pa is dead. Heart trouble. Don't come for the funeral.

We were abnormal, twisted, monsters. Too horrible and broken for anyone to believe we could feel. Only Ival had understood, and now he was gone, they'd taken him, and we would do as I'd promised.

We'd burn down the world.

"Griffin, stop!" One of them stood before us, hands outstretched, a pleading look on his face. And we should have known him, but we didn't.

We looked through another of our eyes, saw a limp figure stir slightly atop a building. And another, her face white as she crouched behind a balcony, her finger pulling on a trigger—

We recoiled, shrieking. The nearest creature ran toward us, but we lunged forward, feelers reaching, and he fell back.

"Griffin, please," he begged. "Look at me! You have to stop this. I know she has you, I know it seems like you can't possibly break free, but she's going to hurt our friends. *You're* going to! Please."

"There is fire in your blood," we said, because we could see it so clearly, like a flame burning inside him. Our soldier, the one who had devoured Turner, moved up behind him. He flinched, but he didn't flee. Didn't do anything but hold his hands out to us.

"Yes," he said. "It's what the ketoi call me, my sea name. Fire in His Blood. But I don't care about that. I just care about what you call me."

The soldier stretched out its feelers. It was almost on him now. "Why don't you use your fire?" we asked. "Unleash it against us!"

He shook his head. He looked unspeakably tired, his coat filthy, one sleeve burned away, his face smeared with blood and soot. "You know why, Griffin. You know. Say my name."

It trembled on the edge of my tongue. But the pain was so great, the loneliness, the fear. I struggled to remember something, anything. "Pa didn't want me."

He blinked, and water made tracks through the grime on his face. "I know, darling. But I do."

"Ival?"

A tremulous smile touched his face, even as the umbra closed the final few inches. "I love you."

"So do I," said another voice. And I turned, we turned, and saw Jack, just as he thrust the Lapidem into its cradle on the plinth.

The world exploded as the Mother of Shadows reached through the gem and into us.

Pain and grief.

But most of all, love.

The queen who shared my mind was malformed, birthed too soon. Broken and hurt, and she would never be a Mother of Shadows herself. Never lay eggs, or sing to beautiful children. Never be what she should have been, had Turner not interfered.

But it didn't matter. Because the Mother of Shadows—her mother—loved her anyway.

We cried out and fell forward. Ival caught us—me—and crushed me to his chest as we sank to the ground.

The Lapidem blazed with light within the plinth, ancient magic flowing through it, and through us. I *felt* Ival. Felt his love for me, that didn't care if I was broken. All the pieces of myself I'd laid at his feet over our years together, all the cracks that still showed where he helped me heal, didn't matter. He loved me, beyond my ability to understand.

Then Jack's arms locked around us both, and his lips pressed against my forehead. "I'm sorry, Griffin," he whispered. "I'm sorry your father couldn't love you the way he should have, but I do. I love you, brother, and I want to be a part of your family, but you have to let this pain go. You have to let it go and let us care about you."

We were all linked, bound to the Mother of Shadows and the pain of the newborn queen above us. Tears slicked my cheeks, but I didn't care. I wept for Pa, because he'd never been able to let his love for me overcome his fear of an angry God. And I wept for Christine, whose parents wouldn't embrace the man she loved because of the color of his skin. I wept for Ival, and all the pain bound up in his father and his brother, and for Iskander, whose mother chose duty over family, and never told him why. For Ma, who asked me not to stand by her side when they laid Pa to rest.

And finally for Jack, because some part of us still stood there together, on the orphan train. He turned to me, struggling to be brave, and draped his own coat around my shoulders.

"Stay warm," he said. And walked away into a future where everyone who should have cared for him failed to do so.

The queen didn't move for a long moment. The gem burned like a flame now, and the Mother whispered through it. Because it didn't matter if her daughter was broken, or deformed, or hurt. It didn't change her love at all.

The little queen reached out, her feelers gently cradling the Lapidem, lifting it from the plinth. Her pained cries had died away without my even noticing. She slowly coiled back into herself, hugging the gem as a child might a favorite doll, as a talisman against the monsters in the dark.

A pair of remaining soldiers slid forth from the shadows. They gathered her carefully, supporting her as her stunted wings never would. I could sense workers moving toward us, coming to help now the danger had passed. They'd found Scarrow and begun to tend him, even as he stared at them in a mix of revulsion and fascination. And Iskander, groggily coming around after his fall, with Christine at his side.

The soldiers hesitated, and the queen stirred within their grasp. I looked up, to see her holding the Lapidem out to me. I reached out automatically, and she placed it in my hands.

"In case you have need in the future, my child," whispered the Mother of Shadows. *"You can always call upon us."*

Then they were gone. I sat blinking, held by my husband and my brother.

My husband.

"Ival?" Realization dawned. "You're...you're alive!"

"Clever of you to notice," he said. "I see why you're so successful a detective."

I shook my head, then dragged him down and kissed him. And we held each other and wept, while the city came to life with umbrae around us.

CHAPTER 57

Griffin

"Well, this could have gone better," Christine said a month later.

We stood on the docks of St. Michael, where we'd managed to find passage on a steamer making its way back to San Francisco.

The stab wound still pained her, although she'd never admit it. Iskander's left arm rested in a sling, having been broken when he struck the stone. Scarrow used makeshift crutches, and had insisted on leaving Hoarfrost even with his burned leg still heavily bandaged.

We would never have made it back to Hoarfrost without the help of the umbrae. Although we didn't go quite so far as to hitch them to sleds as Christine suggested, they aided us the rest of the way out of their subterranean kingdom, back to the camp where the sleds and dogs waited.

No one in the gold mining camp knew precisely what had happened on the glacier. We'd woven a wild tale of collapsed caves, falls into crevasses, and a mutiny on the part of Turner and our guides to explain our injuries. None of us had any compunction about slandering Turner's memory, so we'd claimed to have recovered a few valuable artifacts, which were all that remained of the city we'd gone to find. Turner had stolen them to sell to collectors and abandoned us to die on the glacier. When he failed to ever turn up again, his death would be put down just one more life taken by the Alaskan wilderness.

Still, we'd left the area as quickly as possible, taking only the stele with us, once more in pieces after Whyborne melted the frozen mud holding it together. It would cause some comment in the archaeological world, although Christine's dreams of unveiling a primordial city were obviously dashed.

"Our work will still be accounted an interesting find," Whyborne said. "An unknown civilization, linked to the Eltdown Shards..."

"Or everyone will call it a hoax, as they did the shards." Her brows drew down in a scowl. "Bah!"

"So long as the umbrae aren't disturbed, I'll call it a victory," Iskander said, taking her elbow. "Mr. Hogue, it was...an adventure. I hope to see you again some day."

Jack nodded. "Same here."

"Hmph. I suppose you can be forgiven for siding with Turner, as you didn't know any better," Christine said grudgingly. "I shall send you an invitation to our wedding."

"I'd be honored," my brother said with a bow. "I can't promise to attend, but I'll do my best."

"What do you think the museum will say?" I asked Whyborne, once they'd gone aboard.

Whyborne shrugged. "I don't know. Fortunately Father picked up most of the expenses, and we are coming back with *something*. But it's hardly the spectacular find the director hoped for. Perhaps I should consider a paper analyzing the writing on the stele as compared to the Eltdown Shards, just to restore my reputation." A small scowl crossed his face. "But some dratted sorcerer or other would probably take advantage somehow."

"No doubt," Reverend Scarrow said. Pain etched deep lines around his mouth, but he smiled as he held out his hand. "Thank you for your assistance, Dr. Whyborne. The Cabal will be in touch."

"Well *that* wasn't ominous at all," Whyborne muttered as Scarrow limped away. "Why can't everyone just leave me alone?"

I looked up at him. The sea wind ruffled the fur around his hood, his mouth drawn into a small frown. My altered perceptions hadn't left me, but I'd grown used to seeing him with more than ordinary sight. "Because you're *you*," I said wryly.

"A philologist of small renown?" he suggested.

"Try a very powerful sorcerer with inhuman blood, related to the Endicotts."

"And I thought Father's side of the family was a problem." Whyborne hunched his shoulders. "Oh well." Thrusting out his hand to Jack, he said, "Perhaps we'll see you again."

"I hope so." Jack clasped his hand warmly. "You're a fine man, Dr. Whyborne. I'm glad my brother has you to look out for him."

A faint smile ghosted across Whyborne's face, there and gone. "I rather think it's the other way around. Until next time."

We both watched him board. "I meant what I said." Jack turned to me. "I never knew love was real, you know. But now that I've seen it with my own eyes, I can hope to find it myself, with the right person."

"I hope you do," I replied. "Where do you think you'll go now?"

"I don't know." Grief flashed briefly through his eyes. "I thought Nicholas had shown me a new path."

"He did." I shrugged at his startled look. "I don't agree with Turner in the particulars of the matter, obviously. But you've proved your courage, and your heart. I think he was right when he said you can make a real difference in this world."

Jack blinked rapidly, then pulled me into a hug. "Thank you, brother."

I returned the embrace. "You're welcome. Write as soon as you can."

"I will," he promised. "And I'll come to Widdershins for a visit, eventually. I just need some time to think on my own. Away from sorcerers of any stripe."

"I understand."

"Still...I was thinking." We drew apart, and he offered me a hopeful smile. "I don't know why I kept the Hogue name all these years, except out of habit, when they never did anything for me. I'm thinking about changing it back to Flaherty."

A grin spread across my face. "I'd like that."

"I'm glad." He patted me on the arm, then stepped back. "Your steamer is about to leave, and I think Whyborne would put a curse on me if I made you miss it."

I found Whyborne standing alongside the rail. As the steamer pulled away from the dock, we both waved a farewell to Jack. Christine and Iskander had already gone below, and the night was too frigid for any other passengers to brave the deck.

"Are you going to be all right?" he asked, as the aurora danced above us.

"People keep asking me that."

"For good reason." He glanced down at me.

I shifted my shoulders, feeling the weight of the pack on my back. We hadn't yet gone to our room to stow our few personal belongings, and the Mother of Shadow's gift nestled in the pack between my spare union suit and Whyborne's frayed puce scarf.

I hadn't heard her since we walked out of the caves at the base of the glacier and stumbled back to Hoarfrost. But at night, when the memory of Whyborne falling haunted my dreams, the stone's presence gave me an odd comfort. The Endicotts might still want us both dead, and the Cabal's designs were unclear. But we weren't without allies in the world, even if they were shadowy horrors lurking just past the edge of human civilization.

No one else stirred on the deck, save for sailors busy elsewhere, so I put my hand on his. "I am," I said. "It may sound strange, but after encountering the Mother, I want to try writing to Ma again. Cousin Ruth will speak to her on my behalf as well, I'm certain. Perhaps we may yet reconcile."

"I hope so." Whyborne put his other hand atop mine.

"And if we don't, I'll at least have tried. And I feel at peace with that." I looked up at the stars and the dancing aurora. "And with other things. With Pa, and my brother. With Glenn's ghost. With myself."

"I'm glad."

"There is one thing I'm not at peace with, though," I went on in a serious tone.

He cocked his head worriedly. "Oh?"

"Indeed. My husband and I have a room all to ourselves for the first time in what seems like forever, and yet we're standing about on the deck talking."

A slow, hungry grin stretched his mouth. "A complaint I share. Shall we go below and discover the most creative way to fit us both into one bunk?"

"I thought you'd never ask," I said. Taking his hand in mine, we left the arctic night behind in exchange for each other's warmth.

You are cordially invited to the wedding of
Dr. Christine Esther Putnam
and
Mr. Iskander Gregory Barnett
Widdershins, MA

About the Author

Jordan L. Hawk is a trans author from North Carolina. Childhood tales of mountain ghosts and mysterious creatures gave him a life-long love of things that go bump in the night. When he isn't writing, he brews his own beer and tries to keep the cats from destroying the house. His best-selling Whyborne & Griffin series (beginning with Widdershins) can be found in print, ebook, and audiobook.

If you're interested in receiving Jordan's newsletter and being the first to know when new books are released, please sign up at his website: http://www.jordanlhawk.com. Or join his Facebook reader group, Widdershins Knows Its Own.

Printed in Poland
by Amazon Fulfillment
Poland Sp. z o.o., Wrocław